D1624058

ALL
OUR
WORST
IDEAS

VICKY SKINNER

Swoon
READS

New York

Also by Vicky Skinner

We Are the Ghosts

How to Breathe Underwater

A SWOON READS BOOK

An imprint of Feiwel and Friends and Macmillan Publishing Group, LLC

120 Broadway, New York, NY 10271

Our books may be purchased in bulk for promotional, educational, or
business use. Please contact your local bookseller or the Macmillan Corporate
and Premium Sales Department at (800) 221-7945 ext. 5442 or by e-mail at
MacmillanSpecialMarkets@macmillan.com.

Library of Congress Cataloging-in-Publication Data is available.

ISBN 978-1-250-19542-5 (hardcover) / ISBN 978-1-250-19543-2 (ebook)

BOOK DESIGN BY KATIE KLIMOWICZ

First edition, 2020

1 3 5 7 9 10 8 6 4 2

swoonreads.com

For Mom,
who gave me music

JANUARY

AMY

I'VE BEEN STANDING outside my favorite record store, Spirits, for half an hour.

More accurately, I've been standing across the street from Spirits, leaning against the front window of the tutoring center, listening to Spirits run through my favorite Flaming Lips album over the outdoor speaker system, and deciding whether or not to go inside.

I came here to get a job at the tutoring center because when my mother asked me what I had planned for today, and I told her my only plan was to turn in my application to Stanford, she told me that I needed to get a job.

Actually, what she said was, "Carlos got laid off last week, and we need you to get a job. Go downtown. And put a load of clothes in the washer before you go."

There wasn't even a moment for argument, and what would my argument even *be*? If they need help, I have to help. Carlos has been working as a mechanic for as long as my parents have been married, and now he's being laid off?

And of course, the most selfish part of me thought, *What about Stanford?* Because no matter how hard I work for the Keller Scholarship, if I get it, it isn't going to pay for clothes and extra-long sheets.

So I came to the tutoring center to get a job. But instead of actually going inside, I've been staring at the HELP WANTED sign in the window of Spirits. The bright red SPIRITS sign over the door isn't lit up, but it shines in the sun nevertheless. Maybe a job won't be so bad. For just a second, I close my eyes and remember the first time I ever heard this particular Flaming Lips song. I was thirteen, walking through a carnival with Mama, the lights flashing and swirling while this played so loud from one of the game booths that it was almost deafening.

My phone buzzes, and I open my eyes. It's Jackson, my boyfriend, who's currently looking for new track shoes at REI, and who just texted me to *Go for it! What are you waiting for?*

What am I waiting for? I have zero extra time for a job.

But it's not like this is a choice. It's not like we can't afford to eat, but we're not nearly as well off as some of the people I know, including Jackson, so if Mama says she needs me to get a job, then I have to get a job, even if I feel like I might explode from the overwhelming prospect.

So, it's between Spirits and the tutoring center. The tutoring center would look good on my application for the Keller Scholarship, but working at Spirits would be like living in a daydream. Besides, everyone I know will be trying to get a job at the tutoring center because people are still trying to pad their applications, but absolutely nobody I know works at Spirits, which is an argument in favor of, not against, working there.

My feet take me across the street. When I step into Spirits and walk down the first aisle of records, grazing my fingertips across the cardboard sleeves as I go, I feel like I can breathe for the first time in months. Between SAT scores, getting my Stanford application ready, and trying to prove that I deserve the Keller Scholarship, I haven't stopped to smell the vinyl.

There's a boy behind the counter, and I sneak a look at him as he goes through a tall stack of records. He examines each one, his face giving away no emotion, and then promptly files them into one of two stacks. As I pick up a Nick Drake album and scan the back of it, my eyes pop up to the boy again. He's easily more than six feet, has red hair, pale skin, eyes that are just a little too wide-set, and is wearing a faded maroon T-shirt with a breast pocket. I've seen him before, standing behind that counter when I came in to look for new music, but I've skimmed over him the way I skim over most people.

As I'm watching, a girl comes out of a back room. I recognize her, too, from my frequent visits. She looks like she might be in her mid-twenties, but I can see from where I'm standing, right at the end of the aisle, that she has a badge pinned to her clothes that says MANAGER. Half her head is buzzed close to her scalp, and the other half is slicked back. She walks straight over to the boy, slaps a stack of papers on the counter beside him, and sighs.

"I have *got* to stop hiring college kids," she says. "I can't take going through this stupid process every time a new semester starts." She rifles through the papers in front of her. "I know I'm not supposed to be judging them on their musical taste, but dear God, the last girl couldn't name all four Beatles."

The boy laughs. He has a nice smile. And then his eyes flicker up to me, and I look away quick. I don't want him to know that I'm eavesdropping.

"I have to get someone in here on the weekends," the manager goes on, and something strums in my chest. "It's getting too hard for just you and Morgan to be running cash wrap. Don't you have music-savvy friends who want to work here?"

The boy snorts. "Maybe you should lower your standards."

I open my mouth. "Excuse me?" I haven't even realized I've walked up to them until there's nothing but the counter between us. They both look up at me. "Um, you're hiring?"

The boy taps his fingers on the counter and regards me. I don't miss the way his eyes slide down my body in a completely stoic way, like he's just sizing me up.

His manager is regarding me, too, but her eyes are wary. "You want a job?"

I nod.

She bites her lip. "Any experience?"

I have tons of experience. I've spent years tutoring and volunteering, picking up trash on the side of the road, reading to children, and taking handmade blankets to the nursing home. But running a register? Not so much. I've always been too busy making sure my college applications are perfect to even think about a job. "Um. Not exactly. But I'm a fast learner."

The guy smiles, but he looks away when he does it. Is he laughing at me?

The girl reaches across the counter, holding a hand out to me. "I'm Brooke." She nudges the boy with her elbow. "This is Oliver."

I shake her hand, but Oliver doesn't offer his. He just nods at me in greeting.

Brooke puts her hands on her hips. She's curvy and pretty, and she nods her cleft chin in my direction. "The shirt. You listen to the Lumineers or you thought the design was nice?"

I can see in her eyes that my answer is going to tip the scales on her judgment of me. I look down at my shirt. I tug nervously at the hem. "They're my favorite band. I'm going to their show this summer."

Brooke reaches across the counter and slaps an application in front of me. "Fill this out for our records, but you're hired. You in college?"

I reach into my purse for the pen that I keep in there. "Senior in high school."

"Nights and weekends?"

"Sure." Something creeps into the back of my mind. How am I going to fit a part-time job into my schedule? My hand pauses, my pen sliding to a halt.

"Something wrong?" Brooke asks.

"Um. No." I go back to the form and scribble the rest of my information down.

Brooke glances down at the application when I slide it back to her. "Can you start Monday night? Five o'clock? It'll be slow, so we can train you."

I nod, but I'm thinking about Monday already. It's my first day back at school after winter break, and I'll probably have a load of homework. But I can stay up late. Or do it before my shift. I'll find the time. I have to.

Brooke smiles kindly. "Band shirts or solid colored shirts only. Oh!" She snaps and then points at Oliver. "Except Monday is silly hat day."

Oliver, without even lifting his head, groans.

My eyes shift between them. "What's silly hat day?"

"During the week," Brooke explains, "I come up with stupid stuff for customers to do for a discount. Keeps the business up, and the regulars like it." She grins at me. "We'll see you on Monday." She's already moved on to the next task, her eyes traveling along the stacks of records in front of her and then out to the shop, where one or two people are milling around. It's kind of slow for a Saturday morning, but it's still early.

I glance up at the boy, up and up and up at him because he's at least a foot taller than me, and his eyes feel a mile away. He's watching me hesitantly, a record gripped in his hand. His gaze makes me anxious, maybe because he's so tall, but I smile at him anyway.

He doesn't smile back.

"Okay, bye." I wave at both of them and turn to leave, but I freeze when I'm facing the front window. Because Petra Johnson is standing outside the tutoring center talking to my boyfriend.

My relationship with Petra is hard to define. Maybe if we weren't at the top of the class, always competing for grades and the top spot, Petra and I could be friends. But as it is, we're both just a little too competitive, I'm a little too impatient, and Petra is just a little too mean. But if I'm being honest, Petra is the only person at school who understands why I need to make valedictorian, get into Stanford, get the Keller Scholarship, and get out of this place.

But I've never seen her talk to Jackson before, and she's smiling at him like they've been friends all their lives.

"Everything good?"

I turn back to the counter when I realize Oliver is speaking directly to me for the first time. Brooke has vanished. Oliver and I are completely alone at the front desk.

"Yeah," I say, trying to clear my head. "I forgot to give you back your pen." I put it on the counter in front of him, and his brow creases.

"This is yours," Oliver says, and he reaches out the pen toward me. I stare at it for a second. It's a pen that Mama let me borrow, with the name of the hotel where she works across the side.

"Oh yeah." I take the pen, but I turn back to Oliver again. "You guys aren't, like, pranking me with the whole silly hat day thing, are you?"

He almost looks like he wants to smile. His eyes look significantly cheerier. "I wish. Mandatory for employees."

I just nod, hesitant. I keep thinking that Mama was kidding about the job, that maybe I'll go home and she'll say, "What do you mean you got a job? I wasn't being *serious*. Of course Carlos didn't get laid off!" But I know Mama better than that. And my application is already on the other side of the desk, beside Oliver's moving hands. So I turn and leave.

I'm not sure why seeing Petra and Jackson together has me so flustered, but it still takes me a second to step out of Spirits and cross the street to join them. Jackson puts his arm around me without even making eye contact. After almost a year together, this movement comes naturally to him, like muscle memory.

Petra, however, smiles, her perfectly white teeth glistening against her dark skin, and it's not a kind smile. Petra stopped giving me kind smiles junior year, when it became clear that one of us was going to be valedictorian of our senior class and the other would come in close second. Petra perches her hand on her hip, her purse swinging from the crook of her arm and her curly hair blowing in the cold breeze. I look up at her. I have to look up at most people as I'm five foot one. Petra, tall and slender, is closer to six feet, even without her heels.

"Finding more distractions?" Petra asks, her eyes shooting to Jackson suggestively, and I have to clench my jaw not to say something awful.

"You get your Yale app in yet, Petra?"

Her eyes shoot back to me, narrowing. She tries to hide it, but I can see the panic behind them. "I'm not interested in winning against someone who isn't even trying, you know."

I narrow my eyes right back. "Believe me, I've got this in the bag." I sound much more confident than I feel, and Petra isn't buying it. She wants valedictorian so she can walk into Yale at the top of her graduating class. I want valedictorian so I can get the scholarship that's going to get me to Stanford on a full ride.

She makes a little sound in the back of her throat, and then, without another word, walks around me and right into the tutoring center.

Jackson, his arm still around me, stares into the tutoring center, where we can see through the huge front windows that Petra has walked up to the front desk and is now speaking cheerfully to the woman behind it.

Jackson whistles low. "I think she's getting worse."

I lace my fingers through his and we turn to the lot where we parked his car. "Of course she is. It's barely five months until graduation."

"*You* haven't turned into a terror."

I laugh, but something unsettling sits in my chest. Because even though Jackson hasn't said it out loud, I know he's having a hard time dealing with my obsession with getting into Stanford and getting the Keller Scholarship. And now, a job.

Inside his car, I reach over and take his hand again. A job can't be enough to cause everything to crumble. I just need to hold on.

OLIVER

As soon as the girl leaves, I stop sorting vinyl and walk into Brooke's office. "You sure about that?" I ask her, but she doesn't even look up from the paperwork in front of her.

"Did you see her? She's going to train easy, work hard, and probably someday take my place as manager." She grins up at me and I roll my eyes.

"Too skittish. And too . . . smiley."

Brooke levels me with a look. "Just because she's not a walking grimace like you doesn't mean there's anything wrong with her."

Just then, my phone buzzes and I look down at the text that just came in from my mom.

Just booked you a tour at Missouri Baptist on Monday! I wasn't sure what your work schedule is but I'm sure Brooke can work with you.

I hate it when she does that. Not just scheduling things that she expects me to show up to, but also making the assumption that everyone else's priorities are the same as hers and that they'll just go along with it. Brooke is my *employer*, and this tour is two days away. She has every right to tell me I can't take the day off.

"Hey, Mom set me up a tour at a school on Monday. Think I can come in late?"

Brooke grunts and says, "Yeah. Sure. But you have to train the new girl."

I also hate it when Brooke proves my mother right. "No way. You're the manager. You do it."

Brooke scowls at me. "Um. Exactly. I'm the manager, which means you do as I tell you. Go finish with that vinyl because I need you to set up that new display that came in."

I groan. "Can't someone else do it? Morgan is coming in, in, like, an hour."

Brooke smacks a hand on her desk and smiles up at me, wide-eyed. "I'm understaffed, Oliver. Tell the college kids to stop quitting, and maybe you won't have to make the displays."

AMY

I'm standing on my front porch, breathing in the cold, soaking in my last few moments of quiet before going inside. Just one . . . more . . . minute.

Inside, it's a circus.

"This one is mine, and you know it!" one of my sisters screams at the other one. They're fighting over a pink hairbrush in the middle of the living room, and when I close the door behind me, they both turn to me immediately.

"Amy!" Gabriella screams. "Tell Marisa this is my hairbrush! She bought the purple one, remember? The pink one is mine!"

"No!" Marisa screams back. "I didn't even want a purple one! I want the pink one! You take the purple one!"

I walk around them and into the hallway. "Where's Mama?" I ask, because she's usually wrangling my little siblings into their pj's about now.

"Javi's crying because he swallowed a tooth," Gabriella says. "They're in Mama's room."

I turn in the direction of my parents' room, but before I can knock, the door is thrown open, and Hector runs out of the room and directly into me.

"Ow!" I say, but he's already taking off past me. "You stepped on my toe."

"Sorry," Hector calls over his shoulder as he runs down the hallway.

"Mama?" I call, tapping a knuckle against her doorframe. I hear someone hiccupping from inside.

"Amy?"

I push the door open.

"Hi, sweetie." Mama still has her arms around a crying Javier when I come in, but I ignore my little brother. Gabriella swallowed a tooth last month, so this isn't the first time we're going through this little calamity. "How was job hunting?"

I halt a few steps inside her room. I know I don't have any right to be upset that she asked me to get a job, but now that I've had time to let it sink in, to think about how this is going to derail me, I think I'm upset anyway. Upset that this happened, and that I have to help deal with it.

Not to mention, I'm afraid I'm going to hear a chorus of *see I told you so*'s from her and my stepfather, Carlos, when I tell them I got a job at Spirits. They know how much I like it there, and I know they'll be smug about it. They're always trying to get me to do "teenager things," but they don't get that I don't have time for "teenager things" if I'm going to get the hell out of Missouri when I graduate. This job is not about "teenager things." It's about money, plain and simple.

And maybe it's a little bit about music.

I glance down at Javier, still trembling in Mama's arms. "Well. Actually. I got a job at Spirits. Okay, well, it was great talking to you. Bye."

She frowns at me, but I shut the door. Out in the living room, Marisa and Gabriella are still screaming over the pink hairbrush, but now Hector has joined in, taking Marisa's side, and trying to help her wiggle the brush out of Gabriella's hands. I walk over to them and snatch the hairbrush out of the middle of the battle.

"Now you get to share the purple brush," I tell them, and Marisa and Gabriella start screaming for Mama while I take off for my bedroom. I toss the pink hairbrush on my dresser and collapse on my bed, aware of the textbooks I set out before I left so that I could get back to them when I got home. But I'm exhausted.

Mama comes into my room and shuts the door behind her. Down the hall, I can hear Javi crying still.

"Amaría, tell me about your job," she says, and I hate the tone of her voice. She always gets this tone when she has *opinions*, and I don't particularly feel up to listening to the "You should have done this a long time ago" lecture right now.

"Mama, don't worry about it, okay? I have homework to do." I get off my bed like I was going to do the homework I have instead of vegging out, but she ignores me.

"You're mad at me. Why? Because I made you get a job, like a normal teenager?"

I slam my textbook shut. "Okay, first of all, *normal* teenager? That is so offensive. And second, why didn't you tell me Carlos lost his job? You waited a whole week!"

"It wasn't something you needed to know."

I throw my hands up. "Not until you need me to get a job. You totally blindsided me! I have to focus on *school*, Mama. And now, I have another thing to worry about."

"Well, maybe you should be more worried about *this* than about scholarships and class rank."

I scowl at her. "What does that mean?"

Mama crosses her arms. "*Mija*, I'm not trying to start a fight with you. I just . . ." She trails off and sighs, that same sigh I know so well, followed by words I know so well. "Baby, you know you might not get into Stanford. It's not that I don't believe in you, but getting into Stanford is *hard*. Would it really be so bad to have a backup plan? Have some job experience under your belt? What happens if you don't get that scholarship? You know we can't afford—"

I ball my hands into fists. "I'm going to get into Stanford, and I'm going to get the Keller Scholarship, and I'm going to move to California. All I have to do is make valedictorian, and I have been first in my class for two years. Why can't you just be on my side for once?"

She sighs and comes to stand in front of me, setting her hands on my shoulders. "I am on your side, *mi amor*. But I don't want you to be heartbroken when things don't go your way."

She always says it like that, so gentle. But every time, all I hear is *You can't do it*.

Before I have a chance to call her out on this, there are four small children stampeding through my room, shrieking at the top of their lungs.

"Girls!" Mama shouts after them. "Boys! Stop running! Get out of your sister's room!"

The two sets of twins, two girls and two boys that are my half siblings, ignore Mama and continue chasing one another in circles around her legs like we're in a *Tom and Jerry* rerun.

I slam my hands over my ears. "Get out!" I shout at them, trying to get them to at least slow down, but they don't. Finally, Mama snatches up a wriggling Hector and shuffles him out of the room, and the other three kids follow close behind, a choo-choo train on a sugar rush.

I slam the door behind all of them and lock it. I don't want Mama to come back in and remind me how big the chances are that this will all blow up in my face.

And then I lie back on my bed and call Jackson. He answers on the first ring.

"I don't think I can do this," I tell him, and I hear him sigh in that way that he does when I'm upset. A sympathetic sigh.

"What's wrong?" Just the sound of his voice seems to calm some of the unease inside me.

I shrug, immediately feeling stupid for calling him at all. Jackson doesn't need to hear me complain again about the job and about Mama and about everything.

"Why is that everyone else can handle working and school and a social life, and I can't?"

On the other end of the line, Jackson snorts. "Because everyone else isn't pushing themselves as hard as you are. You want to come over?"

I sigh. "No, I have homework."

"Okay. Want to put me on speaker and turn on some music while you study?"

I smile up at the ceiling. Sometimes, Jackson can be so perfect. "Really? You hate my music."

"Just pick something good."

So I turn on James Arthur, put Jackson on speaker, and start studying.

OLIVER

WE'RE ALWAYS LATE to church. It's like a curse or something. Every Sunday, without fail, I sit by the front door of our apartment, waiting patiently for my mom to emerge from her bedroom, dressed in her finest clothes.

I don't really have fine clothes, so I just wear my nicest pair of jeans.

This Sunday is no different, and we pull up in front of the church fifteen minutes after service has already started. Mom's heels clack loudly against the pavement as we rush up to the door, and I hold it open for her just as my phone buzzes in my pocket. I sigh and reach in to get it, fully prepared for it to be Brooke asking if I can open the shop because someone called in sick.

But it isn't Brooke. It's my dad.

"Oli?" My mom stands half in and half out of the church, her face full of concern.

"It's Dad."

Aggravation overtakes the concern. "Now? It's ten in the morning."

"Sorry. Maybe it's nothing. Go ahead without me."

She sends me a look that says we're thinking the same thing: With Dad, it's never nothing. She hesitates, and then she finally turns and goes inside. My phone is still ringing, and now I have no excuse not to answer.

"Oliver," my dad says before I've even said a word. "Bad news, kid. I need a ride home."

I'm a little confused. Usually, when my dad needs a ride, it's at two in the morning on a Sunday, and I can barely understand what he's saying between the alcohol and his Scottish accent, which incidentally gets stronger when mixed with Jack Daniels. And sometimes, it isn't even him calling. My father changed my name to simply SON in his contacts list, and ever since, I've been getting calls from bartenders to tell me Dad has passed out in one bar or another.

Never has my father called me at ten in the morning on a Sunday, and never has he sounded so sober.

"Where are you?" I ask. Out in the parking lot, a nice-looking man and woman are each holding the hand of a toddler as they all three tiptoe across the pavement. I hold the door open for them and then step away.

"Well, that's the bad part. I'm at the jailhouse in Independence."

"What?"

"It's no big deal. Got in a bit of a brawl last night at Hassey's. But I'm good now. I'm out. I just need a ride home."

I grit my teeth and glance back at the church. Mom is alone inside. "Can't you take the bus?"

"No money."

"So, walk."

"Come on, Oli. Just come get me."

"I'm busy right now. I'm supposed to be in service with Mom."

My father laughs into the phone, a breathy laugh that I don't find particularly amusing. "She's still got you doin' that codswallop, huh?"

Does this feel like groveling in his mind? Is this how he asks for things *nicely*? I don't say anything. I'm not going to defend Mom. I don't need to.

His laughter dies. "Oli, come on. Come get me. The world is still spinnin' a little. I don't know if I'll make it home."

I sigh and hang up without answering. He can stew and wonder if I'm going to show up or not. I roll my eyes at the thought. He knows I'll show up. I always show up. I want to not care about my dad. I've been picking him up from seedy bars and strangers' apartments and questionable clubs since I got my learner's permit, and no matter how much I want to, I can never say no to him.

I'm at the station in half an hour. When I get there, my father sits on a bench outside the front door, scowling up at the sun like it's personally offended him. He looks pathetic, sitting there, shivering in his brown leather jacket, his red hair, the hair I inherited, gleaming bright. He's paler than usual, and I'm certain it's the first time he's been hungover on a Sunday morning instead of still drunk from the night before.

When I reach out to help him off the bench, pulling up until he wraps a hand around my shoulder, a police officer props open the glass door of the station. "Fergus," he says, "I don't want to see you back here again." He turns to me and hands me a card. "It's a damn shame," he says, and goes back inside without another word.

My father is already halfway to my car, completely unconcerned with what's going on. I look down at the card in my hand. It's a business card with the name, address, and meeting times of an Alcoholics Anonymous group. When I finally look away from it, my father is pulling impatiently at the door handle of my truck. I press the unlock button on my key ring and then climb into the driver's seat. It's then that I notice the piece of paper in my father's hand.

Without asking, I reach across the console and snatch it away from him.

"Dammit, Oli," he growls, but he doesn't try to get it back from me.

I read over the paperwork, my cheeks heating in anger as I take it all in. I finally slam it against the steering wheel, blaring the horn in the process. "A court date?" I demand. "Are you kidding?"

My father rolls his eyes and puts on his seat belt. "It's not a big deal."

"Not a big deal?" I wave the paper in his face, but I know he's already read it. "This is a court date. That means the guy you beat up is pressing charges against you. You could go to jail just for being a fucking idiot."

My father chews on his nails. "Oli, it's really too early in the morning for *fuck*, okay? They're not gonna put me in jail."

I scoff. "Why not? Because you're such an upstanding citizen? You have a record. Why would they go easy on you?"

His eyes slide over to mine. He makes a weird face, and then he reaches over and snatches the card that's still in my hand. "What's that then?"

I pull out of the parking lot while he reads the card. He laughs and rolls his window down before tossing the card out.

OLIVER

THE APARTMENT IS silent when I get home that night. The apartment is always silent when I get home. I never work on Sundays, but after dealing with my dad this morning, I needed to be at Spirits.

"Mom?" I call out, and my voice echoes in the living room. We've been living in this apartment for almost four years, but Mom still hasn't put anything on the walls.

There's no answer. I take my wallet and keys out of my pockets and drop them on the table by the front door. Mom must be working the late shift at the hospital. Not surprising.

I drop down on the couch and turn on the TV. My stomach rumbles, but there's no way I'm cooking right now, so instead I pull out my phone and order a pizza.

On the coffee table is a stack of college brochures, all of them with my name on the delivery address. I'm almost positive that Mom already went through them before she went to work, and I press the heel of my sneaker on the top brochure to slide it away. Underneath is an almost identical brochure for a different college.

They all start to look the same after a while. On the cover is either a portrait of overly enthusiastic college students, cheering at a sporting event or participating in some sort of club activity, or else there's a picture of the biggest building on campus, surrounded by greenery and blue skies.

When the delivery guy rings the doorbell, my eyes have started to fall closed. I take a deep breath and push up off the couch to answer the door. He doesn't say so, but I see the recognition in his eyes when he looks over my shoulder and realizes that he was here two nights ago, and just like then, I'm completely alone.

"Thanks," I tell him, leaving him a moderate tip.

I turn off the TV and power up my turntable instead. It's better than the late-night talk shows anyway. I sit on the couch and munch on the pizza while my newest album, purchased just after the shop closed today, blares in my ears so loud, I can almost forget the silence ever existed.

AMY

I TUG AT the bottom of my shirt and sit up straighter in my chair. I can hear the meeting going on through the open door of the counselor's office. The person inside is trying to figure out how they're going to graduate when they failed their last required math class. I try not to eavesdrop because I know I wouldn't like it if someone was eavesdropping on my meeting.

I scrape at the pink polish on my nails.

"Amaría Richardson."

I look up in time to see the boy I heard talking to Mrs. Grimes rush out of the office, his head down. I look away from him, in case he's trying to be invisible. I stand up and follow Mrs. Grimes into her office. I don't close the door behind me. I don't have to. Mrs. Grimes isn't actually allowed to say my rank out loud, so it isn't like anyone is going to overhear.

"How are you this week, Amy?" she asks without taking her eyes from her computer. I tap my fingertips on my knee impatiently. She doesn't have to ask me why I'm here. She knows. I'm here every week to check my rank.

"Fine, thank you."

She makes a humming noise in the back of her throat, and I know something is wrong. She squints at the screen, her eyebrows furrowing deeply. Then she reaches across the desk, grabs the marker she always uses to copy the ranks onto a sticky note, and writes a number down. But then she crosses through it, writes another number, and then she sighs and pushes it across the desk toward me.

"Okay, Amy. This is a weird situation, but, um, you're actually tied with another student. So this number is very tentative."

I blink at her for a long time, the sticky note just sitting on the desk between us, until finally, I open my mouth. "Tied? What do you mean, tied? That can't be possible." I reach out and grab the sticky note, which at least says *1* even if it's not really true.

Mrs. Grimes smiles in a weird way. "It's extremely possible. We still have plenty of time before the end of the school year for the tie to break."

My brain is moving in a million different directions, but I can only think about one thing. "But what if we're still tied at the end of the year? What happens then?"

Mrs. Grimes's mouth twists. "You can't be tied at graduation. We'd further evaluate your grades if your GPAs are exactly the same, and we would use your grade points instead of your grade-point average to determine the valedictorian. But don't worry. This won't be a concern come the end of the school year."

And then another thought makes its way to the front of my brain. "Who am I tied with?"

Mrs. Grimes sighs. "You know I can't tell you that."

But she doesn't have to. I'm already out of the chair, the sticky note clenched in my fist, and before Mrs. Grimes can say anything, I've rushed out of the office and into the hallway, following the flow of traffic to get to Petra's first-period class. I know she has economics because I almost took the class but signed up for AP bio instead so I could be with Jackson.

Petra is already in her seat, flipping through her textbook, and I sit down in the seat in front of hers, spinning around to face her.

Her eyes are wide, but then she sees the sticky note in my hand and rolls her eyes. "I wondered when you would be demanding to know if I'm the one you're tied with."

I clench the note tighter. "So it is you?"

She slams the textbook shut, and the girl across the aisle jumps at the sound. "Of course it's me. Who else would it be? I've known since before break. I can't believe you didn't check before you left for the holidays."

I was so happy to be spending Christmas with Jackson that I walked out of school the Friday before break without even thinking about my rank. Obviously, I was too confident, too cocky, because I thought I didn't have anything to worry about.

Clearly, I was wrong.

I'm not going to let her have it. Petra gets everything she wants, and she can have it all. But she isn't going to have valedictorian. Valedictorian is mine. I worked too damn hard. I gave up everything: my social life, my sanity, everything. I'm not going to lose val. I'm going to do everything I have to in order to keep it.

I stand up. I'm not often afforded the pleasure of looking down at people, but I look down at her now and nod once. "Get your salutatorian speech ready."

As soon as I get to first period, I pull out my planner and begin making changes. I can get in an extra hour of studying every night if I cut my sleep schedule short, and I have to make time for my homework in the evenings. I'm doing homework over breakfast way too often, and the feeling of being rushed is causing me to make mistakes. I'm skimming some of my chapters in my readings— completely unacceptable. And now that I have to factor in a job, I have to be more strict with my time, more structured.

I put my planner away and wait for Jackson at our lab table. We've been partners in AP bio since the beginning of the year. I'm organizing my stuff exactly the way I like it when he shows up. He kisses me on the cheek, and just that tiny act makes it all start to well up inside me again, and suddenly, right in the middle of the science lab, I'm biting my lip to hold back tears.

"Ames? What's wrong?" Jackson knows me well enough to ask this quietly. He knows I don't want to draw attention to myself, that crying in front of people is not something I'm interested in ever doing, and all that just makes me want to cry harder.

I lean in close to him and whisper, "I'm tied."

For a second, he just blinks at me. "Tied for what?"

I stare at him, my whole face tight. "Tied for valedictorian."

Jackson's still staring at me, and I can almost see the moment that confusion shifts to realization. "Oh shit, Amy. I'm sorry. How can you be tied?"

I shrug. If I try to explain it all to him, I'm just going to start crying, so I shake my head and turn away. It wasn't smart to bring it up right now anyway. What did I think I was going to accomplish by bursting into tears in the middle of AP bio?

"Ames, I know you're stressed, but everything's going to be okay." It's exactly the kind of thing that I would expect Jackson to say, and maybe on any other day, it would be enough. But today, it feels like empty words.

"I just need to focus," I say, taking my calendar back out and setting it on the table between us. "I know we haven't really been going out much, but I think after final exams, we'll be good to go. Until then, I really should buckle down. Maybe we could have more study dates for the time being?" My eyes aren't on him. They're on my planner, where every day that I'm supposed to be with Jackson has a little *J* in the corner, enfolded in a heart. But most of them have been written over.

Jackson's eyes are scanning the page, and then he sets his finger on a date in a few weeks. "My birthday party." That's all he says, and I realize I haven't even written it in. It's a Friday night, and I'll probably have to ask for the night off from Spirits. Such a strange thought.

"Right," I say, already writing it into the calendar. "Your birthday party. I almost forgot."

He watches me write *Jackson's Birthday Party* really big and bold inside its square and then sends me a close-lipped smile before pull-ing his stuff for class out of his backpack. "You've been busy. Don't worry about it. Bryce has everything planned. All you have to do is show up."

"I've been a little obsessive," I say. It's not quite an apology, but it's not exactly *not* one, either, and Jackson just shrugs.

"I'm used to it."

At first I think maybe I heard him wrong, but no. I definitely heard the bitterness in his voice when he said that. "What?" I say because I'm not sure what else to say.

Jackson sighs, his shoulders falling in that way I recognize that says he doesn't want to get into something. "Ames, don't worry about it, okay? Just, do me a favor, and don't forget that there are things in the world besides class rank."

My breath gets stuck inside me. I can't believe he just said that. "I know there are other things, but this is important, Jackson." I turn away from him, feeling my face go hot, even as I know Jackson didn't intend to be mean.

I see him out of the corner of my eye, bending close to me to say something, but just then our teacher starts to pass out safety goggles, and every time Jackson tries to talk to me, the teacher shushes him.

OLIVER

"Here at Missouri Baptist University," the speaker at the front of the room says, gesturing wildly, "you'll have the opportunity to advance your academic studies while building your relationship with Christ.

Everyone enrolled full-time will be expected to attend chapel, and our services are truly moving. We also have multiple mission trips every semester, and I've got brochures about our upcoming spring mission trip, if anyone is interested." She picks up a stack of brochures and waves them enthusiastically as my eyes travel around the room, from the back of one head to another.

There are only ten people in my tour group, a student-only tour that my mother arranged for me to attend on this beautiful Monday morning, and I'm bored as shit. I should be covering extra shifts at Spirits, and instead, I'm wasting my time here. The guy sitting two rows in front of me has a tribal tattoo on the back of his neck, and I grimace when I see it. I rub the inside of my own arm, where sometimes I imagine I still feel a throbbing pain, even though I got the tattoo back in June.

"If nobody has any questions, I think we're ready for our tour." Our guide smiles wide at us. She's wearing an MBU T-shirt and jeans, and her blond ponytail swings behind her as she motions for us to follow her out of the room. A tour. Outside. Fantastic. I zip up my jacket and follow her out into the main hall of the building we've been in for the past hour. I feel my body seize up when the cold air hits my face.

"So, I want to take you by our dorm halls so that you can get an idea of which dorm you want to apply for."

She keeps talking, but I've already checked out completely. I tuck my stiff fingers into the pockets of my jacket and follow along, even though this entire thing is pointless. I promised Mom I would come take a tour of MBU, and I also promised to look at the brochures and the websites and the applications, and I did it all with a smile on my face so that my mom wouldn't know the truth.

I don't even know if I want to go to college.

When I graduated high school seven months ago, it took everything I had to convince Mom to give me a year off. Gap years aren't all that uncommon. But it wasn't really just a gap year. I needed time to decide about college, and the only way I could get it was to promise to go to all the tours and the meetings and whatever else Mom wanted in the meantime. She thinks I'm just having a hard time choosing between a state school and a private university. But my time is running out. I'm supposed to be sending in applications, and I'm pretty sure none of this is for me, but I don't know how to tell Mom that. I don't know how to break her heart.

What's the best way to say, *I just want to move out, keep working at Spirits, and maybe someday own a record shop of my own, because music is pretty much the only thing in this life I care about besides you?*

When I get home that afternoon, Mom's car is in its assigned parking space, and I hold in a groan. I don't want to face her right now. I don't want to have to lie about how amazing the modern architecture of MBU's campus is or whatever else I'm supposed to say about the place to convince her I care.

Maybe I can just go straight to work. I'm supposed to be there early today anyway because the new girl starts today, and Brooke wants me to help train her.

But that sounds only marginally more interesting than talking to Mom about the highlights of MBU's campus tour, so I go inside.

She's running around, already in her scrubs and apparently looking for her other shoe, judging by the fact that she's only wearing one.

"Honey!" she says, kissing me on the cheek as she whooshes past. It's like getting a kiss from Road Runner.

"Hey, Mom."

Don't ask me about the tour. Don't ask me about the tour. Don't ask me about the tour.

"How was the tour?" she asks. This, she'll stop moving for. She stands in front of me, a smile on her face and her arms crossed.

"Oh, um." I focus on taking off my jacket and hanging it on a hook by the door so that I don't have to look directly at her. "It was great. The campus is pretty impressive. I just, you know, I don't know if it's quite the place for me."

This is the same thing I've said about the last three universities I went to look at upon her request, and I know exactly what she's going to say because it's the same thing she said the last three times.

"Oli, sweetie, I know you want everything to be perfect and that you've taken this year off to make sure you're in the right headspace for this decision, but I don't want you to miss out because you waited too long, okay?"

She says it so gently that guilt settles in my stomach. She's so good at that—being so kind about trying to micromanage my life that somehow I feel bad for not letting her do it.

She claps her hands together. "Well, no worries. We're going to figure this out. But I have to get to work. I'm pulling a double, so you're on your own for dinner."

She says it as if it hasn't been almost a year since the last time we had dinner together, but I don't mention this, either. I figure if I can just keep her happy, just do what she asks, maybe she won't be so upset when I tell her that I'm pretty sure I'm not going to any of the perfect universities she wants me to.

AMY

"THANK YOU FOR coming in. Have a great day!" I smile at the girl in front of me who just bought a Miley Cyrus vinyl, which I didn't even know existed before today, while she wears a hat that has bunny ears sprouting from the top. She smiles back and rushes out of the store to meet her mother, standing on the sidewalk in front of the shop.

When I turn back to Brooke, she's biting her lip. She's wearing a bowler hat, which makes her look totally steampunk. I'm just wearing a baseball cap with a Superman logo on it that I borrowed from Jackson because it was the only thing I could come up with on such short notice. It is, decidedly, un-silly.

"Oh God. I did something wrong, didn't I? What is it?"

Brooke's mouth turns down, and her eyes scan over the register. "You didn't do anything wrong. Actually, you did everything perfect. You *are* a fast learner. It took Oliver two weeks before he could make a sale without screwing up."

"I can hear you!" Oliver shouts from the stockroom, where the door is propped open and he's pulling down boxes.

"Yeah, I know," Brooke mutters before turning back to me. "Why don't you hang out in the back room with Oliver? He can show you how pricing and inventory haul work. I have to fill out payroll paperwork." She grimaces.

I nod. "Yes, ma'am."

Her eyebrow crinkles. "You don't have to call me ma'am. My wife owns this place. She's the *ma'am* around here, not me."

"Oh. Okay."

She disappears inside the office, and I'm left in the store with nothing but the sound of Oliver clanking old CDs and tapes together, and Sleeping at Last playing over the speaker system. I tap my fingertips on the countertop and glance over at the stockroom. Oliver is sitting on the carpet, glaring down pretty seriously at a record. Great. I'll just hang out with Oliver. Oliver, who hasn't spoken a word to me since I got here.

It isn't until he looks up that I realize I've been standing here too long, watching him. I scramble away from the front desk and go into the stockroom. There's something about Oliver, about his silence, that makes me feel like I need to make as little noise as possible. Like he's a bird perched peacefully on a branch, and if I make too much noise, he'll fly away.

I take a seat on the low shelf beside a stack of earbuds in plastic cases, and he hands me something, big and bulky and shaped like a tape gun.

"Price stickers," he says, moving on.

"I don't know how to use this," I say. I almost feel embarrassed, even though I shouldn't. Why should this be a skill I have in my arsenal when I've never had any use for it?

But Oliver doesn't look at me like I'm stupid or roll his eyes or give any indication that my not knowing how to use a sticker gun makes me inferior to him. He scoots a little closer to me and gently takes the gun from my hand.

"Watching?" he asks. I nod, and he dispenses the gun against the CD case. A little orange sticker attaches itself to the plastic. "The sticker gun is only for sale items." He explains the pricing system to me, the way the back room is organized, and I'm amazed at how efficient he is with his words, like he's practiced in the art of saying as few as possible. He pushes a stack of CDs over to me, and I start putting stickers on them.

"Do you go to East?" I ask him, mostly to make small talk, but I also want to know because I go to East, and I've never noticed him in the halls before. Or at least, I don't think I have. I'll admit, I'm not likely to look at faces around school, because I don't care much for being social. I care about getting to class on time and getting my work done.

His eyes flicker to mine and then down again. "No. Graduated from West back in June."

When he's quiet too long, I ask him, "Where do you go now?"

He doesn't look at me, his hands moving quickly over his work. "Nowhere."

I don't feel like I can press him for more information. He turns his back to me, just slightly, and goes silent again.

"Hello?"

A voice in the shop catches our attention, and Oliver looks over at me. "Think you want to handle that?"

I shrug. "Yeah. Okay." No, I want to tell him. I do *not* want to handle a customer on my own after only working here for three hours. But I straighten my spine and go anyway because I'm confident that I can do this.

"Hello, sir," I say to the guy in front of the register who has his fisted hands pressed into the countertop.

"Yeah, I put some vinyl on hold over the phone last night. Came to pick it up." He leans one elbow on the counter and looks around, his eyes flitting behind me while I work with the computer. No one showed me how to do holds, but the system is pretty simple, so it only takes me a second to find the tab where the list is.

The guy is already impatient by the time I ask for his last name, his fingers drumming on the counter and his shoulders tense beneath his flannel shirt.

I'm looking at the screen, trying to figure out exactly how the system is arranged, when he asks, "Do you know what you're doing?"

I can't tell if he asks me this because I'm taking too long, because it's obvious that I'm new, or because I'm a girl. But either way, my fingers stutter over the keyboard. I won't let him trip me up.

"I've got it right here," I say, ignoring his question. "I just need to . . ." I don't know where the holds are kept, so I turn toward the stockroom, ready to ask Oliver. He's sitting on the shelf, across from where I was sitting moments ago, a tape in each hand and his eyes on me, like he's letting me do this alone but is also making himself available if I need help, and a fondness for him sparks inside me.

Before I can even get a word out, the guy in front of me leans across the counter, until I have to back up to get out of his way, and calls out, "Hey, bro. Think you can help us out here?"

I see the hesitation on Oliver's face at the same time I feel the heat in my cheeks. I'm not embarrassed. Just angry. Oliver sets down what's in his hands and comes to the counter. I step aside, but I feel a shock when Oliver puts a hand on my arm to stop me. He doesn't say anything to the customer, just waits.

"We need some help with a hold," the guy explains, just as Oliver seemed to know he would. "She doesn't quite seem to know how to do it."

Oliver's face is blank. "It's her first day," he says by way of explanation, not that he owes the guy one.

The guy scoffs. "Yeah, I think that's obvious."

Oliver just stares at him for another second and then he turns to me. "What's the problem?"

It isn't often that people can make me feel small, even if I am barely more than five feet, but right now, between the way the guy is looking at me like I'm a bug he found in his shower and the fact that I already have to ask Oliver for help, I feel minuscule. "I don't know where you keep the holds."

Oliver nods and then walks over to a shelf at the end of the counter, hidden beneath the ledge. He points. "They're right here. Sorted by last name." He reaches down and pulls the records the guy is asking for, and I can feel the discomfort pouring off him. It makes me like him more. He hands me the records, holding my eye longer than he has since I met him.

When the guy sees that Oliver has handed the transaction back over to me, he grimaces. "Maybe you should do that, man. I'm in kind of a hurry."

Without thinking, I try to hand the records back to Oliver. The customer is always right, right?

Oliver crosses his arms and nods at the computer.

For a split second, I just grip the albums in my fingers, and then I finish out the transaction, which I've already done several times tonight.

The guy across the counter squishes his lips together in a tight frown.

Oliver stands beside me, and while the guy is swiping his credit card, Oliver says, loud enough for the guy to hear, "You're doing a great job."

I look up at him, but his eyes are on the register in front of me, so I look away quick to see the guy rolling his eyes. I offer him a plastic bag, but he lifts his chin, grabs the records, and stomps toward the door.

As soon as he's gone, I expect Oliver to say something, whether in the defense of customers in general or in criticism of the guy that just left, but he doesn't. He just walks around me, back into the stockroom. I follow him in and take a seat on the floor.

Without a word, he hands me the sticker gun. I take it, and we go back to work, silently.

OLIVER

IT'S HARD FOR me to go back to stocking after dealing with that asshat. Brooke always says that I would be great in customer service if only it weren't for all the customers. But I can be cheerful when I need to be. I can smile at a customer and convince them that they're the most important person on the planet if I have to. But I don't like it. Especially not when pigheaded douche canoes come in and talk to my coworkers like they're idiots.

But the new girl doesn't seem too discouraged by the whole thing. She's beside me in the stockroom, smelling like strawberries and humming along with the music like nothing happened.

She's definitely going to be better at the whole customer service thing than I am.

We work in silence for more than an hour, only occasionally having to stop to check out customers, which I almost exclusively let her handle, since she's so much better at fake smiling than I am.

Later, she takes a box of records that I've priced out to the register just as Brooke comes out of the office and leans against the stockroom doorway. I can see Amy behind her, her fingers moving quickly over the keyboard of one of the computers, shifting the CDs and tapes from regular inventory to sale inventory. I didn't even show her how to do that. She just knows.

"Hey," Brooke says, taking a bite of a granola bar. "Didn't you tour Missouri Baptist today?"

At the front desk, I hear Amy's tapping come to a halt. Brooke has shifted so I can't see Amy, but I know she's listening. She asked what school I was going to earlier, but I deflected, for obvious reasons.

I widen my eyes at Brooke, hoping that maybe she'll get the hint. I'm not talking about Missouri Baptist or anything else like that in front of the new girl, so she should probably just stop talking now.

Brooke widens her eyes right back and looks over her shoulder at Amy, who I hear immediately start typing again. Brooke glances back at me and then turns fully to face Amy. "You know what?" she says, so casually it's almost impressive. "Why don't you go ahead and head out? It's almost closing time, and you've had a great first day."

Amy looks over at us, her eyes innocent. "Are you sure? This box still needs to go into the computer, and—"

"Leave it for tomorrow. You're all done." Brooke smiles, like she's doing Amy a favor, when I know she just really wants Amy out of our hair. Feeling guilty, I focus on the box in front of me. I didn't mean for Brooke to kick her out just so we could talk about the one subject I absolutely don't want to talk about.

Amy smiles, big, and I realize that all this time, her smiles have been genuine, and this is the fake one. "Okay, great. I'll just clock out."

Amy disappears inside Brooke's office, and Brooke turns back to me. "Dear God, it's like I shot her."

I shrug.

And then Amy is walking out the front door with her purse slung over her shoulder, and I'm watching her go because it's like watching an alien, this person who doesn't really click into place here. But then I feel bad because I've never felt 100 percent like I click into place anywhere *but* here.

Brooke counts the money in the drawer while I report damages for the day. There aren't many, just a few CDs that a customer dropped and then accidentally stepped on, cracking the cases.

We both work in silence, but every few minutes, I see Brooke glance at me out of the corner of her eye. She writes something down and then turns her entire body toward me. "You don't like the new girl, do you?"

My hand freezes on the paper, the tip of my pen still pressed down. "Why do you say that?"

She shrugs and runs a hand down the side of her head that's shaved. "You're quiet around her."

"I'm quiet around everybody." I don't much like people, a fact that Brooke knows perfectly well.

Brooke is quiet. She stands with her hip pressed to the counter and her arms crossed until I stop writing and look at her. She won't let it go.

"There's something about her that makes me feel like . . ." I trail off, not really able to explain it.

Brooke makes a waving motion to tell me to go on. "That makes you feel what?"

I sigh. "Like she's judging me."

Brooke laughs. "Oh, come on, Oliver. She's not judging you. She was perfectly nice to you her whole shift."

I shrug. "I feel like she's sizing me up every time she looks at me."

"That's because you're a foot taller than her."

"Har, har."

She smiles, something that doesn't happen particularly often, but Brooke and I are easy around each other. "Is that why you clammed up when I mentioned MBU in front of her?"

I roll my eyes and go back to the damages. "I'm not talking about this."

She throws her hands in the air. "What? I didn't say anything!"

I ignore her and keep writing. I've never come out and told Brooke that I don't want to go to college, but I'm sure she's figured it out, seeing as how I haven't made any movements to try to downgrade my hours to make room for classes. If anything, I've been asking for a fuller schedule. If it were up to me, I would work open to close every day. Actually, if it were up to me, I would probably live here.

"You don't have to say anything. It's all over your face. What, you have some sort of special attachment to Missouri Baptist?"

She just shakes her head. "I was just curious about whether or not you've decided where you're going, that's all. Can't I care about you?"

I stop writing again. This isn't about her caring about me. It's about her trying to get me to admit to something. "No," I finally say, just to get her off my back. "I haven't decided yet."

Brooke shrugs. "Okay. Well, I'm rooting for you, Oli. You can go once you've cleaned up the floor. I'll stay and do everything else."

I glance out at the perfectly arranged and organized sales floor. "Um, your new girl already took care of everything."

Brooke glances up with only her eyes. "Shit. I like her."

I ignore her comment and reach into her office to snatch my car keys off the hook by the door and my jacket off the coatrack. "I'll see you tomorrow, okay?"

I'm putting my jacket on when she says, "Hey, if you need to switch a shift so you can go visit some more campuses, let me know."

I just nod at her. I don't know how, but I have to get out of the college visits that Mom is constantly signing me up for. They're just confusing me even more.

When I start my car, Sleeping at Last comes out of the speakers, and I remember it playing tonight while I worked in the stockroom, when I looked up at Amy and caught her watching me.

AMY

IT'S FAMILY DINNER on Sunday.

Family dinner isn't just us—me, Mama, Carlos, Gabriella, Marisa, Javier, and Hector—an already big family. It also includes my aunts, uncles, and cousins, so many of us that we have to cram into the house. Normally, Jackson would be here, but he's hanging out with the track guys tonight.

By the time I've changed into something I know Abuela will approve of and get out to the kitchen, it's packed with family members. Once a month, everyone in my family shows up at our house (the biggest house in the family) and we feast and talk, and usually, I sit somewhere in the middle of the table and try to avoid eye contact so that no one will ask me about school or my love life or anything else I'm loathe to talk about with my family.

Tonight, like most family dinners, I can't escape it.

"How's school, Amaría?" Tía Marci asks. "Made valedictorian

yet?" She asks this absently, just barely paying attention as she passes a plate of Abuela's famous tamales over to the kids table for them to gobble up.

From the kids table, Gabriella asks, "What's a val-dic-toran?"

"It means your big sister is a genius!" Tío Milo calls back, and everyone at the table except me laughs. In my family, I am something akin to a tower of cards: You know you probably won't build it to the top, and it's only fun if the whole thing collapses at some point. To them, Stanford is about as believable as me moving to Antarctica.

Abuela scowls at me. "You better not get pregnant and have to drop out of college like Rosa did."

From the end of the table, my cousin Rosa groans. "I didn't drop out. It's not considered dropping out if you never made it to the first day." She smiles at me, as if we're comrades in this fact, and scoops Mia, her daughter, into her arms to carry her out of the room, probably to change the diaper I can smell from the other side of the table.

"I'm not going to get pregnant and drop out," I say to no one in particular.

"Well not with that attitude, you aren't," Tía Lucia says, winking at me.

"Isn't it hard to get valedictorian?" Carmen, one of my other cousins, pipes up. Carmen went to my high school last year and graduated the year before me, even though no one knew we were cousins, because we never told anyone. She was perfectly fine leaving me to be the social outcast at school while she ran with the soccer girls.

"Yes," I say. My voice has gotten quieter as their questioning has progressed, and I hate that they can turn me into this, a person who wilts before them.

"But when do you hear about the school in California?" Abuela asks. "I asked one of the ladies at the bingo hall, and she said that Stanford only has a five percent acceptance rate! Five!"

Tía Lucia's eyes go wide. "Five percent? Amaría, why aren't you just going to UMKC? It's so close, and the acceptance rate is so high!"

I'm staring down at my plate, at the pork chop that's sitting undisturbed on the ceramic. "I find out sometime in April," I say quietly, because it's not like anyone is listening.

"How are you even going to pay for out-of-state tuition?" Tío Milo asks. "You know that's, like, a lot of money right?"

No, I want to say. *I have no clue how expensive it is to go to one of the best schools in the country.* I haven't told any of them about the scholarship, mostly because I'm afraid I'll fail. I'm afraid I won't get it. And I don't need them knowing about one more failure if I don't end up making valedictorian or getting into Stanford. It's bad enough that my parents know.

My parents are noticeably silent as my family continues to throw unanswerable questions at me.

"You have a backup, though, right?"

"Are your grades really good enough to make valedictorian?"

"What about your boyfriend? Is he going to Stanford, too?"

But I'm not listening to any of their questions because I already have all my own doubts, and I don't need to hear theirs, too.

AMY

"OLIVER! AMY! Back door!"

I sigh and roll my eyes, but when I look over at Oliver, hoping that he'll commiserate with me over Brooke's annoying shouting, he isn't looking at me. Or at least, I don't think he is. Today's discount stipulation is eyewear, and I can't see Oliver's eyes behind his "Tom Cruise in *Risky Business*" sunglasses.

My sunglasses are pink, heart-shaped, and just a little too small as they belong to Gabriella.

I have learned exactly two things in my first few weeks at Spirits: One, Brooke is a grumpy individual who seems to like me; and two, Oliver is a grumpy individual who seems to hate me.

Where Brooke trusts me and gives me challenges to help me learn the ropes quickly, Oliver likes to pretend I don't exist, and if I have to ask him for help, he often does so silently. He hasn't spoken a word to me since my first day.

Brooke stands by the open back door of the shop, her arms crossed and her eyes on a van parked in the alley. She's talking to the owner of the van in quiet tones when Oliver and I join her. "He's got a load of vinyl in the back. Haul them in and sort them, please."

The guy looks rather pleased with himself, and I follow Oliver as he goes to wait by the guy's trunk. I haven't actually dealt with a customer bringing in used merchandise, and I don't know what to do. So, I just do what I always do: I follow Oliver.

When the door finally opens all the way, Oliver lets out a low whistle. The entire back end of the van is crammed with boxes. "That's a lot of music," he says, probably to himself, but I feel a little satisfaction that he's spoken in my presence at all. He rolls up his sleeves and leans forward to pull a box from the van. He loads it onto the dolly, and I scramble to help him.

It takes half an hour just to get all the boxes into the back room, and then we stand in the little stockroom, surrounded by shelves and merchandise. When Oliver finally closes the door behind us, plunging us into silence, I feel a little nervous. I've never been alone with Oliver, not like this, and it feels like a test, somehow. Like I'm getting one shot, and I better not blow it.

We open the boxes one by one, removing record after record, some of them dusty and all of them in less-than-perfect shape. We try not to trip over each other, but occasionally, in all our dancing around to get to our specific shelves, sorting the records first by genre and then alphabetically, my shoulder finds his breastbone or my elbow finds his rib cage.

"Sorry. I'm sorry," I say for the tenth time.

His mouth is a straight line. "It's fine. You don't have to keep apologizing."

"Right. Sorry." I roll my eyes at myself and set another record on a shelf. I'm not sure why there's no speaker system in the stockroom, but there's no music back here, only the sounds of our breathing and the soft hiss as cardboard covers slide against each other. We could open the door to hear the music in the shop, but for some reason, neither of us has.

I glance over at the box he's sorting through. My box is filled mostly with traditional country western music and Broadway soundtracks, but he has a whole stack of dusty Beatles records in his hand.

When he reaches down into the box again, my eyes catch a glimpse of a tattoo on the inside of his arm. I can tell that it's words, can make out the cursive script, but I can't read what it says while he's moving. I grab a handful of records and walk to his other side, pretending to look through the stack while trying to read the words on his arm, which is easy to be subtle about thanks to the sunglasses. He stops moving momentarily, and I finally get a good look.

the things that we have right now are the best things that we've had yet

"Is that 'Molly'?"

Oliver's head comes up, and he turns toward the door, his brow furrowed. "Who's Molly?" he asks.

I point at his tattoo, hidden again by the sleeve of his shirt. "On your arm. That's 'Molly,' isn't it?"

His head turns toward me, and I feel like he's probably looking at me, even though I can't tell, and the longer he stands there like that, the more nervous I become, until I'm on the verge of twitching. I was very clearly wrong about the tattoo. "I'm sorry. I must have read it wrong."

"You know the Front Bottoms?"

I look up at him. He still wears that bewildered expression, and I'm almost not even sure he really asked the question.

But he waits. I shrug. I still have a stack of Brooks & Dunn albums in my hand. "Sure. I'm actually surprised you know it. 'Molly' was only on their first EP. I never hear anyone mention it."

"It's my favorite." He says it almost like a question, and something about the tone of his voice, the way it seems to make the entire rest of him soften, makes me smile.

"Mine, too. I mean, it would be great if their band wasn't named after the female genitalia, but, you know, what are ya gonna do, right?"

He's still staring at me, and I know for sure this time, because he's reached up and pushed his sunglasses onto his head, and then the door opens and Brooke sticks her head in.

"Amy, could you help me up front?"

I step around Oliver to get to Brooke, and just before I close the door, I shoot a look over my shoulder at Oliver, who's still standing in the middle of the room, looking at me like I'm a completely different species.

OLIVER

I INADVERTENTLY WATCH Amy for the rest of my shift, even when Brooke moves me out to the floor with Morgan and I can only see Amy through the open stockroom door. I'm not trying to be skeevy, but I feel like I'm seeing her completely different now. It's not just that she knows my favorite song by my favorite band, and well enough that she recognized an obscure line from it that I just happened to have tattooed on me.

I guess, more than anything, it's this knowledge that I misjudged her, and somehow, she seems more like a stranger than she did before.

So, later, when she grabs her stuff from Brooke's office and comes back out swinging her bag in that overly cheerful way that she does, with her heart-shaped sunglasses still on, even though it's dark outside, I can't seem to take my eyes off her.

"So, I guess I was just wondering what you thought about the idea?"

And then I realize that Morgan is talking to me, and that I have absolutely no idea what she said. I tear my eyes from Amy and look down at her. Morgan has been working here for almost a year, but I don't know her very well. Mostly because I don't know anyone very well.

"I'm sorry, what idea?"

Morgan, who's going through the hold shelf to pull out anything that's been sitting longer than the three-day limit, looks up at me, and I'm thankful when she doesn't look annoyed that I wasn't paying attention.

"Karaoke night. I'm thinking about pitching it to Brooke. Like, sing karaoke and get twenty percent off. We could do it next month. I totally have a karaoke machine."

"Oh, uh." The idea of having to listen to customers sing karaoke all night makes me want to gouge my eyes out. "Sure. I mean, if Brooke thinks it's a good idea." I send Brooke a telepathic message to convey how awful something like karaoke night would be for all of us, but especially for me.

My eyes slide back to the front door, and I realize that Amy is still standing there. In her blue jeans and her black coat and those heart-shaped sunglasses, she stands on the sidewalk right outside the shop, glowing just slightly red from the sign that hangs above the door.

But she's not alone. She's talking to someone.

She's taken her sunglasses off now, and they dangle from her index finger as she angles her chin to look up at the guy she's with. *Is that her boyfriend?* Amy is looking at him in this timid way, like she's unsure of something as the guy speaks to her, his mouth moving quickly. But then she smiles down at the pavement, and the guy steps forward to put his hands on her shoulders.

"Do you think I should talk to her about it now?" I hear Morgan ask me this, but I can't bring myself to look away from what's going on outside the window.

"Oliver?"

"Yeah." I turn to look down at Morgan. She's not as short as Amy, but she's shorter than I am by quite a few inches. "Sure. I think Brooke is mopping the bathroom. You could go talk to her about it."

Morgan bites her lip and nods. She walks around me. Just when

I think she's gone, and I've turned my attention back to where Amy and that guy are still by the door, this time with his face low beside hers, maybe whispering something in her ear, I hear Morgan's voice from behind me. "Maybe we can do a duet or something."

For a second, I stare straight ahead, thinking maybe I heard her wrong. But then I look over my shoulder, and I see that Morgan is actually blushing, like she's embarrassed that she said anything at all. She shrugs. "You know, we've been working together for a long time, but I don't really hear you sing or anything."

I blink at her. "I don't sing." Mostly because I find the idea of singing in front of people to be absolutely appalling, but also because I have a terrible singing voice.

She seems to think this is funny or cute or something because she winks at me. "Okay, Oliver." That's all she says, and then she smiles and turns away from me, vanishing in the direction of the back hallway, where the bathrooms are.

When I turn back around, Amy and the guy are gone.

AMY

I'M ON MY break Tuesday night, trying to fit in some calculus homework, when Oliver walks into the office and finds me at Brooke's desk. It wouldn't be entirely accurate to say that Oliver hasn't spoken to me since that night we worked together in the stockroom, but we definitely haven't had any meaningful conversations since then, and as far as I can tell, he still hates me, our mutual love for the Front Bottoms aside.

"Sorry," he mutters, the door still open behind him. "Didn't mean to interrupt." He turns to leave, but for some reason, this weird desire that I've been harboring to get Oliver to like me, or to at least tolerate me, makes me stop him.

"You don't have to go. I'm just doing homework. Stay."

The office at Spirits isn't big, but it's the closest thing the shop has to a break room, so even though there's barely enough room for the two of us and Brooke's desk, Oliver comes into the room, shuts the door, and drops down into the metal folding chair that's pressed against the back wall.

I go back to my homework. When I feel brave enough to glance over my shoulder, I see that he's playing a game on his phone. I turn back around quick. I'm supposed to be working on this test review for our exam next week, but it isn't helping me figure anything out other than that I really hate calculus.

When I get the wrong answer for the fourth time on a problem, I look at my cell phone, sitting on the desk beside me, considering. Petra gave me her phone number almost a year ago, when we were both studying our faces off for the SATs. When you're trying to get a high score on the SATs, you use every resource you have, even if that resource hates your guts. I haven't used her number since September, after the SATs, when I promised I'd never use it again. And here I am, turning on my screen, scrolling through my contacts, clicking on her name . . .

"What are you working on?" Oliver asks.

I'm so shocked to hear his voice that my phone clatters to the desk. "Just some calculus homework." I don't turn around to see his expression, but when he doesn't say anything, I go on. "I keep doing the same problem over and over but my answer never comes out to the answer on the solutions list. I guess I'm just . . ." *Distracted*, I think. But I don't say it.

I can't stop thinking about yesterday. About Jackson coming to see me after work, driving me to his place. He made me dinner and held me while we watched a movie and kissed me on the couch until we heard his parents' keys in the lock, and even though I knew I should have been doing this stupid calculus homework instead of messing around with Jackson, I ignored it.

And now, here I am, completely unable to focus on said calculus because Jackson is all I can think about.

I hear the chair behind me squeak and then Oliver hovers over me. Before I can even really process what he's doing, he leans down, his face close to mine, and I feel the press of his thumb against my spine as he holds on to the back of my chair. I can't help but glance up at his face, but he's not looking at me. His eyes sweep over my paper, taking it all in with such concentration that it's almost like he's not even here with me at all.

"Problem's right here," he says, stabbing his finger at the paper. Without asking, he gently takes the pencil from my hand and erases what I have on the page, and then, like he's done it a million times, he writes in the correct formula, solves it, and hands the pencil back to me. The solution matches the one on the review, and I look up at him as he sits back down.

It isn't that I've been under the impression that Oliver is stupid. But when he said he wasn't in school, I just assumed that it's because he thinks school is a waste of time. The guy slouches around, silent as the grave, his head down, his shoulders slumped, all the time. And well, he looks like a slacker.

I'm not the kind of girl to give into idiotic stereotypes. I want to smack myself.

I wait an appropriate amount of time, copy the formula he set up for me, and then ask, "So, you're not in school?" It doesn't matter, not really. But I'm curious anyway. I heard what Brooke said the other day, about Oliver touring MBU.

"No."

That's it. Just no. No explanation. I'm not sure what I was expecting. Just as I'm about to go back to my review, maybe finally give up on trying to make any kind of a connection with him, he says, "Where are you going?"

I glance over my shoulder at him. He blinks at me. How can he have a face so devoid of expression?

"I applied to Stanford."

A beat of silence. "Wow."

There's something about the way he says *that*, too, something that tells me maybe he isn't all that impressed.

"Is that stupid?" What is it about Oliver that makes me feel like I should be trying to get his approval all the time? What do I care if he thinks my plans are stupid? This has been my dream since eighth grade, when we had to create a brochure for a school of our choice, and I, of course, chose Stanford.

But he shakes his head, his eyes going back to his phone. "No. California's just far away. I think that's pretty brave. Leaving home like that."

I laugh, more breath than anything else. "Well, I live in a tiny house with my parents and four siblings, so the farther the better."

His eyebrows pull in. "Your real problem is this music." I'm thrown, momentarily, by his change of subject. He gestures toward my phone, sitting on the desk beside me. I've been listening to Pvris since my break started.

"What's wrong with it?"

"There are all kinds of studies that show that this kind of music will scramble your brains while you're trying to focus."

He reaches out for my phone, but I put a hand over it. Is he seriously going to come in here and try to change my music? No one changes my music. "It helps me concentrate."

"No, it doesn't. Trust me." He grabs the one edge of my phone that isn't covered by my hand, and even though he's given me absolutely no reason to trust him, I let him slip the phone out from under my palm.

He clicks around on my Spotify app, backing out of my favorite playlist and searching for something else instead. He finally decides on something, and soft piano chords filter out of the speaker as he sets my phone back down. I recognize the song. The Civil Wars. "Try this. It's better for your brain cells. What do you have to be so angry about anyway?"

At first, I think he's serious, but when I twist in my seat to look at him, he has a little half smile playing on his mouth. It's the first time he's done anything even resembling joking with me. Or smiling. And that need for his approval dissolves into something more pressing. I want to be Oliver's friend.

But like he knows what I'm thinking, he stands up and opens the door. Just before he steps out, he turns back to me. "Did you know there's a tutoring center across the street? I bet they could help you with that calculus."

I sigh and stare at the closed door, and then after a moment, let my head fall to the desk and listen to the song Oliver chose.

AMY

I'VE ALWAYS BEEN proud of my spot as vice president of the student council. Partly because it looks good on my Stanford application, not to mention my application for the Keller Scholarship, but also because it's always made me feel like I'm doing something for this school.

Maybe I don't go to the Homecoming dances, but I've always been one of the people who help prepare for them. I may never get nominated for prom queen, but I'll be the one to design the ballots.

The biggest downside, of course, is that the president of the student council is none other than Petra Johnson herself, and today, ballot counting day for the prom theme, I'm not feeling too proud of being stuck with Petra.

Add on top of everything else, I have to be out of here soon if I want to make it to my shift at Spirits on time, and I'm feeling pretty antsy.

I've been thinking about Spirits all day, realizing slowly, like a cold coming on over multiple days, that Spirits has become the highlight of my week, and being here, in the middle of the chem lab, trying to focus on ballot counting, is a form of psychological torture.

I don't realize I'm causing the table to shake until Petra reaches over and puts a hand down hard on my leg, effectively making my knee stop bouncing and also making me lose count.

"Dammit," I say, tossing down the stack of ballots I was counting.

"Did you start using?" Petra asks, bending over and looking into my eyes, like I just might be hopped up on something right this second. "Because you know people claim those drugs help you focus, but I swear, it's a downward spiral."

I roll my eyes and start counting again without answering her question. When I'm done with my stack, I jot down the number on the clipboard beside me. "I'm just anxious about getting to work, so can you shut up so I can count?"

Petra nods, and I get side-eye anyway.

I slap my stack of ballots in front of her. "My stack says underwater theme. See you later!" I've already got my bag in my hand, and I'm at the door of the chem lab when Jackson appears in the doorway, and I almost run into him.

"Can we talk?" His gaze goes over my head, and I turn to see Petra's eyes glued to us, her hands frozen with the ballots in them. She doesn't even pretend she's not watching us.

"Yeah, come on," I say, taking Jackson's hand, and getting that same thrill in my stomach that I have every time I've touched Jackson for the past eleven months, like there are sparks going off under my skin.

When we're farther down the empty hallway, and I'm trying not to think about the fact that I'm *definitely* going to be late to Spirits now, Jackson stops me and says, "So, I've been thinking . . ."

"Me, too," I interrupt him. "So, don't tell anyone because we're not announcing it until Friday, but the prom theme is officially 'Under the Sea,' so I'm thinking an aquamarine dress to match an aquamarine tuxedo vest. What do you think?"

"I think we should take a break."

Everything comes to a screeching halt.

Jackson's eyes go over my head again, and I recognize the way he's fidgeting, like he's nervous, which makes me nervous, because he's serious about this. "Ames, I love you so much, but you've been so different these past few weeks. All you can talk about is Stanford and valedictorian, and it's just too much stress for me right now. I know you have a lot to worry about, but this is senior year, and I just feel like we're not having fun like we're supposed to."

"But . . . but I was just—"

I was going to say that I was just talking about what we're going to wear to prom, and how can we be taking a break, because we're going to prom together, and Jackson and I have been together for almost a year, and how can he even be saying something like this? Weren't we *just* curled up on his couch, making out and laughing and being completely in love?

But he goes on. "I know you're working hard, but that's the problem. You're so busy with everything you're trying to do that it's like I'm not even here. I barely see you, and when I do see you, you're so distracted."

"What about the other night?" I keep coming back to it, how good things were, how happy we were.

Jackson shrugs. "It was great. But one good night every few months isn't enough."

I feel my chin trembling now, and my mind is going to all these weird places, and all I can think about is how Jackson's birthday is this Friday. "What about your birthday?"

Jackson's eyes get this sad tilt to them, and he looks like he's about to smile, but he just sighs and says, "Maybe you can sit this one out, okay? Look, maybe once things have settled down, we can reevaluate, but right now, you should focus on school, and I'll focus on track, and we'll just take it one day at a time."

A tear finally makes its way down my cheek, and without even hesitating, Jackson wipes it away. He kisses me, soft and gentle, and then walks away, and I'm left standing in the hallway, trying to figure out what the hell just happened.

OLIVER

AMY IS LATE for her shift, and I feel a weird kind of mixture of anxiety and frustration. Brooke thinks I hate Amy, so she always makes Amy shadow me, even though she's way past the training point. She's already been working at the shop for almost a month. I thought it would bother me, but Amy has a weird kind of energy that I like. She's focused and determined and she gives a shit about everything she does.

Or at least I thought she did. Tonight, she's supposed to be helping me get the rest of these records put into the system, but instead I'm doing it by myself and only mildly seething because I really thought I pegged her wrong, but now she's almost an hour late, and that's just so annoying and—

"Sorry I'm late!" Amy stops at the end of the counter, right beside the computer I'm using to catalog. She's huffing and puffing, and she's also holding a pair of slide-on house shoes in her hand that have koala bears on them, and all this is almost enough to distract me from the fact that she's clearly been crying, but not quite. Her nose is red and her eye makeup just a little goopy and her cheeks splotchy.

She swallows. "I, um, had to stay late for this whole prom thing and then, um, and then . . ." She trails off and clears her throat before saying, "I forgot that it was wacky shoe night, so I had to rush by my house on the way here, and then all I had were these house shoes, so I grabbed them but . . ."

Her eyes have wandered down to my own feet. They widen. "Are you wearing . . . ?" But before she can finish her sentence, she's started laughing.

I look down at the cowboy boots I borrowed from Marshal, our weekends-only cashier, last week, and even though they're definitely not something I would have picked out for myself, I don't think they're *that* funny. But Amy has her head thrown back, and seeing her like that, laughing up at the ceiling, makes me smile.

After a second, I roll my eyes and focus back on the computer. "Just go clock in."

She's suppressed her laughter by pressing her fingertips to her mouth, and she just nods before vanishing into Brooke's office, and I forget what I was even upset about.

When Amy comes back, we create an assembly line behind the counter. I'm printing barcodes while Amy sits at my feet, wearing her koala shoes, sticking the barcodes onto the corresponding records. We work in silence, the way we always do.

"Hallelujah" is playing over the speaker system, the Jeff Buckley version, and I follow along with the lyrics in my head as a girl in Crocs designed to look like watermelons walks by the counter.

"God, I love this song." I don't even really intend for Amy to hear me, but she cranes her neck to look up at me. There's already such a big height difference between the two of us that now that she's sitting on the floor, she's bending back far enough that she looks like she's stargazing. Her face twists into a confused expression. "Are you serious?"

"You don't like it?"

She rolls her eyes. She *actually* rolls her eyes. "Loving 'Hallelujah' is such a cliché."

I rip the next price sticker from the machine, but when she reaches up for it, I don't hand it down to her. She wiggles her fingers, but when I still don't hand her the sticker, she sighs and drops her hand.

"You dare blaspheme the work of Leonard Cohen?"

She shrugs. "Isn't 'Hallelujah' everyone's favorite song? It's so unoriginal."

I scoff at her. "No. That's the problem. It *should* be everyone's favorite song."

Her eyes settle straight ahead on the hold shelf. "It's so repetitive."

"That's where the beauty is, Amy."

She blinks at me, and I think maybe it's because I called her by her name. I can't remember ever having done that before. "That's where the flaw is," she finally says.

She looks up at me, and I look down at her, and I feel a weird warmth flood into my stomach. I hand her the sticker. I'm watching her peel it off my index finger when I hear someone call my name. I recognize Mom's voice before I even look up, but a part of me hopes it isn't really her. Maybe just someone who sounds exactly like her.

But when I turn to look over my shoulder, I see her rushing through the shop, cutting through the line that's forming at the register, and making her way toward me in her blue scrubs. She smiles big, her brown curly hair flowing behind her as she comes over.

"Hi, sweetie," she says when she gets to me. She puts a brown paper sack down on the counter between us. "You forgot your dinner, and I didn't want you to get hungry." She smiles so big. Mom has impressively large gums, which in turn make her seem like she has big teeth, which in turn gives her the biggest smile you've ever seen.

I don't look down at Amy to see if she's looking at Mom. Of course, she is. I think everyone is looking at Mom, and she's not even wearing weird shoes, just her orthopedic ones.

"Thanks, Mom," I say quietly, taking my brown paper sack, which just has a peanut butter sandwich and a baggie full of sliced apples.

Mom opens her mouth to say something, but then her eyes travel over my shoulder, and I can only assume that Amy has stood up. "Oh," Mom squeaks. "Hello. Are you new?" Her eyes shoot back to me, and then she gives that giant smile again.

"I'm Amy," Amy says, stepping up to the counter. "I started a few weeks ago."

Mom's smile gets bigger, if that's even possible. "Well, Amy, it's wonderful to meet you." Her eyes shoot back to me, and her smile loses some of its excellence. "Honey, I have to get to work, but I just wanted to make sure you got your application for MBU in? Because the deadline is coming up quick. Remember I told you that you needed to go ahead and get it in before the weekend. Don't wait until the last minute."

I can feel Amy's eyes boring into me, can feel my skin going red the way it does when I'm even slightly compromised, can feel the lie rising up in my throat. "Yeah, Mom. I sent it this morning."

Mom's smile is blinding. "Oh good. Awesome. Well, I'm working until six. Call me if there's an emergency." Mom sends Amy a little wave. "Nice to meet you, Amy. Love you, Oli."

I wait until Mom is firmly on the sidewalk before turning back to the computer. I don't look at Amy, but I can feel her beside me. I can feel her eyes. She doesn't take her seat again, but instead, presses her hip into the counter and looks up at me.

"You're applying to Missouri Baptist?"

I shrug. That's as good as an answer, right? She already knew I was touring the campus, thanks to Brooke and her big mouth.

"My boyfriend's older brother goes there. Maybe you guys would get along."

I keep my fingers moving on the keyboard, make sure I don't give away that that word, *boyfriend*, makes my stomach feel twisty. God, what the hell do I even care if she has a boyfriend or not? It's not like I didn't see them together.

She sits back down at my feet, and once she's settled, she smiles up at me.

It's not like I like her or anything.

I clear my throat. "Where's your boyfriend going, if you're going to Stanford?"

She doesn't reply for the amount of time it takes to scan three records into the system, and when I look down at her, she's staring straight ahead, looking a little dazed.

"Amy?"

She jerks and looks up at me, her eyes glassy. "Yeah? Oh, um. He hasn't decided yet." She tilts her head back until it's resting against the wood of the shelf behind her. "Who knows, maybe he'll go to Missouri Baptist, and the two of you will be friends."

Over my dead body.

AMY

I cried all the way to work, but it doesn't really hit me until I get home. Almost everyone is already in bed, and the house is completely silent, which means that even though I can feel everything—all the stuff I've been forcing down all night at work—rising up inside me, I can't just sit down on the couch and cry, because my mother, so accustomed to listening for the noises of her children getting up in the middle of the night, will hear me. And she'll want to comfort me. She always does.

So, I do what I do when I want to cry. I get in the shower.

Our shower is really loud, and you can't hear much over the sound of the water. So once it's going, I curl up on the bottom of the tub, wrap my arms around myself, and cry. I can't stop hearing all the words that Jackson said over and over in my head.

For so long, my drive was the thing that Jackson liked most about me. But now, it's too much for him. And now we're months from graduation, and he wants to change his mind. What does that even mean for us in the future? Are we completely done? By "take a break" does he mean "break up"?

Either way, it stings.

It stings because I thought Jackson loved me, the real me, the me that follows the rules and stays in on Friday to get ahead on homework and is working damn hard to have a real future that doesn't involve this house and all my siblings and working full-time at J-Mart instead of going to the school of my dreams.

I cry until my fingers are wrinkled like prunes and the water has gone cold, and then I hiccup while I wrap a towel around myself.

But when I open the door, my mother is sitting on the little bench in the hallway, looking at me. She doesn't say anything, just opens her arms, and I sigh as I walk to her and let her hold me.

OLIVER

AFTER WORK, I sit in front of my computer with the online application for Missouri Baptist University up on the screen. I've been staring at it for so long that I'm pretty sure I just saw the first rays of the sun outside my window.

I've typed my name, but that's it. I couldn't even bring myself to type in our apartment number, because I get a sick feeling in my stomach every time I bring myself to look back at the screen.

Because I don't want to go to Missouri Baptist University.

And I don't want to go to University of Missouri-Kansas City.

Or Rockhurst.

Or Avila.

Or any of them.

It's not that I think college is a bad idea.

I just think college is a bad idea *for me.*

Because the more time I spend at Spirits, the more I'm pretty sure *that* is what I want to do. I want to have debates with Brooke about whether or not jazz counts as classical music and wear stupid clothes so that customers can have discounts and listen to Amy talk shit about my favorite song. I want to own my own record store, and why would I go to business school when I can learn from Brooke?

I slam my computer closed. Then I gather all the stupid brochures that are lying around my room, all the paperwork on loans and dorm halls and campus tours, and I throw it all in the trash. And then I take the trash out so Mom won't find any of it.

Back in my room, I put *Grace*, Jeff Buckley's iconic album, on my record player. The only good thing Dad ever did was leave me his record player when he moved out, and my walls are filled from floor to ceiling with vinyl for it.

This is the only education I need.

AMY

I'VE KNOWN JACKSON since we both started at East almost four years ago. And since I've known him, he's always done the exact same thing for his birthday. Jackson's best friend, Bryce, throws him a huge party, as his parents are particularly lenient on the party front, and while everyone dances and drinks and hooks up in dark corners, Jackson sits on a homemade throne, wearing a birthday crown. It's juvenile, to say the least, but it's tradition.

I know Jackson said I shouldn't come this year, but by God, I'm going to show up anyway. I don't have any friends, and people at school don't particularly like me. No one wants to be friends with the girl who never goes to the parties; the girl who always follows the instruction sheets step-by-step; the girl who cares more about her academic standing than she does about her social life. But Jackson has always seen the other side of me. The side that loves loud music and bright colors and the feel of a guy's hands on me. Jackson picked me. He loves me. I'm not throwing away what we had.

I wear a dark pair of skintight jeans and a black lacy top that I know Jackson loves, and do my makeup like I'm trying to start a war. I'm the girl he wants, and tonight, I'm going to remind him why.

The party doesn't start until ten, and close to eleven, I pull up in front of Bryce's house. The party is already in full swing, with people shivering outside while bodies move inside the house. No one really seems to notice when I slip in the door. No one ever really notices me, and for the most part, I'm okay with that. Maybe that's one thing Jackson is right about—I don't really have time for people right now. But I can make time for him. I know I can.

Bryce's house is four times the size of the house I share with my family, and Bryce is an only child. What it must be like to not have to share a bathroom with four children under the age of ten, not to mention having parents who would let you throw a rager multiple times a year. The closest we get to ragers in our house is family dinner.

Even though I'm basically invisible among the throngs in the house, I still do my best not to stand out. I hug the walls and duck around groups of people playing beer pong and making out and doing shots. I don't want to approach Jackson too quickly. Now that I'm here, amidst the chaos of something that has always made me nervous and now makes me downright panicked, my plan seems like a terrible one.

Not that I even really have a plan. My only plan is to make Jackson miss me. To make him want me. To make him realize what a mistake he made.

But when I round a corner and spot Jackson's throne pressed against the bottom of the staircase, I start to sweat. I've never been good at seduction, or even flirting. Jackson is the one who asked me out a year ago; the one who held my hand, leaned in for the first kiss, asked me in a breathy voice if I was ready to give him all of me. It was never me.

Well, tonight it could be me.

But I need a second to breathe first. I slip into the kitchen through the swinging door, glad when it's completely silent. There's nothing but the thumping of the bass still coming from the living room, making the empty beer bottles on the counter vibrate.

"Amy?" I spin around to find Bryce standing in the open pantry door, two bags of chips in either hand. "What the hell are you doing here?"

I try to play it cool, like I'm supposed to be here. "Oh, you know. Friday night. It's the night to party."

Bryce's eyes narrow. "You never go out on Friday night."

Damn. I decide to shift focus in hopes that he'll let it drop. "I heard you guys won the basketball game last week. Everyone said it was a good game. I bet you played really well."

Bryce tosses the chips on the counter and rushes toward me. He immediately latches onto my elbow and turns me in the direction of the back door. "Amy, you can't be here. I know Jackson told you not to come, and I don't need your drama fucking up my party."

I dig my heels in. "Wait, wait, wait. Bryce, come on. No drama. I promise. I just need to tell Jackson happy birthday, okay?" I pry his fingers off my arm and am surprised when he lets me. Bryce is almost twice my size and is on the basketball team and the football team. There's no way I could get him to let go unless it was his idea.

"Why didn't you tell him at school?"

I shrug. "I didn't see him." And by that I mean that Jackson has been avoiding me all week.

Bryce's eyes shoot to the kitchen door.

I put up my hands. "I have an economics test to study for anyway. Just let me stay long enough to tell Jackson happy birthday, and then I'll leave. Promise."

Bryce chews on the inside of his cheek. He finally sighs and says, "Okay, fine. But I didn't see you, and for God's sake, don't do anything stupid. Let Jackson enjoy his birthday."

I give him the brightest smile I can muster. "Thanks, Bryce."

He rolls his eyes. "Whatever. I'm only doing this because Jackson has been all bummed out since he dumped you."

I wince at the words "dumped you." Bryce scoops up the bags of chips he abandoned, and I'm alone in the kitchen again.

It takes a second for Jackson to notice me when I emerge from the kitchen. His eyes flit over me as he takes in everyone around him, and then they snap back like elastic. Pride and something hotter stirs in my stomach.

I have to wait before I can approach him. The entire basketball team is draped across the stairs, laughing and screwing around. But they have to leave sometime.

One of them claps Jackson on the shoulder, and he looks away from me to join the conversation. The guy points, and then the entire team disperses, like a flock of birds. Amazing.

I step up to the throne as soon as they're gone and curtsy. "Your Highness."

Jackson's eyebrows crinkle, and his mouth pops open. "Amy."

"I couldn't miss your birthday."

He just stares at me, so long my pulse starts to race. "You shouldn't be here. We broke up."

I tap my finger on the armrest of the dining room chair, right next to his hand. "Aren't we still friends? Can't I still wish you a happy birthday?"

His face goes blank, but I don't wait for him to answer. I'm afraid that he's going to say something I don't want to hear, and I'm not going to give him the chance. Instead, I lean forward and plant my mouth on his.

For half a second, his mouth is still under mine. But like a switch someone flips on, he reaches up, buries his hands in my hair, and kisses me back. His response is so sudden, so unexpected, that I lose my footing, and next thing I know, I'm sitting on his lap, letting him put his tongue in my mouth.

I pull away with a sigh, and for a second, Jackson's eyes meet mine, deep and intense, and I know I've reminded him of how good we can be together.

But still, when he finally speaks, he says, "*Dammit*, Amy." He pushes me off him gently, until I'm standing in front of his throne, feeling suddenly naked in this room of prying eyes.

A few people have already noticed that something is going on, but for the most part, everyone is too busy partying. I feel my face flush when I turn back to Jackson and see him wipe his mouth, like he just did something shameful.

"I'm sorry. I just . . . it's your birthday. I just wanted to—"

"I told you not to come," Jackson says, looking everywhere but in my direction. "I told you I need space."

I feel tears threaten, but I bite them back. "I don't want to be on a break. I just want to be with you."

He sighs, his jaw going hard, and when I glance around, I realize more people are looking. "Ames, you should go home."

"Could we maybe go somewhere and talk?" I'm ashamed at the way it sounds like I'm pleading with him.

And I'm even more ashamed when his eyes settle on me, hard, and he says, "No, Amy. This is my party, and you're not supposed to be here."

I have to look away from him when his voice rises. Jackson doesn't get mad easily, doesn't argue unless he feels like he has to. But he's mad now, and I regret everything. I had this perfect image in my head of how this night would go: I would kiss Jackson, and he would whisk me off to someplace private where we would remind each other how in love we are until the party was completely forgotten about.

No, this is definitely not how I imagined it.

The room has gone quiet now, and I don't notice until it's too late, until everyone is listening, watching us like we're a TV show, their eyes springing back and forth between us. Only now, they're all on me as I struggle to choke back tears. I will not cry in front of all these people.

"You're really breaking up with me, aren't you?"

His jaw moves as he looks down at the floor and then up at me from under his eyelashes. "Yeah. I am. I'm sorry, Amy."

Something inside me cracks, and I am ashamed and embarrassed that so many people are witnessing my utter destruction.

I'm trying to regain the feeling in my legs to walk out of here, away from Jackson, but then I feel something tug at the pocket of my jeans, and I turn to find Bryce with my car keys dangling from his fingers. He tosses the keys to one of his friends, another guy on the basketball team, and then the keys are being tossed from person to person, eventually out of sight. I sigh and turn back to Bryce.

"Come on," I tell him. "Get my keys back."

He just shakes his head and crosses his arms, and I can hear the start of laughter moving through the room. I glance around, hoping I can catch a glimpse of whoever has them. I look at Bryce, ready to make another plea, but he's taken a step toward me, his voice low when he speaks. "I said no drama. You should figure out a ride home." He turns away, disappearing into the throng of people that's gathered around us now.

"Bryce!" I shout. My whole body is shaking. He has to be kidding. He isn't going to make me walk home. It's freezing outside, literally, and my house is miles from here. "You can't just take my keys."

Bryce spins around and leans against the doorjamb beside him. "Yes, I can. You're on my property. Shouldn't have come around, Amy." And then he's gone, and so are my keys. That's not even my car. It's my parents' car, and they're going to kill me when I tell them about this.

My first reaction is to turn back to Jackson. I wait for him to tell his best friend to give me my keys back. I wait for him to offer me a ride. I wait for him to do *something*.

He stands there, looking at me. "Bryce," he says, his eyes flickering over to where Bryce has disappeared in the crowd, but his voice is so quiet, his plea so pathetic, that he might as well have not spoken at all.

I turn and rush through the crowd, pushing against anyone that gets in my way until I can throw open the front door. I rush down the steps, but on the last one, I slip. Ice coats everything now, and I scrape across it, landing in a heap on the snowy front lawn.

OLIVER

"READ 'EM AND weep, fellas," I say, laying the cards in my hand down flat on the table between me, Brooke, and Marshal.

Marshal rolls his eyes. "Dear Lord, what cliché poker film did you just walk out of?"

Brooke snickers, but I just ignore them. They can laugh all they want, but I just won an old Cat Stevens record off Marshal and a Rolling Stones vinyl off Brooke. Overall, a good night.

"You have the best poker face of anyone I've ever met," Marshal says.

Brooke scoffs. "You have no idea, man. Oliver could convince the Pope that God wasn't real. Straight fucking face the whole time. Best bluffer I've ever met."

I scowl at her. "Is that supposed to be a compliment?"

She shrugs. "Sure. Why not?"

"I'm great at bullshitting? That's a compliment?"

She shrugs at me again, and I don't miss the glance she shares with Marshal.

I roll my eyes and put my albums down. "Whose deal is it?"

"Yours." Brooke tosses the deck at me, and I groan when the cards scatter.

"Why do you have to be such a pain in the ass?"

She bites her lip and scoots closer to me. "Oh, Oli. Just admit that you love me. Why else would you have stuck around as long as you have?"

It's true that I love Brooke, the way you would love any boss that you've worked with for three years, the way you love the person who has somehow become your best friend while you weren't paying attention. And of course, the way you love someone who is almost ten years older than you, not romantically interested in someone of your gender, and also a giant pain in the ass.

I don't have a great hand. Two pair.

Marshal shifts and then curses when his elbow smacks into a shelf of CDs, causing them all to clatter to the floor. "Why can't we set up the poker table out there?" he asks, pointing a finger over his shoulder to the open door of the stockroom, out to where the shop lies empty and quiet.

Brooke scoffs. "And let a passing customer see that we're gambling inside our business?"

I snort. "We're playing for vinyl. Not exactly high-stakes poker."

Brooke scans the cards in her hand. "Whatever. When you're in charge of managing your wife's business, you can decide where and when you want to have your poker games. I'm not taking any risks here."

Brooke and her wife, Lauren, used to run the shop together, but now Lauren goes to law school while keeping her title as owner of the place, which her parents left her when they died.

"Well, I don't have any worries then because I'm never getting married."

Brooke laughs. "Oh, give me a break, Oli. You'll meet someone, fall madly in love, and probably marry, to the great disappointment of your parents, just like I did." She says the last part so casually that I honestly believe it doesn't bother her that her parents haven't spoken to her since she married Lauren.

"I'm not the marrying type. Hell, I'm not the relationship type."

Brooke purses her lips and looks at me, her eyes scanning me up and down like she's seeing me for the first time. "Yeah, right. You've got hopeless romantic written all over your sullen attitude."

Completely unbidden, I think about Amy, which I've been trying very firmly not to do. But I can't seem to get her out of my head, and it's only getting worse.

As if he knows exactly what I'm thinking, Marshal pipes up, "What do you guys think about Amy?"

I grind my teeth together and keep my eyes on my cards. I swear to God, if he's about to announce his intention to ask her out . . .

But I guess it doesn't matter, since she has a boyfriend.

"Cute as hell," Brooke says immediately, and I snap my eyes over to her. She thinks Amy is cute? I guess I'm not all that surprised. Amy *is* cute as hell. "But Oli hates her."

I roll my eyes. "I don't hate her. She's just . . ."—*sweet, funny, adorable, smart*—". . . weird."

Brooke smiles at me, but not in a nice way. "She's weird because she's not a brooding piece of work, like you?"

My phone rings. *Saved by the bell.* I pull my phone out of my pocket, fully expecting it to be Mom, calling to let me know that she's home from work, like she always does when she works late into the night.

But it isn't my mom. I sigh.

Brooke nods at my phone. "What's up?"

"It's my dad." I want to not answer. God, I want it. Why does it have to be tonight? Why does it have to be when I'm having fun with my friends? When I'm attempting to have a normal life? Why can't he just stay sober for one weekend?

"Yeah?" I say, pressing my phone to my ear.

"He doesn't like his dad?" I hear Marshal whisper to Brooke at the same time that I hear a familiar voice in my ear.

"Hey, Oliver. It's Carson. Come get your dad, please. He hasn't passed out yet, but he's gettin' close. Barfed on a guy's shoes already." Carson is the bartender at my dad's favorite bar, the one he passes out in with the most regularity.

"Yeah, okay. I'll be there as soon as I can."

Brooke is frowning by the time I hang up. "You have to go?" she asks.

I shrug. "Can't leave him there. Sorry. Here." I toss the CDs I brought from my own collection into the pot and put on my jacket.

"Aren't you here first thing in the morning?" Marshal asks.

"I'm always here," I tell him.

OLIVER

"Need help getting him out to your truck?" Carson asks as I throw my father's arm over my shoulder. He's still conscious, but barely. His eyelids droop but he smiles at me nonetheless.

"Oli, m'boy," he slurs. "You're here. How nice." He draws out the last word so that he sounds like a hissing snake, and he's spitting on me.

"Dammit, Dad. Stop." He smells like cheap whiskey, and if he keeps it up, I will, too. "Thanks, but I'm good," I tell Carson. I've dragged Dad out of so many bars that I have legitimate biceps from hauling his weight.

Out by my truck, I shift him to one side and open the door to the cab before forcing him up and onto the back seat. He isn't wearing a jacket, and I'm almost certain he left it inside the bar, but there's no way I'm going back in for it. I lay him down on his side, just in case he pukes again, and I'm leaning down over him to make sure he can breathe okay when he burps in my face.

"Dear God," I groan. "Did you drink all the whiskey they had?"

He laughs, a strange gurgling noise in his throat.

"Try not to fall off the seat." I slam the back door shut and sigh, my hands still pressed to the side of my truck. My father's court date is in twelve days. If he gets caught doing something else stupid before he can even answer for the last thing, he's screwed. I text my mom to let her know that I have to take Dad back to Independence. Why the hell can't he drink there instead of the northern side of Kansas City?

I get on Highway 70 and head for Independence. Now that I'm sitting still, with my stereo off and the darkness closing in around us as we move farther from downtown, I'm starting to feel a little groggy myself.

My headlights catch a figure on the side of the road. The closer we get, the better I can see that it's a girl, a girl with long dark hair, walking down the road in skintight jeans and wedge shoes.

I'm not sure if it's the hair or the way she walks or the curve of her hips, but there's something about her that's so familiar that I slow down. From behind, she looks like Amy. And then I realize, it *is* her, and my stomach does a weird jumbled thing.

I'm the only car on the road as it's almost one in the morning, and I pull off a few feet in front of her, hoping I'm not going to scare the shit out of her. What the hell is she doing, walking down the highway in the middle of the night? I look in my rearview mirror and realize that she's stopped walking, her eyes on my truck and her hands balled into fists. Shit. I definitely scared her. I push my door open slowly. I don't want her to think I'm some creep about to attack her.

"Amy?" I call out. I put my hands up in the air, the only way I can think to show her I'm harmless.

There's something about the way her body sags, the way her relief is visible, that makes my stomach flip-flop again. She's relieved to see me.

"Oliver?" she calls out, finally continuing her walk toward me.

"Do you need a ride?" I ask before she's even gotten to me. It's freezing, and even though she's wearing a coat, when she's finally close enough for me to see her face, I can see that her cheeks and nose are red. How long has she been walking out here?

I see her moment of hesitation, and all the warm feelings I got when she seemed relieved to see me vanish. She doesn't trust me. I can see it on her face, the way her eyes flit to my truck and then back to me. And I guess I get it. She doesn't really know me. We've only been working together for a month, and we both know the kind of horrors humans are capable of.

Before I have the chance to reassure her, she smiles at me, showing all her teeth in the shadow of my truck. "That would be nice. Thank you."

"You're not listening to music" is the first thing she says to me when we get in the truck. "That's weird."

Of course, that's her first thought. Any time Amy is on break, she either has music blaring out of the speaker of her phone or has her earbuds in her ears, the music up so loud that she can't hear me trying to get her attention.

I point my thumb over my shoulder. "He doesn't like my music." I almost regret drawing her attention to him, but she's going to figure out he's back there eventually.

Her eyes travel over her shoulder, into the back seat. She blinks. "Is that your—"

"Dad," I finish before she can.

She doesn't ask why my father is passed out on the back seat, but maybe it's obvious. She doesn't say anything, and we ride down the highway to the sound of my tires crunching over the asphalt.

"Where's your car?"

She doesn't answer for a long time, and I realize she hasn't even told me if I'm going in the right direction, where her house is. I guess I'm still driving to Independence.

"It's pathetic and embarrassing," she finally says.

I just wait for her to tell me or not tell me.

"I decided to go to this party tonight because . . ." She pauses.

I think she might not continue, but finally, she does. "Because I wanted to try to show my ex that we still belong together."

Her words do weird things inside my gut. "I thought you had a boyfriend?"

She sighs. "I lied. This week, he told me he wanted to *take a break*, whatever the hell that means. I thought if I went to this party and looked amazing, I could get him back. But he just told me to leave instead, and then I pissed off his best friend, who stole my keys and wouldn't give them back, so I just left without my car. My house isn't that far."

My brain tries to process everything at once, but there's too much information to decipher. She went to a party hoping to get her ex back. I have to push past that part. And then some asshole stole her keys? And she's just going to let him? She's just going to walk home and, what, abandon her car? This person is just going to get away with this?

Yeah, not gonna happen.

I slam on my breaks and do a U-turn on the highway. I hear my father groan behind me at the same time that Amy gasps. "What are you doing?"

"We're going back for your car."

"What?"

I speed back the way we came. "You're going to tell me where this party is, and we're going to get your car."

She's quiet for a second, and when I look over at her, she's worrying her bottom lip with her teeth.

"Okay?" I ask.

She nods, her eyes wide, her body turned toward me in her seat. "He lives in Mission Hills."

"Okay, I'm going to need you to explain a few things to me," I tell her, pressing my foot down even harder on the gas pedal.

"Okay," she says, but I hear the wariness in her voice.

"First, how did someone even get your keys? And second, what were you going to do about your car? Just never go back?"

She settles back in her seat, the seat belt retracting against her body. "Bryce snatched them out of my pocket. I didn't bring anything with me but my keys, so it was an easy grab. And he would have given them back eventually." She's quiet for a beat. "At least, I'm pretty sure he would. Maybe not for a few days. But I could just take the spare from my stepdad."

I clench my jaw. "That's bullshit."

She shrugs. "I'm used to it." She looks down at her hands and rubs them together. They're probably frozen solid.

I reach over and turn the heat up as high as it'll go and shoot her a look. "Why are you used to it?"

She shrugs again. "I've never been Bryce's favorite person. I'm not really anybody's favorite person. When you're the goody-goody who's always a week ahead on all the assignments and never goes to the parties, you're either invisible or a target for humiliation."

"Did you just use the term *goody-goody*?"

She sends me a blank look.

I drum my fingers on the steering wheel. Bullshit, bullshit, bullshit. I never would have pegged her as someone who's used to being bullied. "You always seem so confident."

She sniffs and raises her head, and I swear on every beating heart on this planet that if she's crying because of these asshats, I'm going to rip them apart. When I look over, she's wiping her nose on the back of her hand, but she's using her hair to shield her face, so I can't tell if she's crying or she's just cold.

"I'm going to California soon, and when I get there, none of this will matter." She laughs bitterly. "Jackson and me being together was a fluke anyway. My greatest turn of luck. But he changed his mind, and I guess I can't be all that surprised. He was always way out of my league."

I don't look at her. I don't want her to know how preposterous I think that idea is.

"This is his house right here."

There's nowhere to park in front of the big house, which is perfectly fine by me. I pull halfway down the street, park in front of a house that's completely dark, and pop open my door. "What kind of car do you drive?" I ask Amy, one foot already on the pavement.

Her eyes go wide. "Wait. What?"

I don't wait for her to answer. I slam my door shut and make my way around the front of my truck. She scrambles out of the passenger seat and throws a glance to the back seat. "Is he okay alone here?" she asks.

"He'll be fine. What kind of car do you drive?" I ask again.

She catches up to me halfway up the front lawn.

"Oliver," she says behind me, her voice laced with nerves. "Maybe this is a bad idea."

I stop, my boots sinking a few inches into the fresh snow in the grass. "Do you want your car back?"

She blinks. "It's a Honda Civic."

I nod and head for the front door. The music inside the house is thumping so loud that I feel it rattle all the blood in my veins. I stand in the open doorway and watch as no one notices us. People writhe around, and something about the smell of alcohol in the air makes me irritable. I'm already plenty pissed on Amy's behalf, but I've never been one for parties, so this is particularly frustrating.

Over in the corner of the room, I spy what I'm looking for. On top of a long table runner is an iHome. It's plugged into a huge speaker system by a million cords, and without even thinking about it, I push my way into the room, around the bodies coming at me from every direction. I turn quickly to make sure that Amy is still behind me, but she's frozen by the front door, her hands curled in front of her and her eyes sweeping the room. I pause, wanting to go back and get her, but if I can just make this end for her, get her car back and let her go home, she'll be much happier.

So when I'm close enough, I reach out and rip the iPod from the dock, and the room falls silent. Immediately, people start to look around, trying to figure out what's going on. And on the other side of the room, pressed against the bottom of the stairs, I see a guy sitting on a dining room chair with an honest-to-God crown on his head. I recognize him from the day he stood outside Spirits with Amy, whispering in her ear. I hate him already.

"Hello, everyone!" I shout over the din of people trying to figure out who's hijacked their party. "I'm looking for the shit-stick who stole my friend's car keys. My friend's name is Amy, and she drives a Honda Civic. Sound familiar to anyone?" I keep my eyes on Jackson, who's slowly standing from his throne.

Someone grabs on to my shoulder and spins me around, and I'm looking down at a short, stocky guy in khaki shorts and a polo. His hair is all messed up, and his mouth is all swollen, and I'm a little embarrassed for him.

"You Bryce?"

The guy scowls at me. "Who the hell are you, and what are you doing in my house?"

I put my hands up, but not in a way that would make him think I'm ready to surrender. "I'm just here to get Amy's keys back. Give them to me, and I'll gladly leave."

His eyes shoot to Amy, still standing over by the door, watching us. I don't miss the fact that her ex is looking at her, too.

Bryce nudges me, and I want to punch him. "What are you going to do if I refuse? Beat me up?"

I snort. "Look, I'm not much for fighting. I'd rather just let the cops take care of it. How many underage kids do you think you have crammed in here? How much have *you* had to drink, Bryce?"

He doesn't even blink.

"You seem like a charming guy. You can probably get off with a warning on the whole alcohol thing. But the car? Well, technically, if you stole Amy's keys, you stole the whole car. How much time do you think you'd get in juvie for grand theft auto? Oh, wait. Are you eighteen? Make that jail." I don't know if any of this is true, but it sounds legit, and it's putting traces of fear in Bryce's eyes, so I go with it.

But then Bryce makes a kind of horse noise with his big lips. "They're not gonna put me in jail for taking her car keys."

"You willing to risk it?"

He blinks up at me, and the fear is back. Chances are good that if the cops show up, they'll just ask Bryce to give Amy her keys, tip their hats, and move on. But a coward like Bryce isn't about to chance that we might catch them on a bad day.

"Fine," Bryce says, rolling his eyes and reaching into one of the cargo pockets of his shorts. "Here." He dangles the keys in front of my face, and I snatch them away quick.

When I turn back to where Amy is standing, it isn't to find the scared-looking girl I saw a moment before. Amy is looking at me, and she's smiling so big that every light in the room dims in comparison. I can't help but smile back. What is this girl doing to me?

When I get to her, I hand her the keys, and maybe she doesn't notice the way her fingertips brush mine, but I notice, and it sends chills up my arm.

Once the keys are firmly in her hand, she turns and looks at Jackson, and so do I. He hasn't moved an inch since the last time I looked. I see the pride in Amy's eyes when she turns and walks out of the house.

"Are you working tomorrow?" she asks once we're outside. We stand at the end of the sidewalk, and I know that we have to separate, her in one direction and me in the other.

"Yep."

She bites her lip, but it doesn't hide her smile. "Great. I'll see you then." She pauses for a second, rattling the keys in her hand. "Thanks, Oliver." She turns, and I watch her walk away, the snow falling onto her hair, until she's completely covered in shadow.

My truck feels empty when I get back to it, but there's a scent lingering in the air, some kind of floral perfume.

In the back seat, my dad coughs and sits up. "What's going on?" he asks, his eyes fuzzy as he looks out the windshield.

"Don't worry about it," I tell him. "Go back to sleep."

OLIVER

When Amy walks into the shop on Saturday night, she walks straight to the counter and hands me a CD. It's a burned CD, a blank white disc with no writing on it.

"What's this?" I ask, my fingers clutching tight to the case.

"It's a thank-you gift. For last night." She taps her fingers on the counter. She bites her lip, and then those dark brown eyes meet mine, finally. "You're not going to tell anyone about . . . about all that? Are you? It's just because this whole situation is a little embarrassing, and I don't want everyone to know. I didn't even want you to know, but now you do, so—"

"Amy."

She stops, and her eyes widen, the way they always seem to when I say her name, like she's surprised I remember it.

"Who am I going to tell?"

Her eyes shift, going straight to where Brooke is helping a customer with something in the back of the store.

"I'm not going to tell Brooke," I say. What does she care what Brooke thinks anyway? But that's easy for me to say. I've known Brooke for three years. I know she isn't as tough as her exterior would suggest. I know that she has a soft spot for people and loves Celine Dion as much as she loves the Smashing Pumpkins. She's a big old softie. But to someone who doesn't know her, she's just that badass half of herself. It's always the hardness that people see first.

Amy takes a deep breath and nods. And that's it. She walks away from me, into the office to clock in, and I'm left standing at the front desk, the CD still in my hand.

We don't speak for the rest of her shift. She stays behind the register while I stock and help customers, and while normally the shift would have been pretty ideal for me, I'm feeling a little antsy. Amy is trying to be bright and optimistic, but as soon as a customer walks out the door, I see the light in her eyes dim a little, see the way she seems to deflate.

And then it's closing time, and the two of us are standing together in the back office, clocking out on Brooke's computer. I try to keep my eyes off her, focusing only on the click-clacking of her fingers on the keyboard, but in the last three hours, I've found it increasingly more difficult not to look at her.

"Walk you out?" I ask.

She looks over her shoulder at me, her hand on the doorknob of Brooke's office. "Yeah," she says quietly. "Okay."

"Night, guys!" Brooke calls to us as we head out of the shop. She locks the door behind us, and then Amy and I are standing on the sidewalk outside, and it's the first time we've ever been completely alone.

"Did you park across the street?" I ask, pointing at the lot at the end of the shopping center where I always park. She nods. Cars still rush past us, but the shops on either side of Spirits and across the street are completely quiet. In the lot, she smiles at me, her arms crossed and the cold wind making her bangs flutter, her face half blue with shadow. I'm not good at getting to know people or letting them in or being a good friend, but I want to be her friend. I'm also not good at telling people that I want to be their friend.

"Be safe driving home," I say. "The road is icy." I want that to be enough to tell her that I suck at this but that I'm here for her. She just sends me a close-lipped smile and nods.

"Thanks, Oliver. I'll see you later." She turns away from me, walking to her car. I climb into my truck, but I wait until she's turned on her headlights and pulled out onto the road before I take out the CD she made me and stick it in my CD player.

The first song is Jeff Buckley's rendition of "Hallelujah."

I press my head to my steering wheel.

I've liked girls before.

Maybe I've even loved girls before.

But relationships? I suck at getting them started and then have no clue what to do once I'm in one. I've never been with a girl longer than a month.

Even after all that, I've never felt this before, this tight twisting in my stomach at the thought of her. This feeling like I'm counting the minutes until our next shift together. This feeling like I can't breathe.

I sit there in the parking lot, with my heater running high, until the song ends and the next begins. It's Rufus Wainwright's version of "Hallelujah." I scowl and then change to the next song.

It's Bon Jovi's rendition of "Hallelujah."

And then Neil Diamond's.

And Brandi Carlile's.

The CD consists of thirteen different versions of "Hallelujah."

FEBRUARY

AMY

It's the first of February, which at East High School means it's time to start selling Valentine-grams, which are really just ugly carnations with a heart-shaped note attached. They sell for a dollar, and on the first of the month, Petra and I are the first ones to run the table during lunch, since we're president and vice president of the student council.

I've spent half the lunch period selling grams to freshman girls who giggle as they address their sappy "Roses are Red, Violets are Blue" love poems to the seniors on the football team and the cross-country team.

"Heard you had a shitty weekend," Petra says, no malice in her voice. She smiles at the girl bent over the table, scribbling away at her heart-shaped paper. I think she might be transcribing one of Shakespeare's sonnets.

"You weren't there?"

She shrugs. "I have better things to do on a Friday night than go to Jackson's juvenile birthday party."

I don't know if she means this as a jab at me, but I don't take it as one. She's right. We both have better things to do, and Friday night was a complete waste of time. I'm so pissed at Jackson.

It's partially his fault that Oliver felt like he had to go into that party and save my ass. All Jackson had to do was stand up to Bryce, and the whole thing would have blown over. Instead, I walked three miles in the freezing cold, in barely there clothing, and was probably only saved from turning into a human Popsicle by Oliver.

I hadn't stopped thinking about it all weekend.

About Jackson, about the party, about Bryce . . . about Oliver. Oliver, who doesn't even know me, but who stopped to pick me up on the side of the road and who stood up for me when he had no clue what he was walking into. Jackson and Bryce and his guys could have been violent, for all Oliver knew.

And just like that, he appears.

Jackson, not Oliver.

He's right across the table from me, standing so close, my skin crawls. "Hey, Ames."

Goose bumps break out along my arms. I'm still Ames to him. I'm still the nickname he's been calling me for the last eleven months. I don't look up at him. I know I'll give in to him if I look up into those eyes that I love so much. And I don't want to give in to Jackson. He's the one who said it was over between us at the party, so what is he even doing here?

I don't look at him, even though I can feel his and Petra's eyes on me. I focus on rearranging the bills in my lap, turning all the dollar bills the same direction, George Washington staring up at me.

"Amy, come on. Please talk to me."

I don't. I'm not going to.

Out of the corner of my eye, I see him hand Petra a dollar bill, which she slides over to me. I see him reach for one of the heart-shaped pieces of paper and pick up one of the pens sitting on the bright pink tablecloth. I force myself not to look as he writes something on the paper. Jackson has the worst chicken-scratch handwriting

I've ever seen. He hands his gram to Petra. She's in charge of the grams; I'm in charge of the money.

"You didn't put a name or homeroom on this," Petra says, holding the gram out to Jackson, but he doesn't take it. I can feel the weight of his eyes on me, and Petra takes the gram back. She picks up one of the pens from the table and when I look over, I'm not surprised that she's writing my name on it: *Amaria Richardson, Pearson*. I'm not even surprised that Petra knows I have Pearson for homeroom.

I try to grab the gram back from Petra because I know Jackson is only sending me one because he feels bad for what happened at the party, or maybe he just feels bad for breaking up with me, and I don't want his gram. But Petra shoves it right into the middle of the stack so that I don't know which one it is, and I sigh, sending her a death glare.

Rules, she mouths at me. The gram is paid for and written on. It can't be taken back.

"Okay, fine," Jackson says, but then he presses his hand into the table and leans over it, until I can feel his breath on my face. A line is forming behind him, but he doesn't seem too concerned about it. "You can ignore me, but I'm just going to talk anyway."

I look up at him, and just like I thought it would, my heart starts to thump, losing its determination. His skin is so smooth, so flawless, and I want to cry remembering how it feels under my fingertips.

"I really fucked up on Friday. I know that. Bryce acted like a dick, and he knows it, too. I know you're having a hard time, and I'm sorry I made it harder on you. You didn't deserve that. I'm sorry I wasn't a better friend, okay?"

"Jackson," I whisper. I don't know what I'm going to say. Maybe that I love him, maybe that I don't think I can forgive him for leaving me alone at that party, maybe that I'm so confused about what I want, so completely overwhelmed by the plan I set for myself, that just looking at him is enough to make me feel lost.

His eyes fall down to my mouth, and for just a second, I think maybe he's going to kiss me. Which is completely ridiculous because we're sitting in the middle of the cafeteria, and if he kisses me right here, in front of everyone, not only will we get detention, but then we'll both be even more confused.

Jackson's lips, those full lips I always loved to feel against mine, part slightly, and I hear him sigh, an odd sound in that moment that I can't quite decipher.

He blinks and leans away from me, situating his body fully and entirely on his side of the table.

It's like we stepped into a time machine for a second, traveling back to those fleeting moments when we couldn't take our eyes off each other. But now Jackson is back in the present, where we aren't together, where I'm alone.

"You shouldn't have kissed me," he says, looking down at the paper and pens in front of him, like he's just realized where he is. "At the party."

I look away, and I finally feel like I can speak. "I know. It won't happen again." I'm surprised to find that I mean this. Jackson wants to be done, and I'm not interested in chasing around someone who doesn't want me.

So we're done.

Jackson holds my eyes for another second, and then he's gone, and I'm staring at Taylor Morris, who's excitedly holding out a dollar bill toward me.

I stuff it in the money bag and try to ignore Petra's eyes, but I can see her in my periphery anyway.

"You okay?" she asks.

Something pokes at me, and I snap, "What the hell do you care anyway?"

Petra doesn't speak to me again.

OLIVER

"This is literally the best night of my life," Brooke says, leaning against the counter beside me.

I snort. "Dear God, you need to get out more."

Brooke pinches me, looking sullen for a mere second before another song starts up on the karaoke machine, and then she lights up again. "Holy shit!" she shouts in my ear. "They're going to sing Spice Girls!" She's bouncing up and down, and I'm ready to bop her on the head like a Whac-a-Mole.

"Yes, I heard Amy announce it. Can you take a fucking chill pill?"

"Stop being a sourpuss," she says. "Go help Amy manage the list. Look at the line! This was our best idea yet!"

Over on the register, Morgan says, "*Our* idea?"

Brooke shushes her, and I actually do what she tells me to because Amy looks a little like she's drowning as she hands around little karaoke CD cases so that people can choose songs from them. She's been doing this all night, and she doesn't even look tired, but it's probably about time for me to relieve her, so I leave Brooke and move over to the sign-up table.

As soon as Amy sees me, she smiles, and I get that weird feeling in my stomach that I do every time she does that. "Doing okay?" I ask as two girls very loudly and excitedly decide they're going to sing Queen. They hand the CD they were poring over to me.

"Sure," Amy says, her face looking stuck in that position, with her mouth in a wide smile and her eyes alight. "I've never listened to most of these," she says, reaching out for the CD in my hand. I give it to her, and she examines the front of it. "Ace of Base, Oasis, the Cure."

"You've never heard of the Cure?"

Amy shrugs. "I've heard *of* them, but I've never heard them."

I purse my lips, trying to measure my words. "I guess a lot of people only know the music of their lifetime."

Amy freezes, her eyes on the screens against the back wall that are scrolling through the multicolored lyrics of "Wannabe."

She turns, slowly, narrowing her eyes at me. "What is *that* supposed to mean?"

I put my hands up. "It's not an insult. The Cure put out their first album in '79. No one expects you to listen to them."

Amy scoffs. "I know music before my time. Um, hello. The Beatles, Elvis, Michael Jackson, Aretha Franklin—"

She breaks off when the song comes to an end, and the girl who was singing steps off the makeshift platform. She hands Amy the mic, and Amy consults the clipboard sitting on the edge of the table next to us. "Okay, next up, we have Will, singing 'Ain't No Sunshine' by Bill Withers. Everybody in the store, give him a big round of applause!"

When the applause borders on thunderous, I'm surprised to find that even more people have crammed in the door. It's not that big of a shop, but karaoke seems to have the people excited. I'm suddenly concerned that this might not be a one-time deal.

When the guy on the stage, wearing glasses and sandals even though it's on the verge of snowing outside, starts a surprisingly good rendition, I can't help myself. I lean down to Amy and ask, "Do you know this song?"

She scowls up at me. "Are you going to ask me that every time a song comes on?"

I have to look away because I don't want her to see me smile. I shrug. I like that she's gotten defensive; I like that she doesn't mind arguing; I like that her cheeks have flushed just a little, which means I'm getting to her.

"Fine," she says. "You think you know good music? You give me your best, I'll give you mine, and the first person to cave to the other's musical genius loses."

I cross my arms, trying to look intense, like this is a serious matter, because Amy looks serious, and honestly, that just makes me like her even more. Because she takes everything seriously, and now that she's standing beside me, I definitely can't avoid it anymore. I like her. A lot.

"What does the winner get?"

She tosses her hands in the air, while up on the stage, the guy, Will, is getting *really* into the song, which is acceptable. It's the kind of song you get into. There's a girl in the crowd pointing her phone at him, and he winks at it as the song moves closer to the end.

"Bragging rights," Amy says. "Good enough for you?"

I shrug. "Sure thing." And without thinking, I reach out my hand. She looks down at it for a second, and then she shakes it. I make a point not to notice the way it sends tingles all the way up my arm.

I risk a glance at her and find that she's watching me, an odd expression on her face. "You're passionate about something. Who would have known?" Her voice has a strangely reverent quality to it that makes me uncomfortable.

And then, in an attempt to avoid her comment and because I have *completely* lost my mind, I pick up her clipboard and scribble my name at the very top. I'm allowed to do that because I'm an employee, right? I look over to see if Brooke is paying attention, but she's not, so I keep going even though I've just now really processed what I'm doing and my stomach is in knots. I can't believe I'm doing this just to entertain a girl.

When I push the clipboard into her hand, Amy just stares at it for a second, and I see her eyes moving back and forth over the top of the page, like she's reading my name once, twice, and then three times. Like she has to do that to believe it. And then she grins up at me.

Will's song comes to an end, and he passes the mic to Amy, and she looks like a kid about to blow out her birthday candles as she says, "Next up, our very own Oliver York, singing 'Friday I'm in Love' by the Cure!"

Because I know what I'm going to see, I turn and look at Brooke. She's standing completely still behind the counter, her eyes wide as saucers. And just as the music for the song starts, I see her mouth, *Holy shit.* Morgan, still ringing up customers, whoops loudly.

And then it hits me what an absolutely awful idea this is, because Amy is watching me, and she's smiling really big, and I can't decide if I love it or hate it, but it's too late to make up my mind because now I have to sing.

I chose "Friday I'm in Love" because it happens to be the most iconic Cure song, and also my favorite. But I also like it because it requires very little vocal talent. I definitely don't think I have an awful voice, but best not to push it when I have this many eyes on me, when I have Amy's eyes on me.

I don't even have to look at the lyrics scrolling across the screen. I know this song forward and backward. Instead, I scan over the faces of strangers, some of whom watch me sing, some who are actually shopping, and some who are just dancing to the music. It's the kind that's hard not to dance to. I'm stiff, mostly out of total discomfort, unable to move my limbs, but nobody seems to mind. During the interlude, I do a little back-and-forth step on the podium, and I hear Amy laugh over the music.

Throughout the whole thing, Morgan cheers, and halfway through, Brooke produces her phone, which she points at me, but Amy just watches with this look on her face, like she's looking at a complete stranger, and maybe she is because this is definitely not the kind of thing I do.

When the song finally ends, I make sure to take a bow because I've already embarrassed myself so much, what's a little more, and then I walk back to Amy.

"Well, well," she says, biting her lip and in the process biting back her grin. "You have a nice voice, too. I'm learning a lot about you tonight, Oliver York."

I shrug, trying to be casual but I'm still a little mortified. "I was feeling inspired."

"I know that song," she says.

I cross my arms and stand beside her, pretending that absolutely nothing has changed in the last three and a half minutes. "I know you do. Everyone does."

Her narrowed eyes are back, and it takes everything to keep myself from smiling.

"Oh, Oliver," she says. "You're going down."

AMY

"I MUST SAY," my calculus teacher says, standing at the front of our class with our graded exams in her hand. "This test didn't go over as well as I hoped it would. It seemed that a lot of you didn't really understand the concept of this chapter."

I'm feeling antsy, my knee bobbing up and down as she speaks. Why doesn't she just give us the damn tests? I can feel my heart sinking. She's talking to me. I know she's talking to me. I wasn't particularly confident during the test, even though I heard Oliver's voice in my head, the way he explained the problems to me at Spirits. But I took this test right between my last good night with Jackson and his suggestion that we "take a break." How was I supposed to focus?

Our teacher begins passing out the tests, obviously going in alphabetical order. Great. That means I'm going to get mine pretty much dead last. I peek over at Petra but am particularly disheartened when I do. She looks so confident. She's going to get an A, and I'm going to fail, and she's going to get the valedictorian spot I worked so hard for.

Petra gets her test, and I'm suddenly very frustrated that she has such a crappy poker face. She bites back her smile, but I see it nonetheless. I don't know if it's instinct or her innate desire to always brag, but she glances over at me. She can't stop her megawatt smile then.

She doesn't show me her grade. We aren't really friends and therefore don't talk about grades or even really discuss the fact that we're competitors.

A sheet of paper falls on my desk, and I stare at it, letting it sit there, like maybe if I don't touch it, it isn't real. I got a C. It's much worse than I imagined, and even though it isn't a midterm or a final, it's still an exam, and it's still a C, and it's still going to bring my final grade down.

I'm *not* going to cry. There's no way I'm going to cry in the middle of class over a test grade and give people more ammunition against me. I swallow hard and flip my paper over. If I can see the grade on it, so can everyone else, including Petra, one row away from me. I stay there with my hand flat on the desk until I have the courage to look up.

My teacher's eyes are on me, and I can see pity there as clear as I can see the sun shining through the window. She pushes her glasses up her nose and looks away.

Petra, unlike our teacher, doesn't try to hide. She looks at me, her face a mixture of confusion and something else that I can't quite read.

I spend the rest of class trying hard to focus on the lesson so that I won't end up in this trap again. I obviously didn't grasp the lesson we learned the first week back from break, or I wouldn't be having these problems so far down the line. I just need to focus more, pay more attention, give my homework and my reviews the time they need and not only my break time at Spirits.

When the bell rings, I shove my almost-failing test down into my bag and take off, ignoring the looks I get when I push past everyone to get to the door. I want to get to the bathroom before I start crying. I can still feel that C burning in my bag like a ten-pound weight.

"Amy!" Petra is chasing me down the hallway. I stop and wait for her to catch up to me, her curly hair bobbing up and down. I don't want to talk to her, I don't want to talk to anyone, but I know Petra. She's persistent. If I run, she'll follow.

"You should have aced that test," she says. Petra seems to have missed the memo about how we never discuss our grades.

I roll my eyes and turn away from her, away from the bathrooms and toward my third period class. "Did you seriously just run down the hallway to tell me that I suck?"

Petra scowls and follows after me. "No, I just . . ." She gets in front of me, making me stop. "I'm just worried, I guess."

I clutch the straps of my backpack hard and step around her quick. "Well, don't worry about me. I'm fine."

AMY

THE NEXT DAY, I stand in the doorway of the science lab. I don't have bio today, but I'm too anxious to wait. "Ms. Murphy?"

My AP bio teacher looks up when I approach her desk, and I can already tell she's not happy to see me. "What can I do for you, Amaría?"

She's the only teacher who refuses to call me Amy, and I hate her for it. "I'd like to request a new lab partner."

She sighs and puts the pen she's using to grade papers down. I ignore the sound of my classmates filing into the room behind me. "I'll admit," she says when her eyes meet mine, "that I've been waiting for one of you to come and ask."

I can't quite meet her eye. I hate it when teachers bring up the fact that they know about our personal lives, that they're just as much a part of the gossip circuit as the rest of us. "Jackson has a lot of friends in the class. I don't think he'd mind switching." I'm trying to sound considerate, but she sees right through me.

"That's just the problem," she says. "If I pair Jackson with anyone else in this class, they'll use the opportunity to turn it into a funhouse. He works with you. He gets better grades as your partner. And you're not one to play around in class. I'm sorry, but the two of you will just have to finish out the semester as lab partners."

My mouth drops open. "But that's not fair."

She smiles up at me, and I get the distinct impression that, despite her current employment, Ms. Murphy doesn't like teenagers, or maybe even people in general. "You'll find that most of life isn't fair, Miss Richardson. And you have to face the consequences of your bad choices."

By *bad choices*, I'm not sure if she means breaking up with Jackson or dating him in the first place.

OLIVER

I'VE BEEN STANDING in the office doorway for almost five full minutes, and Amy still hasn't noticed that I'm here, she's so focused on her homework. It looks like science this time, not calculus. Her eyes scan the page, whipping back and forth, her pencil tapping against the table as she reads over something again and again. I try not to be proud of the fact that she's listening to a soft Parachute song instead of the loud rock music she usually listens to.

"Amy?"

She jerks so violently her pencil goes skittering across the floor. "Dammit," she says, her hand over her chest. "You scared me."

I bend down to pick up her pencil and set it in the crease of her open textbook. "Sorry. I've been standing here for a while."

She blinks at me, almost like she doesn't recognize me, and then she frowns, but I don't know why. She stares down at the page in front of her. "I'm a little out of it."

"Still having trouble?" I ask, pulling the chair that usually sits against the wall up to the desk.

She shrugs, not looking at me. "Yes and no." A crease forms between her eyebrows, her mouth going hard. She looks over at me. "It's stupid."

I frown at her. "If it's got you this worried then it's not stupid." But I think I get what she means. Amy and I aren't quite friends but aren't quite just coworkers, so there's no reason for her to feel like she can talk to me about anything other than music and our new competition. What happened at her ex's party wasn't enough to make her trust me like that. One weird Friday night experience does not a friendship make.

She hesitates for a long time and then sighs and says, "I got a C on my calculus exam."

"That's bad, right?" It might seem like a stupid question, but I got my fair share of Cs in high school, especially senior year, when it felt like nothing really mattered anyway. But Amy doesn't seem like the C type, and she seems pretty upset about it.

She sighs. "Yes. It's bad. It's going to bring my average down, which is going to bring my GPA down, and I could—" She cuts off, letting the end of that sentence float between us. I don't push her to finish it.

Something occurs to me. "Shit. Is it my fault? Did I explain it wrong the other day?"

She's shaking her head before I finish. "No. What you showed me was fine. I'm just"— There it is again, that hanging sentence. But this time, she finishes it—"distracted."

I feel something crawl under my skin. "By your ex?"

She doesn't answer right away, her forehead wrinkling in thought. "Not really. It's not Jackson. It's actually—" She's killing me. I feel oddly impatient to know what's going on in her head, to find a way to solve her problems. "I think it's Spirits," she says, finally looking at me. "I thought I could handle working and going to school, but maybe I can't. I'm spending so much time here, and I feel like I'm falling behind." She stops, but I can already tell what she's going to say next.

"I kind of think I need to quit," she whispers, and even though I heard the sirens, I'm still surprised by the tornado in my gut. "But my family needs the money. My stepdad got laid off and still hasn't found a new job. It's not much, but it helps."

"You can't quit," I say without thinking.

Her head comes up, and she looks at me curiously, and I think that for such a smart girl, she's pretty oblivious if she can't see how much I like her. I feel like the whole world can see it. "We need you," I finally say, in an attempt to save myself. "Brooke will be upset if you quit. Can't you just, you know, get a tutor?"

She smiles. "It's not that easy. I'm more the type to *be* the tutor, not *need* a tutor."

"So, you're going to skate through with Cs instead of asking for help?"

She bites her lip. "No, I guess not," she says, and I lean forward, putting my hand over her textbook so that she looks at me again, instead of down at it.

"I'll help any way I can."

She blinks at me, her dark eyes a little wide, and I just stare at her.

"I think I'm just going through a rough patch," she says. "It'll pass." She smiles at me, her lips pressed tight together. "I can't quit. The school year is almost over anyway. So, you just come through with that music," she says, turning back to her homework.

"I'll have it tomorrow."

She doesn't look at me, but I keep looking at her.

OLIVER

I'M NOT EVEN sure what I'm nervous about, but here I am, with actual butterflies in my stomach as I stuff the CDs in a backpack.

"Are you humming?"

I turn to see my mother standing in the doorway of my bedroom, her arms crossed and a confused expression on her face. When she frowns like that, it brings out every single wrinkle and worry line on her face, and it ages her ten years.

"No," I snap immediately, and her eyebrows raise. "I don't hum. I just, um, have a song stuck in my head." A terrible excuse.

My mother scowls again. "You've been awfully agreeable lately. Something I should know about? Did you get a promotion? Or an acceptance letter?"

It's my turn to scowl. "I'm always agreeable."

My mother snorts. "Oh, sweetie. You growl at people that get too close."

I scowl harder.

"I'm not criticizing your character. Your grouchiness is what people love about you. I'm just commenting on the fact that you're pretty cheery these days."

I think about Amy's eyes and her lips and that flawless skin that I can't stop thinking about touching. I shrug, playing it off. "Not particularly cheery. Things are just going, um, smoothly." Smoothly. My life is anything but smooth. I spent the last week doing research on how the hell to keep Dad from getting in serious trouble with the courts, time is running out on the lie that is my pending admission to Missouri Baptist University, and of course, I'm way into a girl who's still way into her ex.

My mother taps her fingers on the doorjamb. "If you say so. Have somewhere to be today?"

I stuff some more books in my bag: books on Missouri state law, books on criminal offenses, books about how to get yourself out of the shittiest bind of your life.

"Yeah, I'm just meeting Dad at Charlie's before work." And the knowledge that Amy is going to be at Spirits by the time I get there is really the only thing keeping me going. I feel like I'm one misfortune away from smashing something.

Mom taps her foot, she bites her lip, she crosses her arms.

"Mom, what is it?"

She meets my eye and shrugs. "This shouldn't be on you, Oli. It's not your job to take care of your father."

"Yeah? Well, no one else is going to do it," I say, pushing past her and heading down the hall, my backpack slung over my arm. I know it isn't my job to take care of Dad. I know that it's his own damn fault that he got in trouble, and that he should have to face the damn consequences of acting like a total idiot. But when I think about it, when I imagine my father in jail for being stupid enough to have an addiction that makes him lose all sense of himself, it makes my stomach turn. "I'll be late," I call to my mom, ready to shut the door behind me. "I'm closing tonight."

OLIVER

Dad is waiting for me at Charlie's, the coffeehouse that we sometimes meet at when he has it in him to sober up. This isn't very often. Today, we're going to discuss his plan of action, as his court date is in less than a week, and he can't afford his own lawyer, so he has to accept the one the state is offering him.

I slide into a booth at ten on the dot and wait for him to show up. I scan the books I got at the library yesterday, looking at the places I bookmarked. There's a chance Dad could get off with a fine, but I don't know how to guarantee that. I'm not a lawyer.

Dad falls into the booth across from me with a huff, a smile on his face.

"Oli, boy," he says, immediately picking up the cup of coffee I had the waiter bring for me. He gulps it, his eyes wandering around the café over the top, until he finally drops it back onto its saucer with a clatter. He wipes a thumb under his bottom lip and then his eyes go to the table between us. "Wow. Lots of books you got there. We startin' a book club?"

I stare at him for a long time, unease starting to tingle up the back of my neck. "What's going on?"

He tries to look casual as he slumps down in his seat and looks at me, but I can see the way his fingers tremble, the way he can't quite get his eyes to focus. "Whadda you mean?"

"Are you drunk?" I demand.

His eyes focus then, going wide. He doesn't have to answer. Of course, he's drunk. He probably started drinking as soon as he got off work, before the sun even came up.

"Oli," he says when I start piling the books back into my bag.

"Why can't you take anything seriously?" I ask loudly. People are starting to look in our direction, including our waiter, who's subtly glancing our way while wrapping silverware. "You're going to court in less than a week. You might be in big fucking trouble. And it's like it doesn't even faze you." I rip the zipper on my backpack closed and slide out of the booth, almost stumbling in my anger.

"Oli, just calm down."

I can't help but laugh. I'm hysterical at my own idiocy, thinking I could count on him, even once, even when it's his own shit at stake. "Calm down?" I'm looking out the front window when I say it, seeing people walk by in the early morning sunlight. What it must be like to be on the other side of that window, to not have this to deal with all the time.

"Oli, come on. Sit back down. I'll sober up. I promise." Out of the corner of my eye, I see him reach for the cup of coffee before remembering that he already drained it.

I turn back to the table and smack my hand on the tabletop. My father jumps. In that moment, he doesn't look like a father to me. He looks like a child being reprimanded, and maybe that's exactly what he is. "If you don't give a shit, that's fine. You can rot in jail for all I care."

Hurt flashes in his eyes.

Good.

I turn again to leave, and this time his hand comes up, clutching at my jacket, and I yank my arm away from him before swinging my bag over my shoulder and walking out of the café.

Spirits isn't far, only a few doors down, and as soon as I open the door, there she is: Amy, standing in the gospel section, restocking a shelf. She turns and smiles at me, the low morning sunlight slanting across her face, and I can tell by the unfocused look in her eye, by her practiced smile, that she thinks I'm a customer. And then her eyes focus and her smile gets bigger, and for a second, I can almost forget that I left my dad behind at Charlie's, my dad who'll be standing in front of a judge in less than a week, to deal with his own shit.

"Hey," she says, turning to face me as the door falls closed behind me. "I thought you weren't coming in until later."

I shrug—I'm not about to tell her the truth—and before she can ask me any questions, I reach into my bag and pull out the stack of CDs. I suddenly wish I could go back to being nervous about this moment instead of just pissed off. Why does my dad have to ruin everything good in my life? "These are for you," I say.

"My musical education," she says with humor in her voice. "You're old school. Good thing my hand-me-down computer has a disk drive."

Amy comes into the office while I clock in, but instead of retrieving anything from her purse, she holds out her hand to me. "Give me your phone."

I look at her for a second and then reach into my pocket and hand her my cell. She takes it, clicks around for a little bit, and then hands it back to me. "I created a playlist for you on Spotify. Easier that way. No ancient technology required."

I look at the playlist and snort. "Coldplay? This is *my* musical education?"

She crosses her arms, and even though she tries to look stern, there's a sparkle of amusement in her eyes. "When was the last time you listened to this one?"

I shrug. "I don't know. I mean, I've heard 'Yellow' nine hundred times, just like everyone else."

She sighs, like I'm such a burden, and drops her arms at her sides. The whole movement makes me smile. Her eyes dip for a split second. "Listen to the words. Soak it in. Trust me. Things change over time. The way you appreciate things changes."

I'm not smiling anymore, and neither is she.

AMY

I LOAD THE CDs onto my iPod, the iPod that my cousin, Carmen, handed down to me almost five years ago that barely holds a charge. I listen to the first CD on Sunday morning. Oliver gave me six, *six*, and as I lie in bed, I think some music might be nice. I have plenty of homework to do, but the sun is just barely peeking in through my blinds, and I want to be lazy. I want to listen to these albums so that I can argue with Oliver about the ones I don't like. I stretch and smile to myself. I like arguing with Oliver, I like that little crease of disbelief he gets between his eyebrows when I tell him I don't like something he does, or that I haven't heard of a band he loves.

But really, I'm ready for new music. I'm not giving in to Oliver's ridiculous argument that I don't know enough about music just because I don't regularly listen to anything released before my first birthday, but I'm always interested in bands I don't know, so I'm down with this whole experiment.

I put my biggest headphones on, the ones that fold completely over my ears. They make me feel swallowed whole by my music, and I love that feeling more than anything else. I press play, and I laugh when the music starts in my ears. It's not that the music is bad. But the electric, poppy notes of the first song on the CD aren't what I was expecting. I glance at the case. *Parklife* by Blur. I set the case on my stomach, resting my hands on the bed on either side of me, and close my eyes.

This is my favorite way to take in music, new or old or something I've listened to so many times I know every word. Music is meant to be heard without distractions. As much as I love listening to an album while I do the laundry or while I drive through town or while I do homework, this is my ideal way of soaking in music: uninterrupted, undistracted, unblemished by reality. And I do soak it in.

OLIVER

My mother glances over at me when my phone buzzes on the pew between us. I pick it up quick in case it buzzes again. Since we're always late, we're in the back row, so I don't think anyone will notice if I check a text message. It's from a number I don't know, and it says simply *Brit pop is rather smashing, but you'll have to do better than that.*

I grunt out a sound, more like disbelief than actual laughter, but either way, it's loud enough for the people in the pew in front of me to stiffen and glance back at me. Mom smacks me on the leg and narrows her eyes at my phone.

Sorry, I mouth to her. To Amy, I reply, *you liked Blur?*

Bloody awesome.

I roll my eyes, but I'm smiling nevertheless. *How long am I going to have to endure the Brit talk?*

Um. Excuse me. You brought this on yourself. Where I come from, there are consequences when you blaspheme someone else's musical tastes.

I glance up at Mom. She's looking at me disapprovingly. I shrug at her. Yes, I realize I'm being rude. I get it. Whatever. But it's Amy. And she's texting me for the first time, and there's no way I'm going to blow her off. God will understand.

No more culture shock for you, I answer. *Americans only.*

Booooooooring.

I press my lips together to suppress a smile. Before I answer her, my phone buzzes again.

Sooo my brother might have cracked the Blur case a little bit. Don't hate me.

I don't know what to do about this warmth in my stomach. This isn't me. I'm not this person who wants to smile down at my phone until my mouth hurts. But dear God, if I don't feel the need to tell her I don't hate her. That hating her is an idea so preposterous that it's like she's speaking another language.

No worries about the case. Just shows that it's well-loved.

Shit. Isn't it like Rule Number One that when you're speaking to a girl that you *don't* want to know that you have very intense feelings for that you're supposed to avoid the word *love*? I'm an idiot.

Thanks! Sheesh. I thought you were going to be extra mad.

This makes me pause. Am I so much of a monster that she thinks I'll go off on her for accidentally cracking a CD case? Is she . . . scared of me?

Nah. There's no way. Amy is first in line to call me on my shit at work. Lately, she's dethroned Brooke in the *oh shut up, Oliver* category.

Have you listened to the playlist yet?

I just text *not yet.*

Well what are you waiting for? It's Sunday morning. The perfect time for some music education.

I love the way she's talking to me, like we're old friends. Like we talk with each other this way all the time.

I'm in church, and my mom is currently sending me disappointing looks.

You're in church?!!

Is that so shocking? Am I so depraved?

Stop texting me! I don't want to have to visit you in Hell!

I hold in a laugh. I check my phone over and over in hopes that maybe she'll text me again, but she never does, and I try to pretend like I'm not disappointed.

"Who's so important that you had to continuously check your phone during church?" Mom asks as soon as we're sitting down to lunch. She's eating a salad while I cover my order of French fries with a river of ketchup.

"Just someone I work with at Spirits."

She munches and munches, one of her cheeks full, like a guinea pig. "A female someone?" *Crunch, crunch, crunch.*

I sigh and refuse to meet her eye. "Yes, Mom. A female someone."

She's quiet for a long time before I finally look up at her. Big mistake. She's looking at me with a grin the size of Rhode Island, and I know that if she wasn't going to tease me about Amy before, she's going to now. "Is it that adorable new girl you were with the other day? She's cute."

"One and the same," I say, looking away from her and attempting to sound impassive, the way I might have spoken about Amy a month ago. But I know Mom can see right through me. I'm going soft.

"I would be lying if I said I haven't waited for the day a girl would catch your eye."

I roll my eyes. "She hasn't *caught my eye*. And there have been girls."

She shrugs, lacing her fingers together on the table in front of her and nudging her empty plate aside. "I know, but not a girl that's been really special to you." Her smile fades a little. "Is she a college student?"

I can feel the direction this is taking, but I answer her question anyway. "She's a senior. Got her sights set on Stanford."

Her eyebrows shoot up. "Wow. That's impressive . . . and far away." I see her thoughts play across her face. Things like *long-distance relationship* and *heartbreak*.

"Mom," I say, trying to snap her out of it. "Don't get carried away. Amy's just a friend, okay? She's—she's kind of got a boyfriend." It's the easiest way to describe the situation, not that it matters anyway. Even if Amy wasn't totally hung up on her ex, it's not like I'm going to ask her out, right? In this instance, my mother's wayward thoughts might have a point. If Amy is leaving for Stanford at the end of the summer, what am I doing getting so attached to her?

We both sit quiet for a few minutes, and it feels weird, like we've uncovered something that would have been better left hidden. But my thoughts have been set on a track I can't pull them away from, and I can't stop the words that cascade out of my mouth.

"Mom, did you ever consider *not* going to college?"

She puts down her glass of iced tea, and it sloshes over onto the table. "Of course not. If you want to get anywhere in life these days, you have to have a degree. Do you know what dropping out of school gets you? It gets you a life like your father's. What a waste that would be." She stops, and her eyes shoot to me, serious. "Why are you asking me this? Did you hear something from one of the schools? It's still early."

"No, no," I say, waving my hands around to keep her from spiraling. "It's nothing like that. Just thinking."

She grimaces and crosses her arms. "You have opportunities, Oliver, that other people might never have. Not going to school would be wasting them. This has been your path your whole life, and it would be idiotic to stray now."

I stare down at the tabletop because I can't look at her. My life is a waste. It's idiotic. It's comforting to finally get her opinion on the matter, and to know that I'm going to avoid, for as long as I can, telling her what I've already decided.

AMY

I UNLOOP THE car keys from the hook by the door, but they're immediately snatched back out of my hand.

"Sorry, baby, but I need the car today," Mama says as she sticks them in her pocket. "You'll have to take the bus."

I groan and step out of the way as all my siblings rush out the front door. "You can't drop me in the van? You're taking all of them." I motion at my four siblings, already buckling themselves into their seats and picking fights over the chair backs.

Mama shakes her head, and Carlos rushes out to the van. "Sorry, but the vehicles are accounted for, and Carlos doesn't have time for two stops. He has a job interview today." She sends me a close-lipped smile. "Bus, Amaría. You'll be fine."

So I go wait for the bus. Most days, I can talk my parents into letting me take one of the cars, dropping the kids off at the elementary school if they let me take the van, and if I can't take a car, they're usually willing to give me a ride. But I'm also well acquainted with the bus. I sit at the end of my street and pull out my calculus book and my iPod. I can feel the skin around my fingers refusing to stretch in the cold as I select the playlist labeled *Save Ferris*. One of the CDs Oliver let me borrow that I loaded up last night.

I find myself swaying to a big-band cover of "Come On Eileen" when I realize a truck that rolled to a stop at the end of the street right in front of me seconds ago hasn't started moving again.

The loud trumpet music is still going in my ears, but I'm barely listening to it because I know that truck.

Jackson rolls down the window. "Get in!" he calls to me, but I don't move. "Ames, come on. Get in the damn truck. It's fucking freezing."

I bark out a laugh in the direction of his open window. "Right, because you're so concerned about me being cold." I'm not even sure why I say it. Ever since the party, and our weird encounter at the Valentine-gram table, Jackson and I have been studiously avoiding each other. The only time I've really seen him is in AP bio, and even then, we try to be cordial.

He's silent for a moment, and I'm prepared for him to drive off. "Amy, come on. Let me make it up to you, okay? Get in the truck. I know how much you hate taking the bus."

That much is true. I really hate taking the bus. I hate the way it smells and how the vinyl is somehow always greasy and how loud everyone is, like it's a contest or something. I look down at my calculus homework. There's no way I'll be able to do it on the bus, and the faster I get to school, the faster I can really focus on it without distractions.

I'm doing this for my grade, for my valedictorian status, *not* for Jackson.

I toss my backpack onto his floorboard, and I'm swept into a moment of déjà vu. So many times when we were together, Jackson drove me to school, and I would have a textbook on my lap, my index finger saving my place, just like I do now.

"What were you listening to?" Jackson gestures at the earbuds slung around my neck.

Am listening to, I think. Save Ferris is still playing. I can hear the trumpets under the sound of Jackson's tires moving down the street. He doesn't listen to music when he drives. Just sits in silence or listens to sports radio. Drives me nuts.

"Ska," I tell him, pausing my iPod.

"Never heard of them."

I glance sideways at him. "Ska is a genre. Not a band."

He just nods and puts on his turn signal. Being with Jackson has never been awkward for me before. We've always had something to talk about.

"Have a good weekend?" I ask. Ugh. I hate that we've wandered back into small talk territory, but what other option do I have? It's not like we can talk about *us*—about how I'm pretty sure I still love him; about how I still can't really forgive him for ditching me at his party; about how I'm happy with my new job, even if I only took it for the money and now it's starting to take its toll on my grades.

But if I'm being honest, it's not Spirits's fault I almost failed that test.

It's Jackson's. If we were still together, not fighting, I probably would have aced that test. Calculus isn't even a sore spot for me.

"Yeah, I guess so. Went to the game."

I blink at him for a second. I'm not sure which game he's talking about. Is it football season? Is it the swim team? Does the swim team have *games*?

Jackson chuckles. "The basketball game, Amy. God, have I taught you nothing?"

My heart flutters at his laughter. Sports are a thing I went to when Jackson and I were together that I would never do if it wasn't for him. I don't find sports to be particularly interesting, just like he doesn't find studying and listening to indie rock on Friday nights interesting. He always said that staying home on Friday night was a sin.

"Right. The basketball game. Did we win?"

The corner of his mouth is perked up slightly. "Yeah. We won." His eyes flit to me for just a second. "What'd you do this weekend?"

I think about how I spent all day Saturday going over my calculus test and reviews before work. I think about spending Sunday in my room, listening to that Blur album over and over, until I couldn't imagine ever *not* knowing it. I don't mention any of that to him. Those are two things Jackson really doesn't care about—music and academics.

"Just went to work," I tell him, which is true. Every second I didn't spend at home was spent at Spirits.

"So, you like your new job, huh?"

I shrug. I don't know why, but I feel like I can't show him too much enthusiasm, like somehow he might use it against me. "Sure. It's a paycheck, you know. Carlos has a job interview today, so we'll see."

We stop at the light around the corner from school, and he smiles over at me. "You know that's not the only reason you're doing it."

I feel myself blush and look away from him. It's easy to forget, sitting here next to him more than a week after he's broken up with me, quiet and awkward, that he knows me better than anyone, has known me like this for almost a year.

"It's the biggest reason," I say, looking out the window as what's left of the melting snow drifts by.

My phone pings, and I get a weird feeling in my stomach at the thought that maybe it's Oliver.

But it's not even a text. It's an email.

Your tickets have shipped! the subject reads.

God, I can't believe I forgot. In all the business of Spirits and Jackson and valedictorian, I forgot that I bought tickets to see the Lumineers this summer.

I glance over at Jackson, and his eyes are on the screen of my phone. On reflex, I turn it off.

"I forgot about that," he says, as we pull into a parking space and Jackson puts the car in park.

I bought the tickets for Jackson and me. Even though he hates the Lumineers, hates *all* my music, he still agreed to go with me. But everything is different now. I never accounted for a breakup.

I haven't figured out what to say, my hand already on the door handle, ready to run away. But then he says, "We can still go."

I turn away from the window, back to him. His eyes are so soft, and as much as I want to remember him as being the guy who stood by while his best friend stole my car keys, I can only remember him as the guy who ran his fingers through my hair while I did homework, who called me right before he went to sleep to tell me good night, who brought me soup when I was sick.

"If you want." I watch his mouth say the words, seemingly in slow motion.

I open the door. I have to get away from him. Because Jackson is so good at sucking me in, and as much as I want everything to just go back to the way it was, if I let Jackson suck me in again, I know I'll just get hurt. Because he was right when he said it was too hard on him to be with me, that we were rarely ever together anymore. I ignored it for a long time, the way his eyes were always a little sad, because it was too hard to admit.

It's better this way, if we both focus on what we need.

"Thanks, but I'll find someone else to go with. See you in bio."

Jackson is rushing to get his keys out of the ignition, to get to his backpack in the back seat. "Let me walk you," he says, but I'm already closing the door and rushing through the parking lot. I feel like I can breathe once I'm out of his truck, the air cold and biting. I duck around the side of the building and lean against the red brick wall, looking at the empty tennis court across the sidewalk from me.

Absently, I wonder if Oliver likes the Lumineers. Without thinking, I open my contacts and call him. My stomach is in so many knots from being in Jackson's truck that I'm feeling dizzy.

"Hello?" I hear a shout of music in the background and then it goes quiet, and then it's just road sounds.

"Are you on your way to work?" It doesn't even occur to me to tell him it's me. We've been texting back and forth about music so much lately, I know I'm saved in his phone.

"Yeah. Going in early to set up displays before open. Want to help?"

I find myself smiling down at the wet concrete beneath my feet. "Wish I could, but I have AP bio."

All he does is make a little humming noise, and I'm surprised at how *intimate* the sound is. How it sends a chill up my spine. But maybe that's just the cold.

I plunge forward because I did actually call him for a reason. "Do you like the Lumineers?"

There's a silence, and I realize I might have switched subjects too fast. "The Lumineers are good. Why? Have something awful to say about them?"

This makes me laugh, and I hear the first bell ring inside, so I move around the side of the building, toward the front door, my eyes scanning for Jackson as I go. "No. They're my favorite band. I bought tickets to see them in June, but I don't have anyone to go with. I thought maybe you'd want to."

I hear shuffling, the gentle click of a turn signal, the slide of his hands across the steering wheel. "Don't you have other friends who'll want to go with you?"

I bite my lip. That would be a *no*. "If you don't want to go—"

"I want to go," he says over me, and I feel everything in my chest unclench. "I can pay for the ticket if you—"

"No," I say over him, a little too loudly. I'm almost inside now, and I stop just outside the door. "No, that's okay. I already bought the tickets." I don't mention that my parents bought me the tickets for my birthday.

We're quiet for a minute, and then he says, "What's the last concert you went to?" I'm very aware of how low his voice is, like he's whispering to me, and it makes me stop, makes me pay attention.

"Amber Run, back in September."

"I don't know them."

I gasp, trying to be playful, but something about this moment doesn't feel playful. "They're essential, Oliver. I'll bring you an album next time I see you."

He goes quiet again, and then he says, "Okay, Amy," in a weird way. The steps in front of the school are completely empty now, and I'm fairly certain I'm going to be late.

"Gotta go, Oli. See you at the Valentine's Day party on Sunday."

I don't wait for him to answer because I don't think I can handle hearing his voice all low and quiet like that again, so I hang up and rush inside.

"What took you so long?" Jackson asks when I drop down in my seat beside him in AP bio.

"Nothing," I say, but for some reason, I'm avoiding his eyes.

AMY

VALENTINE'S DAY. THE day when people who are in couples get showered with presents and affection and special favors while the single people of the world, like me, have to just . . . take it.

Homeroom is fourth period, and I'm exhausted by all the love and cheer and human-size teddy bears by the time I get there, only to be reminded that we still have to do Valentine-grams. And it's not even Valentine's Day. That's not until Sunday. But God forbid we don't celebrate at school. Luckily, since I manned the Valentine-gram table more than once, I don't have to do the delivery, which is the job everyone wants anyway because it means they don't have to sit in homeroom.

"Make it quick," Mr. Pearson grunts at the gram deliverers when the time comes, and I set my head down on my desk because I can't watch.

Last year, Jackson asked me out on a gram. *Go to the V-Day after-party with me*, it read, the party after the basketball game that Bryce threw. I get a prickly feeling down my arms when I remember that I still have the gram, in the top drawer of my nightstand.

I listen to people murmur as they read their grams, some people trying to figure out who could have sent grams from secret admirers. There are sighs and giggles, and I could puke.

"Here you go, Amy."

I lift my head and look up at the person blocking the light. It's a freshman whose name I don't remember, and she's holding a carnation out to me, which I take quickly, surprised.

But how could I forget? He wrote it right in front of me.

Sure enough, there's Jackson's chicken-scratch handwriting, so messy that I almost can't read it.

Do you remember Valentine's Day last year? I couldn't stop looking at you, all night.

It's a hard thing to forget.

We went to the party and halfway through the night, Jackson became attached to my hip. Before the night was over, he was whispering in my ear about how he wanted to make me his, about how much he liked me, about how beautiful I was. And then he kissed me.

I take a deep breath and stare at the carnation. It's a beautiful orange-y pink, and I blush, thinking about the fact that Petra was on the other side of the table with me while Jackson wrote this, that she might have read it before tucking it away.

And now I'm more confused than ever. Because he wrote this after the party, he wrote it seconds before telling me that I shouldn't have kissed him. But these aren't the words of someone who's finished with what we had. My feelings are all jumbled. And maybe he's just as confused as I am.

I press the flower to my lips, close my eyes, and pray for clarity, because if he keeps this up, I don't know if I can stay away from him.

OLIVER

My mother and I are silent at dinner, but I know it can't last. She sits up straight, and I prepare myself. I pray that it doesn't have to do with MBU. What if they called her? What if she found out that I never sent that application? The deadline hasn't passed, but that doesn't mean she's going to be completely fine with the idea of my lying to her for the past month.

"Oliver, we should talk about your father."

There are about a million different things that she could have said, but nothing is as surprising as this. My parents never speak. They rarely even acknowledge that the other exists. In my mind, they're so far removed from each other that I can't even imagine them ever being in the same room, much less being in a relationship.

My mother stabs at her salad for a minute. But I can't tell if she's angry at me about something or if she's angry at Dad about something. Chances are good she's equally pissed off at both of us. "When was the last time you saw your father sober?"

If I'm being completely honest, I can't think of a single time in my entire life when Dad was 100 percent sober. For as long as I can remember, being with Dad was kind of like hanging out with a toddler: I can't keep his attention, he often rambles, and sometimes he won't stop touching things.

"Mom, it doesn't matter. Dad's never going to change. You know that."

She nods sagely. "Yes, I do know that." She puts her elbows on the table and steeples her fingertips over her plate. "Sweetie, have you thought about attending school outside Missouri?"

I blink at her. "What are you talking about? I thought you wanted me to go to MBU."

She sighs. "This isn't about what I want. This is about what you want."

I just stare at her, ping-ponging between disbelief and rage. This is about what *I* want? Even though if I, right now, open my mouth and tell her that I don't want to go to college at all, she would flip out?

She sighs. "I'm just concerned that you feel you have to stay here because of him, because of how much *help* he needs, and I don't want you to feel tied down by him."

I grind my jaw together. I shouldn't feel tied down by *Dad*. I can't believe that she's not even processing how hypocritical she sounds right now. Maybe Dad is holding me down, but not any more than Mom is.

"You don't need to worry about Dad," I say as calmly as I can. "I can handle myself."

A crease appears between her eyebrows. "You're eighteen, Oliver.

You can't handle yourself, and you certainly can't handle your father. He just uses you—"

"I don't care," I say between gritted teeth. It's the truth. I don't care. He's my dad. It doesn't matter if the only time we spend together, he spends in the back seat of my truck, passed out. It doesn't matter that when I try to talk to him about something serious, he shows up drunk as piss. None of that matters. He's my fucking dad.

She puts up a hand. She pinches her lips together, and I can tell she's trying not to get upset. "I'm not trying to start an argument with you."

I want to growl at her that it's too late, but I've never been good at this, at arguing with Mom, with letting her know how I feel, letting her know that I feel suffocated here with her, but also feel like I can't leave because then she'll have no one. That I feel obligated to help Dad because she's the one who left him, and now he has nobody, too. That I want to leave Kansas City, but I'm scared to leave them and maybe I'm just scared to leave in general because I'm only eighteen, and I have no fucking clue what I'm doing.

But I'll never say any of that to her.

I push back from the table and put my dirty plate in the sink. "Gotta go," I say, heading for the front door and snatching up my jacket as I go.

"Where?" Mom asks, still sitting at the kitchen table.

"Valentine's party. Don't wait up."

I leave her sitting there, her dinner still in front of her.

AMY

I'VE NEVER REALLY been one for nerves. I've entered academic competitions that I won without blinking, given speeches about historical figures without so much as a stutter, and was even Dorothy freshman year in our school's production of *The Wonderful Wizard of Oz* (don't even get me started on how many people threatened to egg my house the day *that* casting went up), but tonight, when I'm standing in front of my full-length mirror, I can actually feel my fingers trembling as I try to do my hair.

Maybe it's because of that stupid gram from Jackson or maybe it's because I'm about to go to a party at my boss's apartment. Either way, I'm nervous. Extremely nervous.

"You look nice," Mama says from the doorway.

"Thanks," I say, turning back to the mirror. I still have my hands in my hair, trying to tie it up in just the right way. The dress I'm wearing—a black, knee-length dress with roses on it—is one I stole from my mother's closet, and I can only hope she doesn't recognize it. She hasn't worn it since she had the first set of twins.

"Don't you think you're a little overdressed for family dinner, though?"

My hands freeze, and I drop the strands of hair I've been attempting to braid together. "What? Family dinner is next week."

Mama's eyes go wide. I can see her in the mirror, her hands clutching the doorframe. "No. We moved it to this week. For Valentine's Day."

My mouth falls open. "But I asked you last week if I could go to a Valentine's Day party, and you said yes. You never once mentioned that you guys moved family dinner to this week."

"I didn't think you'd have plans *today*. I thought the party would be another day." She makes a weird shape with her mouth. "When you didn't go out last night, I thought you decided not to go."

"But *today* is Valentine's Day."

Mama's lips clamp together, and she crosses her arms.

"Can't I skip this one time?" I plead. "Please. I already told everyone I was going tonight. We have family dinner every month. Please. I'm already dressed!" I gesture toward my dress like she might not have already noticed it.

"Yes, in my clothes. I can see that."

Shit.

"Amy, you know the rules. Family dinner is not optional. I'm sorry, but you're not going to a party on a Sunday night, and on family dinner night, even if it *is* Valentine's Day."

She walks away like the conversation is over, and I'm left standing in front of my mirror, entirely overdressed for family dinner. I pick up my phone and pull up my text thread to Oliver.

Can't come to the party. Long story. Sorry.

I text Brooke next, since it's her party. And then I throw my phone down on my mattress hard, as if that will somehow get back at Mama.

OLIVER

"Do you think we have enough cupcakes?"

I look at Brooke's counters, her kitchen table, and the coffee table in the living room. Every surface is covered in finger foods and bowls of chips and dip, and there are pink and red heart-covered cupcakes everywhere. There's enough to feed everyone in Kansas City, but I keep my mouth shut.

"Honey, it's, like, twenty people. There's enough food." Lauren comes into the kitchen, where Brooke is skittering around, putting more trays of food into the oven. Lauren takes a tray from Brooke, puts it on the stove, and kisses her. "Everything is going to be perfect. It's just a silly party."

My phone beeps, and I pull it out of my pocket, my stomach clenching when I see it's a text from Amy.

Can't come to the party. Long story. Sorry.

I don't realize until my body sags under the weight of my disappointment just how much I was looking forward to hanging out with Amy tonight. A party without her . . . well, it just doesn't seem as interesting.

"You look like someone drowned your puppy."

I look up and find Brooke's eyes on me. I feel like I can't escape those eyes. "What's wrong?" she asks, pressing her hip to the counter between us. I'm glad I'm sitting in a chair on the other side of her bar, where she can't see the screen of my phone.

"Nothing," I say, tucking my phone back into my pocket, and I expect Brooke to let it go.

But she just crosses her arms and says, "Is it your dad?"

I'm about to lie, just straight up tell her that yes, it's my dad. But then her phone beeps, too, and she puts up a finger to tell me to wait and reads the text she just got. But of course, I know what she just got. A text from Amy, same as me.

Brooke's fingers start to move, answering the text, but then her fingers freeze, and her eyes slide slowly up to me.

"Oli," she says. "Did Amy text you that she isn't coming to the party?"

I say nothing.

Her eyebrows curve in confusion. "Is that why—" She cuts off, and my stomach turns. Her eyes go wide, and she says, "Oh shit. You like her, don't you?"

I push away from the bar and walk into the living room, pretending to rearrange plates of snacks. If she sees my face, she'll see that it's gone completely red. "No, I don't," I say, trying to sound stern, but I just sound like a little kid with his first crush.

I hear her step out of the kitchen and come into the living room, and I work to keep my back to her as she comes to stand beside me. "Oh please. You have a big ol' crush on her. Dear God, that's adorable. I've never seen you so much as show affection for a dog."

"I am not showing affection." I turn around to glare at her.

She throws back her head and laughs. "Oliver, you've been sharing music with her. I'm pretty sure that's as close to a declaration of your undying love as you're ever going to get."

I grit my teeth. She's lucky I don't just toss the tray of cupcakes in front of me onto the floor. "That is a very specific situation. That is not a *mixed-tape* situation. It is not a show of affection. Don't you have cupcakes to be stressed out about?"

But she's grinning at me, and I know she's forgotten all about the cupcakes.

"Hey," Brooke says, latching on to my arm and shaking it. "Cheer up. This is going to be so much fun, even if Amy doesn't come. Look, Marshal's here." She gestures at the door just as Marshal slinks in.

He's holding a bouquet of carnations that he hands Brooke, blushing furiously. Dear God.

Brooke smiles and gives him a hug.

"Why the long face, partner?" Marshal asks once Brooke has unhanded him.

While a few more people find their way into the living room, I take a deep breath and decide that coming here tonight was an absolutely awful idea.

AMY

An hour into dinner, I want to pluck my eyeballs out.

"Why are you dressed like that?" my cousin, Lupe, sitting on my left side, asks me, as if I haven't been sitting right beside him in this exact dress for the last hour.

I ignore him, but Tía Marci leans over him to see me. "I think you look beautiful. Perfect for Valentine's Day." She reaches across Lupe like he isn't even there and takes my chin in her fingers. "You look just like your mama when she was your age." She purses her lips. "I think you might have gone a little heavy on the eyeliner though."

I gently pry my face away from her fingers and smile, close-lipped. The less I say, the better off I am.

I glance down at my phone in my lap. Oliver never texted me back after I told him I wasn't coming, and I'm trying not to take it personally. Nothing says he has to text me back just because I texted him. He's probably having a great time at the party, a much greater time than I'm having.

I can feel it coming before it does, the hairs on the back of my neck standing up even as Rosa, across the table, finds my eyes. "How are things with the hottie, Amaría?"

My eyes sweep over the table to Mama. She's the only one who knows Jackson and I broke up.

It's now that Carlos looks around the table, like he's just now realizing that Jackson isn't here. "Where *is* Jackson?" he asks, his voice booming over everyone else's.

"We broke up," I say, because it's not like they're not all going to find out anyway, and the table erupts into noise. I sit back in my chair and let them talk over one another until finally, Mama yells, "Okay, okay, okay! It's done, it's over, let it go!" She sends me an apologetic glance, but I just look away from her.

Into the silence, Rosa says, "Well, that was probably for the best. I mean, it wasn't like he was going to follow you to California, right?" My stomach knots when she says this, and maybe it's true and maybe it's not, I guess either way it doesn't matter, but the fact that she said it at all hurts anyway.

Until Mama says something worse.

Quietly, like she thinks I won't hear her, as if she can't help herself, she says, "*If* she goes to California."

It's not a new comment. It's not something she hasn't said a thousand times in a thousand different ways and tones and languages. But when she says it now, in front of our entire family, something inside me snaps.

I push away from the table loudly, and everyone watches me as I stalk past Mama. But I can't let it go that easily. I can't let her get away with that.

So I spin around, pin her surprised eyes with a glare, and say, "Would it kill you to believe in me?"

She doesn't say anything, and for the first time that I can remember, neither does anyone else.

OLIVER

"I ALWAYS THOUGHT it was pretty awesome that Lauren owns a record store *and* is going to law school," Morgan says. "I mean, how intense is that? I couldn't even handle two majors. I had to drop one of them."

"Yeah," I say, taking a sip of the orange soda and champagne in my cup. It isn't exactly the classiest of drinks, but it's better than tequila shots. "Lauren is doing a pretty good job with the shop. What were you majoring in?" I hold in a cringe because if there was an award for being the worst at small talk, I'd finally have trophies in my room like Mom always dreamed about.

Morgan, tall with a dark pixie cut, sips at her own drink. "I was majoring in psychology and literature, but I dropped lit. It's just been rough trying to juggle school and work *and* my band."

She says it in a way that makes it obvious she wants me to ask her about her band. I didn't know Morgan was in a band. Maybe she's never mentioned it before, but chances are better that she has and I wasn't paying attention.

"What do you play?" I almost care, too. I've always liked Morgan. She's pretty and music savvy and has a nice way of talking. But there's just no *feeling* there.

"I play guitar, drums, and piano. Not all at the same time." She lets out a nervous laugh. Huh. She's nervous. Who knew?

Over Morgan's head, the front door opens, but I ignore it. People have been filtering in all night, but I don't know any of them, so I've stopped glancing over every time someone comes in.

But out of the corner of my eye, I can just make out the shape of the person standing in the doorway—someone very short, with long dark hair—and when I look over, Amy is standing in the doorway in a little black dress, her curly hair flowing around her face, and fuck, I suddenly understand all those awful, cheesy, predictable love songs. Because if I was the kind of person to write awful, cheesy, predictable love songs, I would write one about her right now.

And then, like she knows I'm on the verge of writing ballads, Amy's eyes scan every face in the apartment, and when she finds mine, she smiles so big I think I might die because she was actually looking for me, and I can't even believe that.

I don't realize I've walked away from Morgan until I'm standing in front of Amy. She's closed the door behind her, but she's still taking off her coat.

"I thought you weren't coming," I say, helping her pull her arm out of her coat sleeve.

"Long story," she says, and I can't tell from her tone whether she would prefer I ask her about it or just leave it alone.

"You, um . . ." I point at her. And she looks down at her dress, which I meant to tell her looks amazing on her, but what I say instead is: "You wore a dress."

"Was I not supposed to dress up?" she asks, looking around. And then she looks at me. I'm wearing a faded pair of jeans and an old *South Park* shirt. "Let me guess, you *are* dressed up."

"Funny," I say. "Why don't I go grab us some—"

"Oh no, you don't," Amy says, her fingers clasping my arm so tight I think she might bruise me. I'm not sure I'd complain if she did. "You are not allowed to leave me alone. I don't know anyone here."

"The whole staff is here. You know them." I motion around at Marshal and at Morgan, who's still standing in the living room, where I left her, watching us.

Amy bites her lip and looks around, and I'm afraid she's already regretting being here. "I'm just not, you know . . ."

I raise an eyebrow at her. "I don't think I *do* know."

She shrugs. "I don't know if I'm really friends with anyone but you."

Friends. It's the first time either one of us has acknowledged it. We're friends. "Why didn't you bring a date?" I regret the words as soon as I say them. I know why she didn't bring a date. Because she just broke up with her boyfriend and probably is still in love with him. My stomach turns.

She finally lets go of my arm, and I hate that I made her look sad. But one thing I've noticed about Amy: She's good at hiding it. It only takes a second for her expression to change from tragic to devious. "Did you?" she asks, the corners of her mouth tilting up.

"No," I say simply, and then Morgan sidles up to us.

"Hi, Amy," she says, her eyes flitting between the two of us. She's not quite as good at hiding things.

"Hey, Morgan," Amy says. "Happy Valentine's Day!" she all but shouts.

Morgan flinches. "Right. Happy Cupid Likes to Fuck Up Our Lives Day."

Amy giggles nervously, and Morgan sort of looks at her like she's not really sure what she's made of.

"Did you know Morgan plays guitar, drums, and piano in her

band?" I blurt, because I don't like the way Morgan is looking at Amy. Or at me.

Beside me, Amy says, "That is so cool. I played piccolo in band when I was a freshman."

Morgan looks mildly disgusted, but I smile down at Amy. "Piccolo?"

She grins up at me. "It's a hard job, but somebody's got to do it." Her eyes meet something over my shoulder. "Hey, I should go say hi to Brooke. I'll be back." She pats me on the arm, and just like that, she's gone.

I watch her wander into the kitchen to join Brooke, ignoring the commotion behind me as something begins in the living room. Morgan yanks on my shirtsleeve and says in my ear, "It's Spin the Bottle, come on!" She drags me toward the circle forming on the carpet.

"Spin the Bottle?" I ask, incredulous. They're kidding, right? "What is this, middle school?"

Lauren, arranging everyone on the carpet, looks at me. "I had just figured out I was a fucking lesbian in middle school, so I didn't get to play any of these games. Sue me, okay?"

And even as Morgan tugs me to the ground beside her, my eyes search for Amy.

AMY

"AMY!" Brooke, elbow deep in a cookie tray of egg rolls, beams at me. "I thought you weren't coming!" She shoves the pan into the oven, and my eyes are caught by something hanging on the wall behind her.

"What's that?" I ask.

Brooke glances over her shoulder and then smiles. "It's a Kiss Wall!"

I step around her and approach the large board on the wall. It's bright pink and has little strips of paper all over it, multicolored and folded in various formations. "What's a Kiss Wall?"

Brooke comes up beside me and taps a stack of paper strips on the counter. "It's like a Wish Wall, but you write the name of a person you want to kiss instead."

"What if there's no one that you want to kiss?"

She glances sideways at me. "Are you saying there isn't?"

Just then, there's a cheer from the living room, and I look over just in time to see Morgan lean over and plant a kiss on Oliver. I wait, a heartbeat, two, but they don't pull apart. She wraps her hand around the back of his neck, opens her mouth over his, and the cheering gets louder.

I look away, back at the board, my palms starting to sweat. I reach forward and pick up a slip of paper that's pastel green, but then I just hold it in my hand, trying to ignore what's going on in the living room.

"Hey, Brooke?"

She's already turned away from me to pour someone a drink. "Hmm?"

I've been debating whether or not to do this, and now that I'm standing here in Brooke's kitchen, I know I want to do it, but I'm not so sure it's the best time.

"So, I'm applying for this scholarship, and I sort of need a letter of recommendation from someone who's not a teacher, and I was hoping that maybe you would write it. I know we've only worked together for a month and a half, but, I don't know . . ."

Brooke still has a bottle of tequila in her hand, and I realize that she's lining up shots along her counter. But she sets the bottle down and smiles at me. "Of course I will." She reaches out and squeezes my elbow, and I feel a weird peace spread over me, a sense of belonging that flashes quickly. And then Brooke turns away from me, resuming her pouring.

I turn back to the board, tapping the tip of my pen against the counter. And then, without thinking about it, telling myself it's just a board and means absolutely nothing, I write Jackson's name on my slip of paper, fold it in half, and pin it to the board.

"You put something on the Kiss Wall?"

Oliver is standing beside me, and I feel a little uncomfortable with the fact that I didn't hear him approach. He has a strange look on his face, his eyes glued to the slip of paper I just pinned to the wall.

"You have lip gloss on your mouth," I say. I meant for my comment to be a joke, but when I say it, my voice is quiet, and for some reason I have to look away when he reaches up to wipe his mouth.

"What's going on?" I ask Brooke, who puts a shot glass in my hand before tugging me over to the kitchen table. "What's this?"

"We're playing Drunk Truth, so you better buckle up," she says. I glance over my shoulder in time to see Oliver pinning a folded slip of paper to the Kiss Wall. He wanders through the kitchen and pours himself a shot, throws it back, and then pours another.

"I don't think that's how you play the game," I tell him when he's joined us around the table.

He doesn't say anything.

"What's Drunk Truth?" Morgan asks from Oliver's other side. She loops her arm through his.

Brooke is still passing around shots, and she smiles at Morgan like she's a child. "Confessing your sins. Getting fucking wasted and telling everyone your deepest, darkest secrets."

I don't like the sound of this.

"I get to ask a question. Everyone at the table answers or they do a shot. Your choice. You answer a question, you're out of the game. Everyone else, you do shots until you answer one. Let the games begin."

A few people snicker, but I feel mild panic begin low in my stomach.

"Question one: Who was your first love?"

Everyone scoffs. Apparently, that's an easy one. All I can think about is Jackson, the fact that I gave him my virginity, all the things he said to me when we broke up, that I can't even decide if I still love him or if I hate him.

And then I realize that Brooke is staring at me, her eyebrows raised. Because I'm the first one, and I have to tell the truth or I have to drink. I pick up the shot in front of me and drink.

Everyone cheers, and when I look over at Brooke, prepared to gloat, she isn't looking at me. Her eyes are glued to Oliver, and when I turn, his eyes are glued to me. I can't read the expression on his face, but it's an expression I've never seen on him before.

He picks up his shot glass and drinks. Everyone cheers.

Morgan blinks out at the table. "What if I've never been in love?"

Brooke blinks back at her. She obviously wasn't expecting that. "Drink," she says after a second of deliberation, and everyone cheers as Morgan obeys.

Stories go around the table, more than half telling a story about a girl or boy they were in love with as a child or one of their high school sweethearts. From what I can tell, I'm the only person here who's actually still *in* high school.

"Question two!" Brooke shouts when there are only ten of us left at the table. "Tell us about your last bad breakup."

"That's not a question," Oliver says beside me, maybe a little slower than usual, and I think maybe those shots are getting to him.

"Just answer it, York."

Oliver points at me. "Her first."

I narrow my eyes at him. He already knows about my bad breakup. Well, he knows part of it, at least. I'm not rehashing that for these people. I do the shot.

Oliver snorts and then he throws back his shot, too.

Morgan sighs and wrings her hands. "My last boyfriend dumped me because he said he'd rather fuck my sister." And then, even though she isn't expected to, she throws back her shot.

Around the table, three people do shots and the others tell their stories: stories of cheating significant others, weird sex fetishes, and one long-distance relationship gone sour.

"Question three!" Brooke shouts, even though she doesn't have to this time. No one is cheering. Everyone is watching our game with rapt attention. "Tell us the story of how you lost your virginity."

Nope. Absolutely not. Not happening. My fingertips are starting to tingle, and my stomach is warm, but I throw back my shot anyway. I'm not telling anyone about my first time with Jackson, the only person I've been with.

Again, Oliver hesitates. I wonder what kind of story he has to tell, probably some awkward, fumbling, back-seat prom sex story. I can't keep my eyes from going to Morgan, from thinking about her tongue in his mouth in the living room. My palms start to sweat again, but I'm pretty sure it's the tequila.

Whatever Oliver's story is, he isn't planning to share it. He does his shot, and I have to say, I'm surprised. Don't guys love talking about that kind of thing?

As if to confirm my suspicion, the three remaining boys at the table tell their stories and bow out, leaving two girls, both of which do their shots.

"Question four!" I'm not sure I'm going to be able to hold out any longer. I'm going to have to spill some kind of hideous story about Jackson and me or I'm going to fall over.

"Who did you put on the Kiss Wall?" Brooke is grinning. She's having too much fun with this. I guess this one isn't so bad. The only person who knows anything about Jackson is Oliver, and at the rate he's going, he isn't going to remember tonight anyway.

"Jackson. My ex."

Brooke's smile fades slowly, and I watch her as I step back from the table, stumbling a little against someone who's standing behind me. Brooke's eyes, full of panic now for some reason, move to Oliver, and when I look up, he's looking at me again, and his eyes stay glued to me as he tilts his head and lets the shot of tequila slide down his throat.

OLIVER

My HEAD IS spinning, and I can't decide what I want to do more: strangle Brooke for what she obviously thought was a well-concealed plan to get me to confess my feelings to Amy (it wasn't) or kiss Amy so hard and so long that she'll forget about her ex.

By the time I decide which I want more (kill Brooke), she's asking me to tell the table a tragic story about my parents, so I tell them about how my parents didn't love each other enough to stay together, and that seems to be good enough.

I'm set free.

But looking around, I don't see Amy anymore, and honestly, compared to everyone else, most half tipsy and ready for more, Amy is really the only person I'm interested in hanging out with tonight.

I'm starting to feel the tequila in the tips of my fingers, and I move down the short hallway to the bathroom, thinking maybe some cold water on my face will help, when I hear something from Brooke and Lauren's bedroom.

Sniffling.

Crying.

"Amy?" I push the door open slowly, noting that the lights are off. The light from the hallway rushes in, and I see her there, sitting on the floor, her back against the end of the bed, wiping at her face. "What's going on?"

She gestures for me to close the door, and I do, stepping in and shutting out the light.

"I'm sorry. I'm so sorry. I know you probably regret even inviting me to this thing now."

My heart is pounding. I want her to stop apologizing. I feel her eyes on me, and I stand with my back to the door before sitting down beside her.

"It's okay," I finally say. "This whole thing is juvenile anyway."

I hear Amy laugh. I can't see her whole face, only the portion from the tip of her nose to her hairline. Her eyes, her cheekbones, all striped with light coming from the moonlight through the open blinds.

"I was thinking the same thing. I thought these people were in college. Shouldn't they be hooking up in the bathroom or something?"

"Pretty much. How you feeling?" What I mean is, how drunk is she? I can feel the alcohol in the numbness of my fingers and the warmth in my stomach, but I can hold my liquor pretty well. Amy, on the other hand, is half my size. I want to ask her why she was in here crying, if it was because of her ex, but I'm not good at being pushy, or at comforting people, or at generally being an acceptable human being.

"I'm drunk crying in my boss's bedroom. Doesn't that tell you everything you need to know?" She gives a wet kind of laugh. "I feel like I'm going to hurl. You?"

"Same."

Her foot bumps mine. "Oops. Sorry," she whispers, and I sort of wish I could kiss her. But there's her ex, and her tears, and the fact that as much as I'm starting to feel about her, we still don't really know each other.

We fall into a long silence, and I finally say, "Are you okay?" This time, there's no way she can mistake what I mean.

She shifts and sets her head back on the edge of the mattress. "Just feeling overwhelmed, but yeah, I'm okay. You don't have to stay with me."

"I know I don't have to," I tell her, my voice quiet. I want to stay with her as long as she'll let me. Anything she has to say is way more interesting than anything anyone else has to say.

"Oliver," she whispers. "Why don't you have a girlfriend?"

Because the girls I like often want to get back together with their exes doesn't seem like a very reasonable answer. "I'm not good with people."

"Everyone here seems to like you. You're funny and nice."

"I'm anything but nice." I think the term my mother often uses to describe me is *prickly*.

"You're nice to me."

A sliver of light highlights her dark brown eyes, and it's on the tip of my tongue to tell her that I'm nice to her because I'm fairly certain I'm developing some pretty serious feelings for her.

But I don't say it.

Instead, I say, "What does it say about how nice I am that my best friend is my boss?"

I expect her to laugh, but she doesn't. "What does it say about me that my only friend is my mom?"

I feel a little shaken. "I guess I don't get it. If you're such a social pariah, why did Jackson, popular guy extraordinaire, date you?"

Her eyes finally break away from mine. "When we first started dating, the fact that I'm so driven was the reason he liked me. He thought it was cute how serious I am. But I guess that changed. I guess I've gotten a little . . . intense. He just wants to have fun."

Her voice drips with loneliness, and it makes my stomach ache. "Is that what he said, that you're not fun?"

"Yeah," she finally whispers. Her voice cracks. I'm just about to answer, but before I can, she talks over me. "But I still love him. No matter what I do, I can't stop."

There are so many things I want to say, so many ways that I want to tell her that if he can't see how amazing she is then he doesn't deserve her, but it's like someone bricked over my mouth, sealing all the right words in, until she finally sends me a little smile.

"I think maybe we should go back to the party."

We struggle to our feet, both of us a little off-balance. Amy steps up onto her tiptoes and kisses me on the cheek. "Thanks for hanging with me, Oliver."

I stand there for a long time after she's gone.

AMY

I FEEL LIKE shit Monday morning. It feels like someone is periodically trying to get a nail through my temple with a baseball bat.

"Where the hell were you?" someone demands as I try to remember the combination to my locker, and if I'm being honest, if we weren't in school, I would probably clock the person currently shouting in my ear.

"Fuck," I groan. "Where was I when?"

Petra, looking even more assassin chic than usual grabs me by one shoulder and spins me around to face her. I stumble into the locker next to mine.

"Move," the girl who owns the locker growls, and if one more person demands something of me in a haughty tone, I'm going to lose it.

I straighten up, and Petra looks at me, her mouth hanging open. "Um, hello! Student council meeting at seven this morning? Did you seriously forget? We were supposed to be finalizing prom decorations. Where were you?"

I flinch. Yep, now I remember.

"Fucking fuck," I say instead of actually answering Petra. "I can't believe I forgot."

Petra's mouth is hanging down so low I think it might actually touch the floor. "You *forgot*? What the hell, Amy? Since when do you forget anything? Don't you have a photographic memory or something?"

"God, Petra, would you shut up?" I shout before I can stop myself. "If I had a photographic memory, I wouldn't have a fucking B in calculus."

Her eyes go wide, and a few of the people walking by slow as they pass, probably trying to figure out if this is about to descend into a fight. I can't look at any of them. I feel like I'm going to puke.

"Are you—" Petra starts. She leans into me, examining my face. I swat her away. "Are you hungover?"

I groan, pressing my forehead to my locker door. After the game of Drunk Truth last night, there were many more cocktails to be had, gleefully prepared by Brooke, until I eventually had to call Mama and tell her I was sleeping on Brooke's couch. Of course, I didn't tell her *why*. "Just leave me alone, Petra, okay? Look, just—can you just send me the notes or whatever you need me to do for prom setup, okay? And just leave me alone?"

I walk away from her, leaving my calculus book behind in the locker I can't open.

"Amy, wait," Petra calls out after me, and then I feel her hand on my elbow again, yanking me back. Dear God, why won't she just let me go? "Come here."

I don't really have the strength to fight her, so I let her drag me down the hallway, and then I'm very confused when she sits me down on a bench in the courtyard and starts digging around in her huge purse.

"Petra, can you just—"

She holds up a hand to shush me and then pulls a bottle of Gatorade and a bottle of pills out of her purse. She thrusts both of them at me. "Take four if the headache is really bad," she says, crossing her arms.

And then she just watches me. Until I finally open the Gatorade, shake four ibuprofen pills into my hand, and throw it all back. The Gatorade is strawberry-lemonade flavored, and that doesn't even surprise me.

When I've gulped down the entire bottle of Gatorade, Petra takes it from me, tossing it into a recycling bin close by before stuffing the bottle of ibuprofen back in her bag.

"Thanks," I say, which, I realize, is the first time I've ever thanked Petra for anything. She doesn't say anything back at first, and I'm reaching for my bag that I dropped on the ground beside my foot, when she says, "You're slipping."

I turn wide eyes on her. "I am not. What, just because I got a bad grade on a test and missed a StuCo meeting?"

"I thought this stuff was *important* to you."

"It is," I say. I can't believe she's even saying any of this to me. "Why are you on me right now? It's none of your business what I do with my life."

She stands, slinging her bag over her shoulder. "I'm not interested in winning against someone who isn't even trying."

All I can do is stare up at her. Ever since Petra and I discovered two years ago that we were at the top of our class, it's always been her and me. We're the ones who volunteer the most, do all the extra credit, take extra summer classes. It's always us.

She looks at me for a long moment, and then she turns and leaves me sitting there, my head still pounding.

OLIVER

I LAUGH WHEN Amy walks into the shop that afternoon, her eyelids sagging, wearing a They Might Be Giants T-shirt for band shirt night, and looking like she hasn't slept in a month.

"Would you shut the hell up?" she growls at me, which just makes me laugh harder.

"You're cranky. How are you still hungover?"

She stops at the counter to glare at me. "I'm not still hungover. I'm just really tired." Brooke comes out of the office, whistling, and Amy points a deadly finger at her. "And *you*. I blame you for this."

Brooke grins. "Why, hello, sunshine. Is someone having trouble handling the consequences of their life choices?"

Amy groans and leans against the front counter. "I hate both of you."

Brooke shakes her head. "You can work in the stockroom today. Try to stay upright."

Amy rushes into the stockroom and slams the door behind her, and I don't realize I'm smiling until Brooke slides past me, sending me a knowing look as she passes. I bite back my smile.

It isn't until an hour later that the phone rings. Brooke is in her office and Amy hasn't emerged from behind the closed door of the stockroom, so I reach for the cordless.

"Spirits. This is Oliver. How can I help you?"

There is immediate screaming, and it takes me a shocked second to realize that it's children in the background of the call.

"Hello?"

Then a woman's voice finally breaks in. "*Cállate, niños!* Sorry about that. This is Amy's mother. Can you tell her that her stepfather is on his way to get the car? He needs it."

I'm already moving toward the stockroom door. "Sure, I'll just let you talk to—"

"No, no. Just give her the message. She'll have to take the bus home." And then she hangs up, just like that.

I stare down at the phone in my hand and then at the closed door in front of me. I can hear music playing behind it, and when I push it open, Amy, looking more full of life than she did when she came in, is bent at an awkward angle, looking sideways at a shelf of old CDs that are about to be put on clearance.

"Amy?"

She pops up quick and smacks her head on a shelf above her.

"Shit," we both say at the same time, but oddly, after she's recovered, she smiles at me. "Hey. Do you need me out front?"

I lean against the door and shake my head. "No. But your mom just called. She said your stepdad is coming to get the car."

She looks at me, her face blank. "Seriously?"

"I could take you home."

Amy's eyebrows go up, her mouth taking on a funny shape. "Really?"

I shrug. "Sure. Why not?" It's not as if I have anywhere else to be, and even if I did, would I care? Why would I let Amy take the bus home when I have a perfectly good vehicle?

Her eyes seem to smile, along with the rest of her. "Okay. Thanks, Oli."

I try to ignore the way my heart pounds when she calls me that.

AMY

I WAIT FOR Oliver on the sidewalk. I glance over my shoulder at the tutoring center. It's been closed for hours, the lights off behind the big front windows. I turn back around in time to see Oliver waving to Brooke, letting the glass door fall shut behind him.

We walk to his truck in silence, and when we climb in, I immediately have a flashback to that night, to his father unconscious in the back seat while Oliver tries desperately to pretend he isn't there. He hasn't spoken about his dad since, and I'm too terrified to ask.

Oliver cranks the ignition, the heater blasting, and before he even puts his seat belt on, he roots around in his console for a CD. After a second, he closes the console and reaches over and pops open the glove box, also stuffed with CDs. And then he leans into the back seat and produces a box from the floorboard and opens it to reveal even more CDs. I suddenly have an image of him sleeping in a bed made of stacks of thick jewel cases.

"Oh! I have the Amber Run album!" I say just as he's getting ready to put a CD in the stereo, and I almost feel bad that he went through all that trouble. Before he can say anything, I'm digging around in my bag, pulling out my favorite Amber Run album and shoving it at him. "Put this in."

He doesn't seem offended by my command, just takes the CD from me and pops it into the stereo. "So, what are you reading?"

For a second, I'm not sure what he means, until I realize I took my copy of *Ethics* out of my bag when I was rooting around for the CD. Oliver adjusts the volume on the stereo low so we can talk over it, and then puts the car in drive.

"Oh. It's Plato. I'm writing an essay on it for this scholarship I'm applying for at Stanford." I lean my head back against the seat, looking over at him. "Have you ever heard of Plato's Cave?"

I see his hands grip the steering wheel and release it again. "I don't think so. Tell me about it."

"Well, there are these people who sit in a cave, facing a wall. There's a fire behind them, and the only thing they know about reality are the shadows that are projected onto the wall in front of them from the cave mouth behind them. And when they're introduced to the real world, it's scary. They don't know what's real and what's fake. To them, what's fake is reality. The shadows."

Oliver lets out a little rueful chuckle. "Makes sense."

I look over at him, his hair ruffling slightly in the breeze through the barely cracked window. He's so cute, his red hair and the dimple in his chin and the freckles scattered across his nose. Those freckles travel all the way down his arms, peeking out at me from where he's shoved the sleeves up on his hooded sweatshirt all the way to his elbows.

One hand over the other, he takes a wide turn. "This song is nice." He reaches out to turn it up, but I almost don't want him to. I want to ask him a million questions about his home life, mostly because the only thing I know is that his mother is maybe nicer to strangers than anyone else I've ever met, and that his father might be passing out in his back seat on a regular basis.

We drive in silence for a little while. I direct him toward my house and watch downtown Kansas City fly past as Amber Run's smooth melody flows through the cab. The song reaches a crescendo, and my heart starts to beat loud in my ears, adrenaline pumping through me. I feel like I'm alive inside the song.

I feel a strange flutter in my stomach at all the sensations together—the cold biting my cheeks, the heat pressing against my fingertips, the open, clear sound of the electric guitar.

We stop for a long time, too long, and I open my eyes—when did I close them?—to see that we're sitting at a stop sign. There's a honk behind us, and when I look over, Oliver looks away from me and slams on the gas, rocketing us forward so fast, my stomach flips.

The song ends as we're pulling into my neighborhood, and I don't know what comes over me, but I say, "I'm not ready to go home. Can we just keep driving?"

For just a second, the truck slows, coasting right past my front door, but then we're moving forward again, turning at the end of my street onto the intersecting street, the music still playing loudly over us.

We drive as the guitars continue, and I think maybe I haven't been this happy in a long time, this content. We drive all the way back to the shop, moving through downtown Kansas City as the sky goes from pink to purple to black.

Oliver looks over at me sharply, and then, without warning, he yanks the steering wheel, and we pull over in front of a closed bank.

"Why did you pull over?" I ask, worried that we were about to run out of gas or lose a tire or something.

"This requires a lot of attention," he says seriously, turning up the music.

Pride bursts in my chest. "You like Amber Run, huh?" I demand, my heart racing. I've never known anything like this before, this utter excitement at knowing that there's someone else in the world who loves the same bands that I do.

We sit there for the entire rest of the album, both of us staring out the front window as cars drive by. From where we sit, I can see the glowing sign of Spirits down the road, a red beacon in the winter night, like a buoy on the ocean. I smile and close my eyes, listening until the last song ends.

Without a word, Oliver pulls back onto the road. The album starts over again, and we move in the direction of my neighborhood. When we slow again in front of my house, Oliver reaches forward to take the CD from the player, but I reach out and put a hand on his arm to stop him. "Borrow it."

Oliver hesitates, his eyes sliding down to where I'm touching him. I pull my hand back and his eyes find mine across the expanse between us. "You sure?"

I nod. "I trust you. Return it when you want."

He doesn't say anything as I turn, climb out of his truck, and slam the door shut behind me.

AMY

I KNOW I'VE run out of options. I don't like giving up, and I don't like surrendering, admitting when I can't handle something on my own. As far as I'm concerned, I can handle everything on my own. I've been doing it for as long as I can remember.

But when I get my calculus exam back on Friday, and see that I got a C, I know I have to get some help or it's all over for me, my pride be damned.

That's how I end up standing outside the tutoring center on Saturday afternoon, trying to make myself go inside. I glance over my shoulder at Spirits, and I can't help but feel like everything's all wrong now that I'm on the other side of the street. This side doesn't feel right anymore. It feels like switching lives with someone.

"Why are you just standing out here?"

I whip around. I shouldn't be surprised to find Petra standing in front of me, holding the door of the tutoring center open with one arm and leaning out onto the sidewalk.

I'm not about to tell her that the reason I'm standing out here is because I'm way too nervous to go in. "I need calculus help," I finally tell her.

Petra's eyes narrow. "Are you serious?"

I turn to leave. I'm not going to stand here and be berated by Petra because she thinks she's better than me.

"Wait," Petra says. "I know you got a C on the calc exam."

I turn back to her, feeling anger vibrate in my jaw like a dentist's drill. "How do you know about that?"

She shrugs. "Someone in StuCo saw your paper and sort of told everyone else. Everyone . . . everyone was sort of making fun of you at the meeting."

I feel sick to my stomach. It's no secret that no one at school likes me. To everyone, I'm a brownnoser and a teacher's pet and whatever else they have to throw at me. But I had no idea that people were keeping tabs on my academics. I figured that was just Petra.

"I don't participate," Petra says, and there's something so genuine in her expression, maybe it's pity, that I think I believe her, even though Petra hasn't exactly been known for her kindness toward me in the past.

"Whatever."

"Amy," she says when I turn away again. "Look, I'll tutor you one-on-one, okay?"

I look back over my shoulder at her, still standing there, her hair blowing in the wind, her skin gleaming in the sun, and her eyes just a little desperate.

"Amy, come on. I have an A-plus in calc. Are you going to turn that down?"

I hate it when she's right.

"Meet me at my house tonight. I'm done here at five, okay?" She pats her pockets like she's looking for something, but I wave her off.

"I know where you live, Petra. I'll be there at six." I know I should be grateful that Petra is doing me a huge favor, but all I feel is shame.

AMY

ONLY A FEW neighborhoods separate Petra's house from mine, but it might as well be an ocean. I don't really give in to envy, but I never fail to notice that her entryway is bigger than my bedroom and my sisters' bedroom put together.

Petra closes the door behind me and then gestures toward the dining room, which is bigger than our living room. She has a notebook and her calculus book sitting on the corner of the table, lined up perfectly against the edge.

"Do you like cream puffs?" she asks as I sling my backpack onto one of the chairs. They're probably antique or something, and I'm suddenly very nervous about potentially damaging one of them. I move my bag to the floor, making sure that it isn't resting against the table leg.

"Um," I say in response.

Petra appears through the kitchen doorway with a tray of cream puffs in her hand like she's about to begin feeding her guests at a grand party. I take a cream puff because I'm starving.

"Thanks," I say, taking a napkin from the fancy holder in the center of the table and placing my cream puff (homemade, I suspect) and napkin on the tablecloth.

"Okay," she says, sitting up straight in her chair. "Let's go over your calc test."

An hour later, I have a headache, and Petra is rubbing her eyes like she's a toddler who needs a nap. Half the cream puffs are gone, and I haven't missed the fact that Petra hasn't eaten a single one.

"Okay, do you want to move on to the next section or—"

The front door flies open, and next thing I know, there's a pre-teen in a leotard tearing through the house, rushing through the dining room and into the kitchen before I even have a second to process what's going on.

"Petra?" a woman by the front door calls out.

I know Petra's mother from field trips that she chaperoned and after-school activities that she showed up to in her minivan. She's just as tall and beautiful as Petra, but in the same way that Petra's mouth is always slightly down-turned, her mother always has a smile on her face.

"We're in here!" Petra calls out to her mother at the same time that Petra's little sister comes back into the dining room, munching on what looks like Hot Fries.

"Who are you?" she asks around the food in her mouth.

Petra rolls her eyes. "It's Amy, you dork. You don't remember Amy?"

The girl shrugs and walks back into the kitchen just as Petra's mother comes into the dining room. "Amy," she says. "It's so nice to see you again. How have you been?"

I smile up at her because it isn't her fault her daughter is trying to steal my future right out from under me. "I'm good. Petra's just helping me with some calculus homework."

Petra's mother sighs. "Petra's always off helping everyone. That tutoring center runs her ragged. She's always there. It's a wonder she has any time for her own homework much less being valedictorian!" Petra's mother, completely oblivious to the wide-eyed look that Petra is sending her, puts her hand on my shoulder.

I grit my teeth. "Yeah, I know. Isn't that great?"

Petra rolls her eyes as her mother's hand falls away from me. "Mom, we're kind of in the middle of something."

Petra's mother claps her hand over her mouth and turns to leave the dining room, sending us a friendly wave as she goes.

"I'm guessing you don't often discuss your academic competition with your mother," I say as soon as she's gone. "Wouldn't want her to know you might not make val."

"Yeah, except I'm going to make val, so why would I even bring it up?"

I slam my calculus book closed. "What makes you so sure? We're still tied." Probably. I haven't been to the counselor's office since the day I found out we were tied, since I'm always rushing from last period to Spirits and am usually doing homework before the first bell.

Petra stops rifling through her own textbook. "You're too distracted. You're trying to divide your time between looking good for Stanford, trying to get Jackson back, and working at that record store. You're trying to juggle too much, and all you're doing is making it easier for me to make val."

I tap my pen against my notebook. I hate that she looks so smug, closing all her books with her shoulders pressed back and her chin high. "Okay, genius. You want to be my life coach? Give me some pointers."

She gives me a firm look, lacing her fingers over her notebook. "You're really serious about this?"

I feel my stomach twist. I don't know if she means serious about being valedictorian or serious about wanting her advice. In the end, it doesn't really matter. The answer is yes.

She narrows her eyes at me, and I feel the hairs on the back of my neck stand up. I can tell I'm not going to like this. "I think it's time for you to let go of Jackson."

I sit back in my seat with a huff. "I'm not—"

"I'm serious, Amy," she says more forcefully. "Boyfriends are a bad idea, but pining for ex-boyfriends is even worse. It makes it impossible to think straight."

I don't know what to say to that.

"And you have to quit your job."

Petra's words stop me short. "No, I can't quit. I'm working there while my stepdad finds a new job." But it's more than that. It's something burrowing under my skin. Spirits is the only place where I feel like I belong and it stopped being about Carlos a while ago.

Petra drops her head in her hands. "So what you're saying is you want this but you're not willing to sacrifice anything for it?"

That makes rage simmer beneath my skin. "I've given up my social life, my free time, my relationships—"

"—just to fail," she finishes for me.

We stare at each other for a long time.

"I'm not going to fail." I reach down to put my book in my back-pack, my hands trembling either from adrenaline or from anger.

Petra blinks up at me. She opens her mouth to say something

else, but a loud crash emanates from the kitchen, and I use the opportunity to see myself out.

OLIVER

I CAN'T SAY I've completely forgotten about Dad. There's no forgetting Dad. Ever. But I have mostly managed to keep my mind off him since the last time I saw him. I heard secondhand that he was sentenced with what seemed to me like a lifetime's worth of community service hours. Much deserved, in my opinion.

And that's why I should have been expecting to run into him. Of course, I should have. Because I should have known that he would pop up in my life when I was least expecting it, once I'd let my guard down.

And when I'm least expecting it is when I'm hopping on the highway to get to the hardware store on the other side of town, and there he is, standing on the side of the road with a garbage bag and a trash poker.

I think about stopping. I think about pulling over right now and telling him that he's the thing I'm most ashamed of in my life. I think about pulling over and telling him to grow up. To grow up so that I can figure out what the hell I want to do with my life without taking his needs into account. I want to tell him that he should have stood up to my mother all those years ago, stuck around, let me be my own person, so that I don't have to feel like a piece of shit now for wanting to do what *I* want.

I keep driving. Because I would never say those things to him, no matter how pissed off I was.

But then a little thought starts to wriggle its way into my brain.

I don't want to be like him. I don't want to need something like alcohol to keep my mind off my dissatisfying life. I don't want to be hopeless and directionless and a complete waste of space.

And maybe that's why Mom is right. Maybe the key to never becoming Dad is going to college, even if it's right here in Missouri, where I would never really be able to escape the things that have been keeping me here all this time.

Maybe I should apply to MBU and just be done with it.

Maybe Amy would look at me differently if I was a college guy. Maybe she would look at me the way she looks at her ex.

Maybe she would love me if I had any clue what I was doing.

AMY

ON FRIDAY NIGHT, I stand in front of my mirror and stare. I've been doing this for the last half hour, trying to decide if this is really what I want to do. Do I want to spend my Friday night at a basketball game in hopes that I might see Jackson there? Do I really want to waste prime studying hours?

All I can think about is the way he looked at me across the table when he bought that gram, the way that being close to him still sends butterflies alive in my stomach, like I'm living in my own personal fairy tale. That's the way it's supposed to be.

I can't get valedictorian with Petra around, and I can't make Stanford accept me.

But I can get Jackson back.

I've forgiven him for being an asshole at his birthday party, and

I can't stop thinking about what he wrote on that Valentine-gram, can't stop thinking about how both of the grams are now in one of my drawers, constantly reminding me every time I open it just how much I miss him.

I don't understand the majority of the rules of basketball. I know that the players are trying to score a goal, that the goals are worth two points, and that *traveling* is a call the referees make, but I don't actually know what traveling is. Also, I know that Jackson would play basketball if he was any good at it, but he's really only good at track.

Half an hour later, I'm standing beside the bleachers, still invisible to everyone in the gym, deciding whether I can do this or not.

I take a step toward the court and peek over the bottom of the bleachers. I see Jackson immediately. He has on his pilot jacket, with the wool collar, and he looks amazing. And he's all alone.

I take a deep breath. If I'm going to do this, if I'm really going to make a play for Jackson, at least one more, I need to do it now, before I lose my nerve. I step around the side of the bleachers just as our team scores a goal, and the crowd erupts. I watch Jackson jump to his feet, clapping loudly and then cupping his hands around his mouth to yell, "That's it, Number Twenty-Three!"

I guess that means Bryce just scored.

When Jackson settles back down on the bleachers, his eyes scan the sidelines, almost like he's looking for someone, and they land on me. For a second, it's almost like he doesn't recognize me, like I'm someone who's been gone and now looks like a completely different person, even though we saw each other in first period this morning.

And then, surprisingly, he waves me over, and I have a flash of the week before we started dating. I had walked into our history class, looking for a place to sit since my normal seat was taken, and he did the same thing, waving me over, accepting me when it seemed like maybe no one else could even see me.

"Where is everyone?" I ask, sliding onto the bleacher beside him. He usually has an entourage at these things.

Jackson rolls his eyes. "Tony's parents are out of town and his brother is in town from Berkeley. He offered to buy beer, so people are kind of having a party at his place." Jackson leans toward me a little but keeps his eyes on the court, and I don't know if he wants to be closer to me or he's just trying to see around the cheering father sitting in front of us. He smells like Old Spice and dryer sheets. "What are you doing here, anyway?" he says when the court goes quiet, and a foul is called. "You hate basketball."

"I don't hate basketball," I lie. "I just don't understand the appeal of it."

In the eleven months that we were together, Jackson never attempted to explain the rules of basketball to me, and he doesn't try now. "God, it's cold," I say. My fingers are going numb. I flex them to get the blood pumping, but they're still cold as ice. The gym has always been a little drafty, and it's snowing outside.

"Here," Jackson says, and before I really know what's happening, he's cupped my fingers between his hands and has his mouth pressed to them, blowing warm breath onto them in puffs. I watch him blow and then rub his hands together around mine. He used to do this for me all the time, when we were lying in bed together and my fingers had gone cold.

"What are you doing?" I whisper, because it feels like speaking too loud will ruin everything.

He stops, lets his hands drop and mine stay suspended between us. "I don't know," he says. "Habit."

That's what happens when you do the same thing with someone for almost a year. You form habits. We stare at each other, and I get this strange feeling in the pit of my stomach. Because this is how it's supposed to be. It's supposed to be Jackson and me, together. I can feel it, and I know he can, too.

"I'm going to the concession stand," I say, hopping up. Part of me hopes that he'll offer to come with me. I imagine us walking along the sidelines, out to the lobby where the Booster Club sells candy and drinks, confessing to one another all the emotions that still exist between us. But he doesn't. He goes back to watching the basketball game, and I walk to the concession stand alone, tucking my jacket around me. It's a little too big for me. It fit last winter.

I stand in line behind a group of rowdy girls, keeping my eyes straight ahead and trying to decide what I want.

"Can I have a hot chocolate and a bag of M&M's please?" I say to the basketball mom as soon as I get to the front of the line. I want to hurry up and get back to Jackson, but the cold is killing me, and some hot chocolate will definitely warm me up. She sets the cup and the bag in front of me and smiles. I reach into my jeans and fish out the money to pay and then take my hot chocolate and M&M's. The candy is for Jackson. His favorite.

I try to move quickly while also trying to keep my hot chocolate from sloshing out onto my hands. Unfortunately, I'm so focused on my hot chocolate that I don't realize Jackson isn't alone until I've made it up the stairs to our spot on the bleachers, until I'm standing in front of him, the M&Ms outstretched.

I freeze. Jackson and some girl are both looking down at the candy in my hand, and then they both look up at me. My brain takes in details it refuses to process: Jackson's jacket draped across the girl's shoulders, their fingers entwined on Jackson's thigh.

And then it hits me like a truck.

The girl's face is completely blank. She obviously has no clue who I am. But Jackson's face has an emotion written all over it: shame.

I'm still just standing there, blocking the people on the rows behind us, my hand wrapped around the bag of candy until finally, I let it fall to the bleachers with a *thunk*. And even though it doesn't make any sense, it feels like being broken up with all over again. Even though nothing really happened, my mind keeps playing back the moment that Jackson held my hands against his mouth.

And then my hot chocolate goes the way of the candy, splattering liquid all over me and Jackson and the guy in the row in front of us before I turn and rush down the stairs, back to the floor.

"Amy!"

I'm already halfway through the lobby. I can't stop. What happened to my perfectly crafted life? What happened to my plan for my senior year? What did I do to deserve this?

"Amy, please!"

I finally get to my car, but when I have to stop to fumble with my keys, Jackson catches up with me. "Amy, don't go."

I throw my car door open with so much force that it bounces on the hinges and slams shut again. "Don't go? Are you kidding? And what should I do instead? Stay here so I can watch you snuggle with your new girlfriend?"

His eyes move down to my pants, where hot chocolate spans from my knees to my shoelaces. "Can't we just be friends?"

I grind my teeth together and throw open my car door again. "I don't have time for friends."

OLIVER

I FIND DAD passed out in a stone courtyard, between two tall business parks, at three in the morning. There are two benches in the center of the courtyard, facing each other, and my father is stretched out on one of them. His cell phone lies on the concrete beside the bench. He must have dropped it after he called me.

I shouldn't be surprised. Why should my father give up drinking just because some judge told him to? Why should picking up trash on the side of the highway have any kind of permanent effect on him whatsoever? Why did I think he would ever have a real reason to give it all up?

I press a hand to his chest. It rises and falls slowly, so I take a seat on the other bench. It's cold, the way only three in the morning can be cold, but oddly, it feels nice. I suck in a breath, my lungs burning against it.

This late at night, it feels like the world is moving in slow motion, or the gravity of the Earth has shifted, and you could float away into the atmosphere if you just spoke loud enough.

My eyes travel through the courtyard, painted orange and yellow in the lights from the buildings around us, finally falling on a strange metal sculpture right in the center. It's long and metallic, a series of flat pieces of metal that curve around each other, one on top of the other, like nesting dolls. I step up to it, touching my fingers to the metal, the cold almost painful against my skin.

And then, on the highway in front of me, a car races by, and the whole sculpture vibrates, sound waves moving through the metal and coming out like a groan that's haunting. I smile up at it, goose bumps rising on my arms.

It makes me think of Amy. I'm not even sure why. Maybe because everything makes me think of Amy.

I walk back to my dad and nudge him awake. He groans and swats my hand away. I shove him. "Dad, you gotta sit up."

Like me, my father is tall and thin, much too heavy for me to attempt to drag him back to the truck. I'd probably need a dolly for that. My father gets to his feet, but I have to throw one of his arms over my shoulders to get him to stagger his way to my truck, which is parked illegally against a curb. Almost as soon as I get him in the passenger seat, he falls asleep, and I strap him in like a two-year-old.

I make my way out of the city, stopping at a red light just as we pass from Kansas City into Independence. I sigh and set my head against the seat. The music coming through my speakers is enough to almost put me to sleep. It's an album that I'm thinking about loaning to Amy, a Norwegian pop singer that she might love enough to give up the contest.

I glance out the passenger side window at an old church. I guess I've never noticed it before. The sign out front proclaims it's a Catholic church. Out of the corner of my eye, I see the light turn green, but there's no one behind me, so I stay where I am, trying to make out the images in the shadow-covered stained-glass windows.

"What is this shit?" I hear Dad grumble, and then I hear the sound of tires squealing behind me before something hits us.

MARCH

OLIVER

IT'S ALMOST ALL worth it when Amy sees my cast. Maybe that's a horrible thing to think. After all, we did (ironically) get rear-ended by a drunk driver in the middle of the night, but I can't help being mildly thankful when Amy walks into the shop that night, her eyes finding me like they always do when she comes to work, and then going wide when she sees the cast on my arm.

"What happened?" She takes my plastered arm in her hands gently, like she might injure it further with the slightest pressure. "Did you slip on the ice? How long have you lived here? Don't you know how to maneuver a February snowstorm?" She isn't even looking at me. She's running the tip of her finger over the elephant and the kitten Brooke and Lauren drew on it while I was at their place last night.

"Not quite. Car accident."

Her mouth opens in horror. She hasn't let go of my arm, and I can feel my whole body starting to quiver slightly. She's standing so close to me.

"A car accident? Oh my God."

"Amy, I'm okay."

When she looks at me, I feel my stomach flip. Even though Amy and I are friends, and even though I knew before now that she cares about me, I didn't really get that she *cares* about me. That maybe if something happened to me, it might actually mean something to her.

I can smell the floral scent of her shampoo when she pushes up on her toes to hug me, and I can feel the warmth of her along my body. I wrap my good arm around her, pressing my fingertips into her spine, gently.

She finally lets me go, and we both look down at the cast on my arm. She doesn't say anything, but I know she's waiting for the explanation.

"I went to pick up my dad. He was sort of . . . passed out." I leave it at that.

"Again?" she hisses.

Something inside me cracks open when she says that. I can't even really say why. Maybe it's because she was paying attention. When was the last time someone paid attention? And I don't mean Brooke noticing that I have feelings for Amy. No, it's more than that. I never told Amy specifically about my dad, but she gets it anyway. She saw him in the back seat that night. She figured out what was going on.

Because she cares.

"Do you want to go for a drive tonight?"

She sends me a wary look. "Is your car okay to drive?"

"Oh. Yeah. The bumper's a little ugly, but it's fine."

She smiles and nods. "Okay. New music for the competition?"

"There's something I want to show you."

She blinks up at me, and something flashes across her face, something that makes me feel like maybe I've said something wrong. But then her smile comes back.

"Sounds great. I could use a stress reliever."

I feel my good mood deflate slightly. "Everything okay?"

She looks away from me, and she doesn't have to answer. I can see it, the way you can see the rain clouds coming from miles away to cover up what's left of the sunshine.

"Your ex?"

A part of me is hoping she'll say no, of course not, not her ex. It's that damn calculus, it's her family getting on her nerves, it's the unbearable wait to hear from Stanford, anything but her ex, but when she looks up at me, I know I've guessed right.

"He's seeing someone," she says quietly.

I know the right things to say. Things like, *Man that sucks* or *How does that make you feel?* But instead, I say, "Amy, you deserve better."

Her dark eyes meet mine, and I can see that they're a little teary. I'm surprised at the way seeing her like this makes my chest ache, makes me want to hold her. Her chin starts to tremble, and I reach out and press my thumb there, feel her smooth skin under mine.

"Can someone tell me where the bathroom is?"

I pull my hand away from Amy's face and we both look over to see a teenage girl leaning across the counter, wiggling madly.

"It's in the back corner behind the posters," Amy says, pointing in the direction of the large restroom sign hanging from the ceiling. When the girl is gone, Amy looks back at me. "I should clock in," she says.

As soon as she's gone, Brooke saunters over. I pretend to be recording damages. "I'm starting to think you broke that arm on purpose," she says.

OLIVER

In the passenger seat of my car, Amy uncaps a black Sharpie with a *pop*. "Okay, hand it over," she says.

I roll my eyes but gladly set my arm on the console between our seats. Amy immediately bends over it with a smile. As she moves from one side of the cast to the other, her fingers brush the sensitive skin on the inside of my arm, and I hold in the gasp that rises up in my throat. She's writing quickly and doesn't notice what she's doing to me.

I've got big, big plans but I can see them slipping through.

"'Maps'?" I ask, recognizing the lyrics from one of the Front Bottoms's more popular songs.

Amy shrugs. "I like it. Besides, the cast covers your tattoo."

After a minute of listening to Walk the Moon (Amy says they're fine, but definitely not worth admitting that I'm the greater musical genius) sing between us, she says, "So where are we going anyway?"

"Just something I saw the other day. Made me think of you." I know that by saying this, I'm probably revealing too much.

Out of the corner of my eye, I see her look at me, but I keep my eyes on the road because if I look over at her now, I'm going to tell her that the moment I met her was the moment I came alive, and I think that just might ruin our night.

"Oli, what's going on with your dad?"

Finally, she's asking me. I don't even hesitate. I've spent so many years trying to only share parts of myself with people, the parts I think they can handle, but I want Amy to know all my parts.

"He's an alcoholic. My parents split a few years ago, but Dad was drinking well before that. He got arrested a couple months ago for a bar fight and got sentenced to about a thousand hours of community service. I just feel like I don't really know what to do about him. I don't want to cut him out of my life, but I also don't want to be his babysitter. And I *definitely* don't want to end up like him."

I can feel her looking at me while I drive. Clumsily, thanks to my cast. "That might be the most I've ever heard you say at one time," she says, and I laugh.

AMY

OLIVER PARKS DOWNTOWN, in a no-parking zone, but it's after ten, and I don't think we're going to get a ticket. It's just cold enough that when we get out of the truck, the wind makes me shiver hard, and I pull my coat close around me.

While I'm busy worrying about how cold I am, Oliver has led me into a courtyard. There's fresh snow covering every inch of it, including the benches. It's like we've stepped into a painting, our footsteps leaving ruts in the canvas.

And at first, I think this is all it is. Surely Oliver brought me to this quiet place, surrounded by stone buildings, because it's peaceful, and he knows just how desperate I am for peace lately. But then I hear a quiet sound, like the ringing of large bells in a clock tower in the distance. I stop, and beside me, Oliver stops, too.

"You hear it?" he asks. He points at something directly in the center of the courtyard. From where I stand, I can make out the shape of it, a rusty statue made up of half-moon shapes, pointed up at the sky, spooned on top of one another, like stacked shields.

"What is it?" I ask, taking a hesitant step toward it.

It shouldn't really startle me when Oliver grabs my hand, wrapping his long fingers around mine and pulling me toward the statue, but something about the way his hand seems to envelope the entirety of mine makes my heart pound loud in my cold ears.

When we're closer, the sound of our feet in the snow, the sound of my heart pounding loud in my head, is covered by a different sound. It's a moaning sound, like a choir singing out the cry of tortured souls. Snow has collected on some of the parts of the metal slabs that curve slightly, creating ledges.

"What is it?" I ask. "Where's the sound coming from?"

Oliver nods toward a plaque that sits low to the ground beneath the statue. "It's some sort of scientific explanation about how it creates sound waves from the air around us. I'm not much of a science brain, so I don't really understand it, but I think it's pretty cool."

I reach out and touch it, feel the way the metal vibrates under my fingertips, until my skin is humming along with it. After a minute, my arm goes numb, and I finally take my hand off it. We stand for a moment, listening to the way the sound seems to explode from inside the curves, sound overlapping itself.

I turn and look up at Oliver, but he doesn't look back, and I'm thankful for it because for just a moment, it's nice to look at him without him looking back. To see the way the snow falls in large flakes into his red hair, the parts of his ears that stick out just a little too far, mixing in with the freckles along his cheeks. Oliver is beautiful, a fact I've been very aware of, but now, watching him close his eyes and listen to the notes coming from the installation, like if he listens hard enough the notes will evolve into words, he's something more than beautiful.

"Tell me something," I say, and watch as his eyes pop open and find me. "This feels like the place for secrets. Tell me something about you." *Something no one else knows*, I want to add, but I don't want to push him. I don't want to break whatever we're doing here.

He looks at me for a long time. If we were back in the shop, maybe this could be a joke. Maybe this could be something we did with half smiles on our faces. Maybe he could answer with something silly. But we're here, and sometime in the last few seconds, a heaviness has settled between us, a heaviness that's drawing me toward him.

"I can't," he says then, his eyes falling away from me. "It'll change things."

I don't know what that means, but I'm not ready for this Oliver I've never met before, serious and unguarded, to vanish. I take a desperate step toward him. "You can trust me," I say, and he looks up at me, his eyes wide like I've startled him. So, I say it again. "You can trust me, Oliver. I promise." I want him to feel what I feel right here, in this cold courtyard, surrounded by falling snow and the kind of quiet only winter can bring on its back.

Because being here with Oliver, being anywhere with Oliver, makes me feel safe in a way I've never felt before. Like I can close my eyes and breathe and no one is going to laugh or tell me I'm doing it wrong.

I feel a scared kind of dread in my stomach when I think he'll shut down now, never open up to me, never tell me something that can only be whispered. I wait for him to shake his head and walk away from me, for his wall to go back up.

Instead, he says, "I don't want to go to college."

I don't say anything at first. I'm not sure what I was expecting. I guess I thought it would be worse, bigger, truly the kind of secret that changes everything. But this secret feels like something else entirely.

Why is this something that had to wait until this moment to be spoken aloud?

"Why would that change things?" I ask when I can finally find the words to speak again. "What would it change?"

I see the way his jaw works beneath his skin as he regards me, and I sense it again, his internal battle about whether or not to shut me out again.

Finally he sighs, stuffing his hands in his pockets. "People like you, valedictorians and people with four-point-oh's, they don't hang out with people like me, who have no clue what they want to do with their lives. Your only goal in life is to go to college, and I couldn't give a shit about college. Where does that leave us?"

I blink at him. Is that how the world works in his mind? "Oliver, I don't care if you don't want to go to college."

His eyes land on me. "You don't?"

I throw my hands up. "Of course not. Just because I want to go to college doesn't mean I expect everyone to. If we were all the same, that would make us pretty boring."

He bites his lip, and I find myself staring at the spot, dark pink where his teeth have released it. I watch his mouth curve into a smile. "I guess I imagined you sitting with all your Top-Ten-Percent friends, talking about the stupid boy you work with, who doesn't even want to go to college because he's such a waste of space."

I just stare at him, his words shock me so much. Is it the fact that he imagined me hanging out with other people like me, even though I've told him I don't have any friends at all? Is it that he thinks not wanting to go to college is such a crime that he assumes I'll feel the need to berate him to other people? Or is it that he can somehow deem himself a waste of space based on something so insignificant?

I want to tell him that he's *anything* but a waste of space. That in the last two months he's made me feel like my life will be emptier without him, without Sprits, without the way I feel when I'm there.

But I don't say that. Instead, I say, "Do you want me to tell you a secret?"

His eyes shift back and forth between my own and then he nods.

"I've never in my life felt like I belonged anywhere. I'm moving to California because I'm hoping I'll belong there."

A crease appears between his eyebrows, like a question mark.

"I've never felt like my home was really my home. Not after my dad left, not after my mom had my brothers and sisters. Kansas City has always felt like this place that I endure."

His lips part, his breath escaping in a cloud of steam, before he says, "That's it. That's the feeling. Like there's no such thing as home."

I just nod, too. He understands. He gets it. He feels it, too. Of course he does.

His hand comes up, slowly, and I think maybe he'll touch me, a hand on my arm or a fingertip across my cheek. But he doesn't. His hand falls to his side again, and I shiver, like he's taken the heat away without giving it to me in the first place.

"Let me play you something," he says, and it feels strange in this moment, bringing up our stupid contest when the air around us feels heavy with earnestness. But I don't stop him. He takes out his phone and picks a song, and I wonder if he chose it before we came here or if it's a spur of the moment decision.

Maybe it should be awkward, standing right here, with the moan coming off the statue still loud beneath the careful chords of the music coming out of Oliver's phone, which he holds up between us, flat on his palm. But it isn't awkward. It's lovely.

I don't tell him that I already know the band, Nothing But Thieves, and that I've listened to this song on a dozen different occasions. Because standing here with him, the cold turning the tip of my nose numb, I'm certain I've never heard it like this.

The song is short, only two and a half minutes, and when the singer's voice cracks with desperation, I feel an odd urge to cry. I press my hand to the sculpture again, and somehow, it feels like it's vibrating with the song. When I look up at Oliver, I could swear his eyes are watery, too, but I'm certain it's from the bite of the cold wind.

When the song is over, I smile up at Oliver. "You're not going to win tonight."

He laughs and tucks his phone back into his pocket. "I should take you home," he says, his voice a whisper, and then we're slipping our way back to his truck, and even though his secret isn't the scar he thinks it is, he's right. It changes things.

OLIVER

I JERK AWAKE on Friday morning when I hear someone knocking on the front door. The sun is up, but I can tell by the odd way that it's slanted into my room that it's way too early for someone to be visiting.

And yet, they knock again.

I climb out of bed and stumble into the living room. The house is cold and silent, Mom's bedroom door shut. She worked another night shift at the hospital, and I can't remember when her shift ended so I can't tell if she's asleep or if she hasn't made it home yet.

I should have known when I heard the banging exactly who it is. The apartment I share with my mom never sees visitors. No girls, no friends, no coworkers. I'm not even positive that anyone knows where I live. And so, I should have known exactly who it is.

I sigh, looking out at Dad from the open doorway. "What do you want?" I ask him, surprised that he even knows the world exists before noon. I'm not sure he's ever seen it.

Well, except for when I had to pick him up from the police station.

Dad grips the doorjamb, and I don't miss the way he slips his foot into the corner of the doorway, just in case I'm tempted to slam the door in his face. "I just want to talk to you, Oli. Can I take you out for breakfast?"

And that's how I end up sitting across from my father at Charlie's, watching him devour pancakes, dripping with syrup.

"What do you want to talk about?" I demand. I have an omelet sitting on the plate in front of me, but I'm not feeling much like eating. In fact, the smell of the eggs is making me queasy.

My dad's fork drops to his plate. "Oli, I'm—" He breaks off and looks away, at the cast wrapped around my arm. "I'm sorry about what happened. It was my fault, and I know that. I know that you shouldn't have been there, picking my ass up off the concrete." He grits his teeth, and when he speaks again, he chokes over his words. "I didn't mean this for you, Oli. It kills me that you got hurt. That I put you in harm's way." He digs his fingertips into his chest, his shirt wrinkling around them. And when he looks up at me, there are tears in his eyes.

I steel myself against it. What else can I do? Dad has been hurting me my whole life. When he got so drunk he stumbled home from the bars every night, when he got so drunk he started fights, when he got so drunk Mom couldn't bear to look at him. He was always hurting me. How is this, this stupid cast and the dented bumper on my truck, any different than it was before?

My father's bloodshot eyes find me, and he moves fast, reaching across the table and gripping my hands over the top of it, so hard it hurts. "I can't lose you, Oli. I can't. You're the only good thing in my life. Tell me what to do. Just tell me what to do to fix this."

I look down at where he has a hold on me. One of his big hands spans across half the words Amy wrote on my cast. I think about her looking up at me in that courtyard, the same courtyard I carried Dad out of, snowflakes landing in her long eyelashes. I want to be back there with her, in that place that was just the two of us, where we could whisper secrets to each other that no one else could understand.

I pull my hands out from under his, sliding them back toward me on the tabletop. "You need help," I tell him. "You want to fix this? You want to see me again? You go to A.A. You see a counselor. I don't care which. But you need help. Or this is over for good."

His eyes go wide, and his surprise mirrors my own, even if I refuse to show it. I wasn't planning to serve him up an ultimatum, but here we are. And I mean it. I've done a lot for him. I've spent the past ten years being his crutch, his very reason for living, as he tells me again and again. But I'm tired of being responsible for him. I'm tired of being the only adult in this relationship. So it's time for him to buck up or find someone else to pick him up from Hassey's.

Dad's hands fall to his lap, and I see the conflict on his face. What was he expecting me to tell him? That what he's doing is enough? That he doesn't have to change? That life can go on as it always has, even after I got my damn arm broken trying to get him home in the middle of the night?

Yeah. That's exactly what he was expecting.

But for the past few days, my mind has been flashing back to the look on Amy's face when I told her I don't want college. I was expecting revulsion, I was expecting disappointment, disgust, even confusion. But instead, she looked at me with respect, and it felt so damn good, and it's enough. For now, it's enough that someone like Amy respects me and my choices. I don't need Dad's approval, too.

Maybe I don't need Mom's, either.

AMY

I'M CLOSING WITH Oliver tonight. It's my first time closing with just him, instead of him and Brooke, and I'm a little jittery. He's focused, his eyes flitting in between the computer in front of him and back down to the sales slips in his hands as he goes over the transactions for the day to make sure everything adds up.

We've barely spoken, and I can't help but feel like I've done something wrong, even though I don't even think I've had the chance to. Maybe I should have just left it alone the other night. Maybe I should have just let him have his secrets if he wanted them. But all I can think about is the relief in his shoulders when he told me about not wanting to go to college. Those same shoulders are bunched up an inch higher than usual tonight, and I want to know why.

"Hey," I say, stepping up to him.

He doesn't take his eyes off the screen, but he says, "Hey, what's up?"

"Are you okay?"

At this, his eyes finally flit over to me, his hands faltering on the sales slips. "Yeah, I'm fine, why?"

He blinks down at the slips in his hand for a second and then he puts them down and looks at me, and I can see in the skin around his eyes just how tired he is. He opens his mouth, shuts it again, opens it again, takes a deep breath, closes it. "Just thinking," he says.

"About what?"

He bites his lip and lets it go. He shrugs, and I know he's not going to tell me. I don't know what happened between us out in the snow, but I don't think it's going to happen again, right here. He's closed back up. We stand there for a long moment, until the music changes and the heavy sounds of an electric bass breaks between us.

"You better get to work before I write you up," he jokes, and I laugh, turning away from the register. I start walking the aisles, straightening displays and reorganizing stray vinyl, but I can feel him watching me.

Moments later, when the music changes, I laugh.

"What's so funny over there?" he asks.

I shrug. "Isn't this, like, the sex song?" I ask, listening to the chords of Marvin Gaye's "Let's Get It On" over the sound system.

Oliver stops working and narrows his eyes at me. "The sex song?"

"Yeah, you know, in the movies, any time a character is looking to get lucky, they play this song. It's like a *thing*. Although, I don't think that's particularly realistic. If I was going to choose a song to have sex to, this probably wouldn't be it."

Behind the counter, the register opens with a ding. "I wouldn't know," Oliver says quietly.

He's still not looking at me, and it's starting to make my stomach turn. I want him to talk to me. I know he's stressed out from dealing with his dad and the car accident and all that, but I just want him to look at me the way he did the other night. I want him to see me.

So, I walk up to the counter and lean my elbows on it. "Okay, Mr. Know-It-All. What's your sex song?"

Oliver's entire body freezes. "I don't have one."

I sigh and turn my back to him, leaning against the counter, facing the other direction. "Oh, please, Oliver. You have a song for every occasion, and you don't have a song for when you're going to hook up with a girl?"

He's quiet and still, making no noise whatsoever, so I look over my shoulder at him. Finally, his eyes are on me, and I regret trying to be casual because something about seeing Oliver like this, intense and serious, after weeks of finally seeing another side of him makes me nervous. I don't want to say the wrong thing, and now I feel like I have.

But then he says, "You want a sex song? I'll give you a sex song."

I smile at the way he says it, so determined. I like this Oliver much better. He disappears into Brooke's office and comes back out with a set of headphones and his phone in his hand. He's scrolling around on the screen by the time he's standing right in front of me, his hand outstretched, offering me the headphones.

"Oh," I say, taking them and looking down at their sleek lines. "These look expensive."

He stops scrolling. "It's cool," he says, pushing them toward me with a nudge. "Put them on."

I hesitate, and before I get the chance, he's reached out, taken the headphones, and clamped them over my ears. I arrange them so that they're not caught around my hair and then jump up on the counter, letting my feet dangle between us. When I'm up here, we're the same height.

The music starts.

I hold on to the edge of the counter and listen to the singer's voice, sliding over the notes so cleanly it gives me goose bumps. I don't recognize the song, but I know the singer's voice to be Ed

Sheeran's, and I can't help but smile at that because it's so unexpected. Ed sings Oliver's sex song.

The song is only mildly sexy, a sad song, about a girl crying and a boy wiping away the tears, but Oliver was right to choose it. Something about it makes warmth run up my arms, and perhaps it's not just the song itself, but just knowing what the song is *supposed* to make me feel. Knowing Oliver wants me to feel sexy, wants me to feel the drumbeat in my blood and the slide of Ed's voice on my nerves, and that alone makes my skin hot. I let my eyes slide closed, focusing on Ed's crisp harmonies.

But then I feel a tingling on the surface of my skin, an awareness in my pores. I open my eyes, and Oliver is right there, so close I can feel his breath on my lips. His eyebrows furrow, like being this close to me is painful. His hands slide along the tops of my thighs, and I gasp just before he leans forward and swallows the sound with his mouth.

If I thought my skin was hot before, it's nothing compared to the way it burns as Oliver's hands move to my hips, as he pulls me against him and then wets my lips with his tongue. Every touch is unexpected and yet somehow not surprising at all, gentle and soft and aching.

I think maybe I should pull away, maybe we shouldn't be making out on the counter where anyone could see through the windows, but I have Ed Sheeran in my ears, and Oliver smells like lemon hand soap, so I open my mouth and keep kissing him.

The song fades into the next one, and Oliver pushes his hands into my hair, halfway knocking one of the earphones off with his long fingers. We kiss through two more songs, and when the album ends, and I can hear the muffled sounds of our lips, I finally inch away from him.

He sighs and smiles, his eyes still closed. It's amazing and terrifying. "Did I win the contest?"

I can't help but laugh at that and then give him a playful shove. "Absolutely not."

He helps me off the counter and we don't speak again as we finish closing up the shop. We don't speak as he walks me to my car or as I climb into my driver's seat, and I don't look back when I drive out of the parking lot.

OLIVER

THAT NIGHT, I lie in bed and listen to the Lumineers. I listen to them because I know they're Amy's favorite and right now, everything is Amy.

Her skin under my fingers, the pressure of her mouth, the smell of her shampoo.

I've always been disappointed by the thought that, in the event of a near-death experience, my brain is supposed to supply some spiritual kind of montage of powerful life moments. I never really thought I had any of those.

Now I know, if I'm seconds from death, I'll think of Amy and her mouth, and I'll die happy.

AMY

THAT NIGHT, I lie in bed and listen to the Lumineers. I listen to them because they're my comfort band, and I think what I need right now is comfort.

But I can hear Ed Sheeran in my head. I can feel Oliver's fingers in my hair. I can see the green of his eyes when he pulled away from me.

The two Valentine-grams Jackson gave me are sitting beside me on my bed, and I ruffle my fingertips over them and glance at the wilted carnation in the vase beside my bed.

What the hell do I do now?

OLIVER

EVEN THOUGH I tell myself it's time to chill out, I check my phone again. I've probably checked it at least four hundred times since last night, and just like the last three hundred ninety-nine times, there's no message from Amy.

I'm not sure what I'm expecting exactly. Maybe I should be the one messaging her. Maybe I should just grow a pair and tell Amy that I've never been in love before, but I'm fairly certain this is what it feels like. Because what else could this be?

"Would you put your phone away?" Mom hisses when she sees me checking it again. That makes four hundred one. I roll my eyes and put my phone in my pocket. The Sunday sermon is almost over, based on how much shouting our pastor is doing, so I figure I can probably do without checking again until we get back outside.

"What are you so jittery about?" Mom asks when she sees me checking my phone again at lunch. I'm not sure if Amy is at work today. I could go by there. I could text Brooke and ask if Amy's there, if she's acting any differently.

"Are you checking your application status?" Mom asks, and I'm so startled by the question that I just stare up at her with wide eyes.

Shit, shit, shit. It's already March. College acceptance letters are probably being delivered in peoples' mailboxes already. And now that email acceptances are a popular thing, of course Mom thinks I'm checking for mine . . . because my mother still thinks I actually applied.

Shit.

"Uh, yeah," I lie because I can't decide if it's worse to lie to my mother or have to tell her that I'm checking my phone every fifteen seconds because I made out with the girl of my dreams last night, and I'm waiting for her to say something about it.

God, I should have just said something last night. I should have told her how I feel about her. But no, after that kiss, I acted like a chickenshit and made that stupid joke about the contest. There's something wrong with my brain.

Mom nudges me with her elbow as we walk out of the restaurant. It's a sunny day, all the snow from Friday night completely melted and nothing but dark spots left on the concrete.

"Don't worry so much," she says. "There's no reason why you wouldn't be a shoo-in for a place like MBU."

I can think of one reason.

AMY

I HAVEN'T REALLY had any deep or meaningful conversations with Mama since I freaked out at family dinner. Mostly, we've spoken in passing about what's for dinner or who's taking the car in the morning, and not much else. But she chooses tonight to finally knock on my door. I only stopped by the house for a second to change because it's eighties night at the shop, and I didn't want to wear my crazy makeup and neon paraphernalia to school, and since there's nobody else in the house, I guess Mama decided it's a safe time to approach.

"Off to work?" she asks from my open doorway.

"Yep," I say, being mildly rude and turning up the volume on my computer, where music is already streaming so loud I can barely hear myself think.

Mama leans against my doorjamb and sighs. "Are you going to ignore me forever?"

I roll my eyes and go back to applying my hot pink eye shadow. "I'm not ignoring you. I've been busy."

"Too busy to talk to me?"

I shrug. Sort of. I've been too busy for everything and everyone lately, and I haven't really been interested in getting into it with Mama. There's a reason I never said anything to her about how I've been feeling. I'm absolutely awful at confrontation, especially when it comes to her.

Mama comes up behind me and pulls the scrunchie out of my side ponytail, attempting to smooth out the bumps I left there since I'm already running late.

"Baby, I didn't want to upset you. I'm just concerned."

I do my best not to make eye contact with her in my mirror. I start in on my eyeliner. "It's not your concerns that are upsetting me, it's your doubts."

She pulls her hands away from me, letting my hair curtain down around my shoulders. "Baby, it's not that I doubt *you*. I just know how this goes. Stanford is a hard school to get into. And even if you do get in, the chances you'll get this scholarship—"

I jerk away from her, and she looks like I just slapped her. "I know all the obstacles. I don't need you to remind me. I have a hard enough time having faith in myself without your contribution."

Her eyes look pained at that, but I don't know what else to say, how to make her see that I need someone to believe in me.

"I have to go to work," I say when she continues saying nothing. I'm halfway to my car when I realize I never finished my eyeliner.

OLIVER

IT FINALLY HAPPENS after work. Amy and I are walking through the parking lot when she says, "Oli," and my stomach twists up in knots. Of course. I knew the second she walked in and didn't look at me that this day wasn't going to end well, but I wasn't prepared for the way she says my name, like she's going to try to let me down gently. God, I hate that. "I think last night was a bad idea." She keeps her head down when she says it.

"Because of Jackson?" I knew this, of course. Knew it almost a month ago, when we were sitting in Brooke's room, and she was crying. I knew she still had feelings for him. But I guess I wasn't ready for it to be a reason for us not to be more than friends.

"I'm not trying to get back together with him," she says, and I should feel something like relief, but instead there's just tension in my stomach, just the clench of waiting for the other shoe to drop. "But I don't think it would be fair for me to pursue something else when I still feel . . ." She trails off and then sighs, her arms falling to her sides. "While I still feel something."

She isn't really making sense, but I understand in the curve of her mouth and the wrinkle in her brow what she's saying. She's confused.

She doesn't know how she feels about her ex and maybe she doesn't know how she feels about me, either.

"It's okay," I say.

She blinks up at me with those dark eyes. "It is?"

I shrug. "Sometimes friends do stupid stuff like make out at work. That's what happens when you're exposed to Ed Sheeran."

She laughs, and the knots in my stomach loosen a little. Yes, I want to kiss her again. Yes, I'm pretty sure that I'm in love with her. And yes, I thought that kiss meant something. I thought maybe it meant the beginning of something real between us. But I can handle all that stuff on my own as long as Amy keeps laughing the way she just did.

Amy stops beside her car, shivering a little, even though it's much warmer than it was last time we walked like this. "Friends, huh?"

"We're friends, aren't we?"

She keeps her head down again. "Oli, I'm pretty sure you're my best friend."

I walked into work today hoping and praying that Amy would want me. That she'd tell me that kiss was the greatest moment of her life, the way it was for me.

But hearing her say that I'm her best friend is easily a close second.

And then she says, "Hey, Oli? Do you have dinner plans next Sunday?"

AMY

AT FAMILY DINNER on Sunday, I yawn so loud, the sound actually drowns out the noise of my siblings fighting with my cousins, and Mama and Abuela yelling at them to stop.

Beside me, Abuela nudges me with her elbow. "Why are you so tired, *mija*? You're not sleeping?"

No, I'm not sleeping. Because I'm studying calculus problems every night until I fear my eyes are going to burst. I can practically feel the blood vessels in my eyes pulsing.

"Just a lot to do," I say, hoping she'll leave it at that. But Abuela has never been one to let anything lie.

Just then, the doorbell rings, and the entire table goes silent. Carlos, sitting at the head of the table, looks around at my aunts and uncles, my cousins, my siblings, me. His thick eyebrows turn in. "Are we missing someone?" he asks.

"Actually, I invited someone." I push away from the table and go to the door, peeking through the peephole out of habit. Oliver is standing on my porch, and I'm staring at his distorted face through the peephole, even as he reaches out and rings the doorbell again.

"Is it Jackson?" I hear Carlos ask someone at the table, or maybe everyone at the table.

I step back and open the door.

For a second, Oliver and I just stare at each other.

"Hi," I finally say when it appears that he's going to say absolutely nothing. From the table behind me, I hear Mama call out, "Who is it, Amaría?"

I'm not even sure how to answer that question. It's simple enough. What is Oliver to me? My coworker? My friend? The guy I made out with on top of a counter at work?

Before I even have the chance to answer, I feel hands wrap around me, two around my leg and two around my waist and Gabriella and Marisa are peeking up at Oliver from behind me.

"Oh my gosh!" Gabi shrieks. "Are you Amy's boyfriend?"

I flinch in horror and reach down to pry their fingers off me. "Gabi, Mari, get away from here! Go back to dinner!" But they haven't even had a chance to go before the boys have approached, one from each side. "No!" I shout before they can open their mouths and add to the already awkward situation.

They scatter, but then it's Mama walking over from the dining room, opening the door enough that she can see out onto the porch.

"Hello," she says, gripping the door and smiling out at Oliver that way she only smiles at teachers and complete strangers. "And who are you?"

The way Mama looks Oliver up and down makes me certain I made a mistake inviting him. It occurred to me seconds after I invited him that it might be a mistake, but all I could think about was having to face family dinner alone and how much easier it might be if I had Oliver at my side.

"Mama, this is Oliver York. We work together at Spirits. Oliver, this is my mom."

Oliver reaches out to shake Mama's hand, but she still looks skeptical, which makes me want to bark at her because Oliver is probably the only person in my life who isn't completely full of shit.

But Oliver just smiles and steps into the house, closing me in between his tall body and Mama's short one. I move out of the way and send Mama a look to tell her to back off as Oliver comes all the way inside. He's glancing around the house, and finally his eyes land on the dining room, where my entire immediate family is crammed around our tiny dining table. He walks toward them with an expression on his face that I've never seen before, either amazement or utter fear.

The table goes quiet, and then, like a bomb going off, it erupts into noise again. People are shifting to make room for Oliver, Mama is bringing out the piano stool from the living room, the one we've kept even though the actual piano has been gone for ages, and Oliver and I are being herded toward the table with extreme fervor.

We're barely seated before people start throwing questions in Oliver's direction—*What's your name? Are you in school? Do you have a job? Where do you live? How many brothers and sisters do you have?* Oliver tries to answer the questions as politely as he can without giving too much away: Oliver York, taking a year off, works with Amy, lives on the other side of Kansas City, closer to Independence than the Kansas-Missouri line, no brothers or sisters.

It's this last answer that makes everyone go silent, and when Oliver elaborates (no aunts or uncles or cousins, just him, his mom, and his dad, who doesn't live with them), everyone goes quiet, shocked.

"Just you and your mom at home?" Mama finally asks. "Doesn't that get lonely?"

I want to kick her, but she's too far away from me. "Mama," I say, because I'm used to her asking *me* inappropriate questions, but to ask Oliver? Really?

Mama ignores me, and so does Oliver. "Yeah," he says finally. "The house is always quiet, but this is the hand I've been dealt."

For the first time, I see honest sadness in Oliver's eyes. Honest regret. It never really occurred to me that maybe Oli is lonely. Sure, we talked about the fact that he isn't much of a people person and doesn't really have friends, but I didn't think that meant he's completely lonely, or even that he's sad about it.

As several conversations kick up around the table, I lean over to Oliver and say in his ear, "I'm sorry about all this."

His eyebrows go up. "I was going to be at home by myself,

eating leftover pizza and watching March Madness. This is better." He shoves some food in his mouth and smiles. "What is this, by the way? It's delicious."

I glance down at his plate. "*Lengua*. Cow tongue."

He stops chewing for a second, then shrugs and keeps eating.

OLIVER

WALKING INTO AMY'S family dinner is like walking into a circus where you're expected to participate even though you have no idea what's going on. After dinner, everyone gathers around Amy's tiny coffee table in the living room, taking seats in chairs, on tables, on the floor, anywhere they can reach, and then they just keep talking. They've already been talking for more than an hour, but no one ever seems to run out of things to say.

After Amy is finished helping her mother with the dishes, she takes a seat beside me on the floor, pressing her back to the wall and nudging me with her shoulder. I nudge her back. All I can think about is that soon, I'll have to go back to my own house, back to the quiet, to the loneliness. It starts to make anxiety rise in my chest, but then Amy scoots closer to me.

"Thanks for coming," she says.

We fall into silence, letting everyone else's conversations overlap our own. "Your family is so big and so—"

"Mexican?"

"I was going to say exciting."

"That's just the nice way of saying they're loud."

I tap my fingers against my knee. "Forgive me if this is a terribly offensive question, but Amy Richardson isn't exactly a traditional Mexican name."

She nods, her eyes roving the room. "My name is Amaría. Amaría Richardson. My dad is as white as they come." She snorts, and I'm a little mesmerized by her. Amaría. Beautiful. She keeps talking without looking at me. "Carlos isn't my real dad. But he's been around since I was a kid. My dad lives in L.A., and I see him once a year."

"Just once?"

"Yep." She somehow seems to be opening up and building a wall between us at the exact same time.

"Does that bother you?"

She wraps her arms around her knees and presses her chin to them. "I guess not. Carlos has always been there when I needed a dad. I guess if I move to California, I'll be seeing Dad more. Maybe."

"I wouldn't even know what it's like to have a real dad."

Amy rolls her chin on her knee. "What about the dad you have?"

I shrug and look down at my worn-out sneakers. "He moved here from Scotland when my mom got pregnant. And then he kind of fell apart and started drinking. I'm all he has. And my mom, too, I guess."

"That's a lot of pressure."

I shrug. "You're under a lot of pressure, too. Valedictorian? First one in the family to go to college?" I only know this last part because Amy's grandmother kept saying it over and over during dinner.

Amy looks around, probably to make sure no one is listening. No one appears to be. "No one thinks I can do it." She says it with a wry smile on her mouth.

"What do you mean?"

She doesn't say anything for a long time, but then finally, she leans in even closer to me, our faces so close, I could barely lean forward, and we would be kissing. "They're always talking about how hard it all is, how expensive college is, how hard I have to work, as if I don't know. They don't really think I can make it happen. Maybe I don't really think I can, either."

"Bullshit," I say as quietly as I can, so nobody but Amy can hear me. "You can do anything you want. I've seen it."

She doesn't answer, just looks at me for a long time, her expression unwavering.

"What are you guys whispering about over there?" Amy's mother asks loudly.

I look over at Amy, and she smiles at me in a conspiratorial way. When she smiles like that, she lights up the whole room, the whole world. What would I do if I wasn't right here next to her? How could anything else matter?

When I'm finally able to tear my eyes from her, I see that Amy's mother is standing up from the couch, her hands clasped in front of her. "We actually have been waiting until tonight to tell everyone the good news. Carlos just got a new manager job at Rudy's Auto Repair."

The room kicks up in conversation and praise, and I smile over at Amy because I know this is something that's been sitting on her shoulders since I met her. She looks like she's about to join in the celebration when her mother looks over at her, the entire living room spanning between us and her, and says, "I know it's been hard to fit a job into your schedule. If you need to quit now, you can."

The feeling I get is what I imagine it's like to be struck by lightning. Amy can't quit. She's only just started. She's only been at the shop for a few months, and she loves it there, and Brooke loves having her there, and what would Spirits even look like without her?

I turn to Amy, ready to make a case for the shop, but she's not looking at me, and no matter how long I sit here, waiting for her to say something, she just stares down at the carpet.

AMY

THE NEXT DAY, I'm leaving eighth period, my last class of the day, when my phone rings. It's Brooke. I pause in the middle of the court-yard, afraid that she's calling to fire me for some reason. Ever since Mama told me I could quit, which I know she only did because I've been so mad at her, I've been on edge about Spirits. Because I know quitting is the right thing to do so that I can focus on Stanford and graduation.

But if I'm being honest with myself, I just don't want to. I love Spirits, and I'm not sure I can handle the stress of everything else without it.

"Amy!" Brooke practically shouts in my ear, her voice full of enthusiasm. Well, that's a good sign. "Sorry. I know you're not working tonight, but I thought you'd want to know that Oli's mom is throw-ing him a surprise party for his birthday next week, on Wednesday. Not this Wednesday, next Wednesday. I know, Wednesday is a weird night for a party. I have to have Lauren cover at Spirits for me, but luckily, the only two people his mom invited are Marshal and me because, well, Oli doesn't actually have that many friends, but she doesn't really know you yet, so I thought I'd extend the invitation. It's Wednesday at his place, and I can give you a ride if you don't know how to get there. We have to be there at six forty-five, and Oli is show-ing up at seven."

I stand in the center of the quad and stare down at my shoes. "You just said a lot of words really fast."

"I'll text you the info." She hangs up.

"Wednesday at six forty-five," I say, racking my brain, trying to figure out if I have any other responsibilities that day. It's a gymnastics and karate day for the twins, so I'll definitely have to take Brooke up on her offer to give me a ride, since my parents will have to split in order to get all the kids to their activities on time. "Wednesday at six forty-five," I say again.

From behind me, someone says, "What's Wednesday at six forty-five?"

I whip around to see Jackson behind me, leaning against the flagpole.

"Birthday party," I say, and then suck my lips in between my teeth because why did I just tell him that? It isn't any of Jackson's business what I'm going to be doing on Wednesday at six forty-five, and he certainly shouldn't be eavesdropping on my conversations.

Jackson smirks at me. "Anyone I know?"

I think about Oliver walking into Jackson's party and demanding my car keys back. "No."

I see confusion flash across his face, like he can't believe that I'm not going to tell him who it is. Or perhaps he doesn't believe that I might have friends he doesn't know about. And I'm not positive that's an unwarranted belief.

"I should go," I tell him, pointing over my shoulder. "I have to get to the library to get some homework done. Big test on Friday in AP bio."

"Right," Jackson says, nodding, even though I'm pretty sure he forgot all about the test. "Can I walk with you?"

I hesitate, feeling everything inside me go a little stiff. "Don't you, like, have to, like, meet your girlfriend or something?"

Jackson sighs and then starts walking in the direction of the library, even though I never actually said he could walk with me. "Look, Ames, I'm sorry you found out that way. I didn't mean for that to happen."

I scoff, trying to sound more casual than I feel. "It's fine, Jackson. We broke up two months ago. You're certainly allowed to date whoever you want." I can almost completely convince myself that I mean what I'm saying, but of course, in my head, I'm thinking, *It's only been two months* and *is that all it takes to get over someone you were with for almost a year?*

Jackson puts his hands in his pockets as we walk, and we're back to where we were right after the breakup—quiet and awkward.

My phone buzzes, and I look down to see a text from Oli.

Do you think going to AA meetings with my dad will prevent me from becoming an alcoholic?

It buzzes again.

Like preventative medicine?

And again.

Like, going to AA is the equivalent to getting a flu shot?

I scroll through the messages and laugh.

"What's so funny?" Jackson asks, his eyes sliding over to the phone resting in my palm, and, for reasons I can hardly even understand, I slip my phone into my pocket so Jackson can't see it.

"Nothing," I say, just as I see a blur out of the corner of my eye. And then someone's arm is being looped through mine, and I'm looking up at Petra.

But her eyes aren't on me; they're on Jackson.

"If I could just steal my study partner," she says to him with a tight smile on her face.

For a second, Jackson looks a little stricken, but then he stops walking, and like she's on a mission, Petra keeps moving.

"You're not doing a great job avoiding your ex," she says once we've moved far enough away that I know Jackson can't hear us, and between her words and her arm through mine, I feel like I've been swept into another dimension. As far as I can remember, this is the first time that Petra has ever touched me, and looking down at her arm hooked through mine, I wonder how I ended up here.

OLIVER

WHEN WE WALK into the A.A. meeting, I'm expecting people like my dad, middle-age men who look hopeless and rundown, but the room is full of people of all ages and genders. There are even people my age.

A nice woman in a sweater-vest takes the podium at the front of the room and smiles. "Welcome, everyone. It's so nice to see you here. Hello to all our familiar faces and hello, also, to our new ones. There's a few of you." Her gaze lands on us, and I glance around to see if maybe someone else is here for the first time and making it obvious. Everyone is looking at us.

"I'd love to hear from some people today. Is there anyone who has a story to tell? Has it been a good week or a difficult one?"

We sit in silence for a moment but then someone volunteers, stepping up to the podium to tell us she had a drink this week with a friend but didn't relapse. Another goes after her to say that he's made it exactly three months and feels better than ever.

I'm not sure how long this is supposed to go on, having never been to an Alcoholics Anonymous meeting before, but a glance at the clock tells me it's been forty-five minutes—forty-five minutes of stories, some of them triumphant, some of them not so much.

The woman in the sweater-vest makes her way to the podium and smiles out at everyone. "My name is Pam. Most of you know me. I started drinking just after my son was born, and I didn't stop even after I got pregnant with my middle daughter and then my youngest daughter. I started with the excuses: I was stressed from work, one glass a day was good for my health, and next thing I knew, I was waking up in bed with someone I didn't know in the middle of the night, still drunk, only to find that I'd left my kids at home, alone. I've been sober now for seven years."

I feel like maybe I'm supposed to applaud her, but no one else does, so I don't. She smiles at us and then taps the podium gently. "Well, if no one else has any stories to share then I'd like to—"

To my complete surprise, Dad stands up.

"Oh, one of our new faces," Pam says. "We're so happy to see you. Do you have something you'd like to say?" She gestures at the microphone in front of her and takes a step back to let Dad approach it. He sends Pam a strange, close-lipped smile and then starts to speak into the microphone, his accent larger than life.

"I'm, uh, Fergus. I was seventeen when my family came here on holiday. I'd never had a drink in my life. I was a good boy, through and through. And then I fell in love. I fell in love with a beautiful American girl, completely lost my mind over her. We had a passionate summer together and then my parents shipped me back to Scotland, wiping their hands of the whole experience. But my girl was pregnant, so as soon as I turned eighteen, I got a work visa, moved across the ocean, and now here I am. Only, my parents hated the whole arrangement, so they disowned me. No money, no family, nothin' but my pregnant girl, so I got a job, she went to college, and everything was all right. I loved them more than anything in the world, my wife and son.

"But she wanted it all, yeah? She wanted the fairy tale. She wanted a big house and a successful husband and fifteen kids, and I couldn't afford any of that, so I started to drink. And then we really couldn't afford anything, so I started borrowing money so I could drink more. And then, one day it was all gone. I woke up from a drunk stupor to find that my wife didn't love me anymore, my kid didn't know me, I'd lost my job, I'd lost everything. She kicked me out of the house, and I saw my kid every once in a while. But what reason did I have to live? What reason did I have to be sober every morning? So that I could be clearheaded to see how far down the fuckin' toilet my life had gone? I didn't want to see it straight. I didn't want to see that I had nothing.

"So I stayed drunk. And the only time I got with my kid was when he was picking me up off the side of the road or scrapin' me outta some bar. But he got hurt. He was picking my sorry ass up in the middle of the night and some *other* drunk slammed into him and broke his fuckin' arm, gave him a concussion, and I can't fucking take that back. And I can't take back the years that I spent knocked out on my ass or wasted as fuck, but I can try from here. I still don't have anything, but my son is alive, so that's a reason to keep my nose clean."

I feel like I've been run over by a truck.

Pam smiles at him and then smiles out at me from behind the podium. Dad takes his seat beside me and pats me on the knee like we're buddies, but I can't stop looking at him. I can't stop trying to figure out why I've never heard this whole story before.

After the meeting, Pam comes to talk to us. "I like to personally greet all our new faces," she says. "I just want you to know that we're always here, and that you can always feel safe here." She grins in my direction. "You must be the son." She gestures at my cast, and I wave it awkwardly. Her eyes are back on Dad. "I wish you the best. And hopefully we'll see you back here very soon."

OLIVER

DAD IS TRYING to figure out what he wants off the dinner menu, and I'm trying to decide if the thoughts going through my head are really something I'm thinking about blurting out right here in the middle of Charlie's. He finally decides on pancakes, even though it's almost eleven at night, and I decide on a cup of coffee.

The waitress wanders off, and my father and I are left in a kind of quiet that we've never been in before. Even when Dad was pretty solidly drunk, he's always been a talker. He's always been the one who hates the silence. And now here he is, staring down at the table between us like it's going to erase everything that's happened in the last two hours.

I have never known this much of my father, and I'm not sure that I want to know. Life is more complicated when he's more than just a fuckup. When he's more than just the consistently drunk father who also consistently ruins my life.

And now everything is different. And I can't even explain why, but I have an immediate urge to tell him the truth about school. It's almost April, and when the school year ends, I can't keep up this charade with Mom. So, what harm could it do, to tell him everything right now, after everything he just said in there?

"I have something to tell you," I say, and from the way Dad looks up at me, his eyes tired and the bags under them looking like they need their own zip codes, I know he's just as afraid as I am. So I take a deep breath, and I plunge in. "I'm not going to college."

He looks at me for a second like he doesn't quite know who I am, and then he leans back in the booth, his body sagging. "Fuck," is all he says, the word barely a whisper, and for some reason, even though I know that's not a particularly good response, it gives me the momentum to keep talking.

"I never applied to the school I told Mom I was going to. And when I don't get a letter from them, she's going to know I didn't apply, and I'm just going to be one more disappointment in her life."

Dad leans forward again, planting his elbows on the table and covering his mouth with one hand. "Fuck, she's gonna kill you," he says, and I sigh because *duh*. Of course she's going to kill me. But doesn't he have any other advice for me? From one disappointment to another, he's got to have something. He taps on the table between us, clicking his teeth together. "When you gonna tell her?" he asks.

I bang my head on the table so loud my coffee cup rattles on its saucer. "Fuck if I know. Maybe I don't have to tell her. I can say they offered me a free ride so she doesn't ask about money. I can just pack my shit at the end of the summer and just pretend I'm living on campus. Maybe she'll never ask about it."

My father is silent, and when I lift my head, he's sending me a look like, *You know you're an idiot, right?*

"Okay, yes, it's a stupid idea," I shoot at him. "I get that. But I have no fucking clue what to do."

I'm not expecting it, but for just a second, he doesn't look like the person I've become so used to sitting across this table from. He looks like an adult. He looks like a father. He looks like someone who has something to say, like someone whose opinion might mean something.

"Oli, if this is really what you want to do, and to be honest, at this point I don't think you have much of a choice, you're buried so deep in it, you need to tell your mum. You need to tell her what you want and you have to be prepared to lose her respect. You have to be ready to lose her for the life you want for yourself. We've been holding you down long enough. It's time for you to do something for yourself."

By the time he's done speaking, my hands are trembling. When Dad stood up to his parents, they cut him off. They disowned him. My father said no, and this is where it got him. Every time Mom told me if I didn't stay on track, I would end up like my father, it always felt like the ultimate threat. And maybe Dad fucked up, but at least he tried. At least he had the balls to stand up for what he wanted.

"Thanks, Dad."

He blinks at me, probably because I've never thanked him for anything in my life.

OLIVER

I'M NOT SURPRISED that Mom is throwing me a surprise party. If there's anything my mom is terrible at, it's keeping secrets, especially when that secret requires calling your boss and changing your schedule so that you show up at work only to find that your boss isn't there and you don't *actually* have a shift to work and now have to drive all the way back home. Subtle.

So I'm not surprised when I walk up to the apartment and it's almost comically dark. Mom didn't even leave the front porch light on, and I'm pretty sure that light has been left on permanently since we moved in. The entire apartment is dark and silent, and I know it's because everyone inside is collectively holding their breath.

And I'm not surprised when the light goes on and there's a meager exclamation of "Surprise!"

I am, however, surprised to find four people in my living room instead of three. Because I know Mom didn't invite Amy. And there's no reason she should be here, in my living room, dressed like she's about to go on a date, in a shiny silver top and a black skirt that hugs her in all the most distracting places. But she's here anyway, and I can't take my eyes off her as Mom smiles at me and then a cake is produced. My favorite, chocolate with white icing.

I blow out the candles, and we sit around the dining room table, eating pizza, and I'm trying to be part of the conversation, but I can't stop thinking about the fact that Amy is wearing heels. And hoop earrings.

Mom clears her throat. "So, Amy," she begins. "Oli tells me you're going to Stanford."

Amy chokes on the pizza in her mouth. Brooke slides a soda in her direction, and Amy gulps it down before answering. "Actually, I haven't gotten in yet. I'm still waiting to hear back."

Mom waves Amy off. "Oh, I'm sure you'll get in," she says. "You seem like a very smart girl. And so pretty." As if that has anything to do with getting into college. Mom glances at me in the absolutely least subtle way, and I roll my eyes. Across the table, Amy's eyes have gone wide, and a blush is spreading across her cheeks.

"You know," Brooke says, her mouth half full. Unlike Amy, she hasn't dressed up. She's wearing a black tank top and ripped jeans, and I wish beyond every wish that I could be as comfortable as she looks now. "We've been thinking of moving the shop to Cali. The hipsters out there are way more into vinyl than anyone in Missouri. Plus better work for Lauren when she's out of law school. We wouldn't be able to do it any time soon. We'd have to find a building and all that junk. But if it happens, you're a shoo-in for a store manager position." She nudges Amy with her elbow, and Amy looks discombobulated again.

"Oh," is all she says, and I honestly can't tell if it's an *oh* like that's a terrific offer that she'd love to take Brooke up on, or *oh* like Amy has no plans to be in any way associated with Spirits as soon as she leaves for California. She probably plans to cut all ties. She won't have time for people back in Kansas City once she's gone.

My pizza suddenly seems unappetizing.

"Oli, why don't we go ahead and open your presents?"

I still have pizza in my mouth, but I take a sip of soda to wash it down and accept a gift my mother hands me. It's a box covered in striped wrapping paper. I smile at Mom, figuring I probably know what's in it. Mom gets me a band T-shirt every year for my birthday without fail. Inside is a Civil Wars T-shirt.

"Thanks, Mom."

Mom leans over to hug me, and when she sits back, her eyes are glistening. "I can't believe my baby is already nineteen. Where did the time go?"

She does this every year, too. "Aw, Mom. Suck it up." I smile over at her, and I can't help but think maybe, just maybe, when I finally get around to telling her I don't want to go to college, maybe she'll be on my side, maybe she'll understand.

I go back to my gifts, opening a set of KISS bobbleheads from Marshal and a Death Cab for Cutie poster from Brooke.

"Your mom said to get you something for your dorm room," Brooke says, motioning at the poster.

Beside her, Mom grimaces. "I was thinking more along the lines of a lamp or a sheet set."

A skinny envelope sits on the tabletop, and I reach for it, my stomach hopping up into my throat when I see there's a stack of bills sitting inside. Mom grins at me. "That's for when you're ready to do your dorm shopping. I figure we could go soon and get everything you need."

I stare down into the envelope, feeling an urgent and sudden need to just spill everything, to tell her I'm not going to college and I'm not going to live in a dorm and I'm certainly not going to take this money. But when I look up and see everyone's eyes on me, I know this isn't the place to spit everything out. My eyes find Amy's, and she sends me a sympathetic smile. She, at least, knows, and that's enough to comfort me as I shove the envelope in my back pocket.

"Thanks, Mom."

Mom stretches to reach across the table and pick up the last gift left. She scans the wrapping, which is just pieces of tissue paper layered over one another. When she doesn't see a card or a tag, Mom scowls. "Who is this from?" she asks, as if there are at least a hundred other people it could have come from.

"Oh, I brought that," Amy spits out. "It's really nothing special." Amy looks embarrassed, but I reach out and take it. I know the weight of a CD case in my hand, and my mind is already on that mix she made me of "Hallelujah" covers while I rip the tissue paper off.

All that's written on the mix is the Front Bottoms.

When I look back at Amy, her face is buried in her hands, and I can see the blush that's spread all the way to her ears and down her neck. "It's so stupid," she says, her words muffled by her hands.

"It's not stupid," I tell her, even though I don't know exactly what it is. It doesn't really matter. If it came from Amy, it's not stupid.

She bites her lip. "It's just a mix of my favorites. Nothing special."

Maybe it's not the best party etiquette, but I take the CD into the living room, where Mom still holds on to her huge stereo from the nineties on an antique side table. I pop open the top and put the CD in, and when the music starts, I wave everyone into the living room with me.

Amy hesitates, hovering between the dining room and the living room, watching us as the notes I know so well, the reverberating notes of "Molly" blare from the stereo. On another day, Mom would tell me the music is too loud, that I'm going to shake the paint off the walls, but today, she just leans against the wall and smiles at me.

I reach out for Amy and pull her into the living room with me as "Molly" dissolves into "Flashlight," a song that's fast and pumping, and Brooke is already dancing through the living room with her eyes closed. As the chorus picks up, the drums and the guitar screaming loud, we bounce around the living room, clapping our hands and making room when Marshal joins us, the four of us dancing until we're out of breath and our downstairs neighbors probably hate us.

When the CD ends, the apartment falling quiet again, we all collapse on the couch, and I'm pressed between the arm of the couch and Amy, her leg against mine from hip to knee.

"Thank you," I say to her as Brooke and Mom start to discuss whether or not we're done with the snow for the rest of the year.

"It's nothing," she says, her eyes sparking in the light of the living room lamp. "I probably should have given you some new music instead so that you could finally bow before me, The Queen of Music."

She grins at me, and I pinch her lightly on her knee. She shrieks and punches me in the arm, and I'm happier than I've been since, well, ever.

OLIVER

It's close to eleven when everyone starts to grumble like they're ready to leave.

Mom is the first one to go.

"No one has to leave," she says, putting her hands up to stop us when Brooke and Marshal move toward the direction of the door. Mom has changed into her scrubs and is fastening her watch to her wrist. "I didn't mean to break up the fun. I just really have to get to work."

"No, that's okay," Brooke says, tucking her hands into her back pockets. "I have to get to the shop and help Lauren get closed up. Sorry, Oli."

"Yeah, sorry, Oli," Marshal says, "but if I don't get home before my roommate brings whatever girl he's met back to the apartment, he'll lock me out all night, and I've been sleeping in my car too much."

I just nod, trying hard not to dwell on the fact that everyone is going to leave, and I'm going to be left in this unbearably silent apartment. I'm getting ready to shut the door behind all of them when Brooke scowls at me. "Where's Amy? I was going to give her a ride home."

I look over my shoulder, but Amy is nowhere to be found. I turn back to Brooke. "She was going to the bathroom earlier. Maybe something's wrong."

Brooke sends me a weird look, but she doesn't move. She crosses her arms and then her mouth curls into a smile. "You know what? Marshal and I are going to head out. Why don't you go ahead and give Amy a ride home yourself when she gets out of the bathroom?"

My stomach flutters at her suggestion. I know she's just screwing with me. That she's loving it, in fact. But if I'm being honest, the idea of being alone with Amy, of getting to be the one to drive her home, makes my skin heat with excitement.

"Yeah, I'll just, uh, take her home. I'll give her a ride. That's not a problem. I can do that."

Brooke grins at me, cocks one eyebrow, and then she and Marshal are gone. I shut the door and stare at it for a long time, waiting for Amy's footsteps behind me. But she never comes, and after a few minutes, I make my way down the hall to the bathroom. I'm not entirely sure of the best way to approach the situation. Will it embarrass her if I knock on the door and ask her if she's okay? Probably.

But when I get to the end of the hallway, the bathroom door is open, and the light is off. I stop, thoroughly confused, and then I hear something in my bedroom, the telling clatter of CD cases smacking together. I'm already smiling by the time I get there. And there she is, looking like the greatest thing I've ever seen in my life, in the dim light of my bedside lamp, standing in front of my floor-to-ceiling shelves, rifling through my CDs and vinyl.

AMY

WHEN I TURN slightly away from Oliver's music collection and see the shape of someone in the doorway, I screech and drop the CD in my hand. Oliver steps into the room, already laughing.

"Sorry. Didn't mean to scare you."

He bends down to pick up the CD at my feet, straightening and handing it to me, his eyes fixed on mine.

"Is it okay that I'm in here?" I ask him. "I didn't mean to snoop. I just saw all the music and . . ."

He sends me a strange look, his mouth twisting. "It's okay that you're in here."

I replace the CD in the spot I took it from and run my fingertips over the cases. "This collection is pretty amazing." I've been looking at it for who knows how long and still have only looked through half of the CDs and vinyl that line the walls of Oli's room.

He follows me slowly as I scan my way down the wall. "This is what happens when you abuse your employee discount."

"Yeah, I guess so." I stop moving and realize that I can't hear voices in the living room. Damn. Did I piss them off by disappearing? "Oh God. Is everyone mad at me?" I ask.

Oli shakes his head. "Everyone left."

"Everyone left? Because of me?"

His mouth quirks up on one side. "No. Brooke and Marshal had to get somewhere, and Mom had to leave for her shift at the hospital."

I sigh and lean against the shelf beside me. "Brooke was my ride."

Oliver's gaze settles on me, steady, and it's a little unnerving. "I'll take you."

The reality of the situation starts to tingle under my skin. We're completely alone in Oliver's apartment. Everyone is gone, and Oli's standing so close to me that I can feel his breath on my face.

We stand in silence for a long time, until finally Oli says, "Do you want me to take you home right now?"

I don't want to go home. I don't want to leave him yet. Just the thought does something to my skin, makes it ache, makes my chest feel tight.

"Can I stay instead? Hang out? Listen to some music?"

His mouth opens, but he doesn't say anything for a long time, his fingers tapping their way along the shelf beside him, like they can't stay still. Maybe he wants to be alone, but he isn't sure how to tell me so. He's used to the quiet, to being on his own, and maybe he needs that again now.

"It's okay," I tell him quickly. "I don't have to stay. It's just quiet here, and I thought maybe—"

"Stay forever," he says, and I laugh, my stomach fluttering.

I know Oliver likes me. Or at least, I know he's attracted to me. He never would have kissed me that night at Spirits if he didn't like me in one way or another. But when he says things like that, things that make me feel wanted, well . . . it does something to me, like I can feel all my insides going soft. This isn't the same Oliver I knew two months ago. He's not the boy who wouldn't speak to me, who could barely look at me. He's the boy who sat across the dining room table and told me my gift wasn't stupid while his mom watched. I wanted to tell him then that he makes my heart go sore when he does things like that.

I nudge him with the toe of my shoe, and he reaches out and pulls a CD off the shelf beside him. "Music?" He pops open the case without even looking at it, and I smile at his confidence that every

CD on his shelves is worth listening to, that whatever he blindly chooses will be good enough to share.

I slide down to the floor, stretching my legs out in front of me, and watch him go to his computer and pop the CD in. He's so deliberate with his movements.

"How are these organized?" I ask, tapping one of the shelves by my hip.

"Genre, then artist's last name or band name, then release date."

I smile up at him as he comes back to me. "You are such a nerd."

Music filters from the computer, where a screen saver is already flashing across the screen, pictures of Oliver and his mom that I watch go by again and again as Sleeping at Last flows into the room like syrup. Oliver drops down onto the floor beside me, and I try to ignore the feel of his hip pressed against mine. He perches his arms on his knees and looks over at me.

I close my eyes and lean my head back against the shelf behind me. It's amazing what music can do to me, like cold and warmth at the same time flooding from one end of my skin to the other. I take a deep breath, like I could breathe it into my lungs.

"The last time I listened to Sleeping at Last was my first day at Spirits," I say.

"You can't quit," Oliver says, and I sigh because I knew he would bring it up. We haven't spoken about what my mother said to me at family dinner, but I know Oliver has to be thinking about it as much as I am. Carlos being out of a job was the only reason I've stayed even though fitting Spirits into my life is hard, but now that Mom is telling me it's okay to quit, well, my stomach feels all twisted just thinking about it.

"This girl—she's been tutoring me in calculus—she told me I

should quit, and I can't pretend like I haven't thought about how it would make everything so much easier. But if I'm being honest, Spirits kind of feels like home. Is that stupid?" I laugh a little to myself, but when I look up at Oli, he isn't laughing, or smiling, or looking amused at all.

"That's not stupid," he says.

I press my hands into my face. I feel like an idiot for saying all this to him.

"Amy," he says, and he looks like he wants to say something, but for a long time, he just doesn't. And then he says, "I need you there." His eyes travel all over my face, and I feel a tug in my chest, in my hands, in my whole body, pulling me toward him.

I kiss him.

Oliver reacts so suddenly, it startles me when his hands go into my hair, when he turns and presses as much of his body to mine as he can, when he angles his head and kisses me like he's trying to memorize my mouth.

His mouth moves down to my neck, and I clutch his shirt, trying to keep myself grounded as everything becomes Oliver and the notes of a piano and the friction of the carpet on my legs. We make our way up to the bed, keeping contact anywhere we can: our lips, our fingers, our kneecaps. His weight pushes me down into his soft mattress, and I try to catch my breath, gasping anytime he moves from my mouth to find a fresh spot on my skin he hasn't kissed yet.

His fingers find their way to the edge of my shirt, and I can feel his hesitation in the way his fingers flex against my hip. I grab hold of his fingers and send them up my stomach. He sighs into my neck, but then his mouth finds mine again as my shirt is shoved up under my arms and Oliver shudders against me.

When the CD plays its way through the last song, and the room plummets into silence, Oliver presses his forehead to mine. "We should probably slow down," he says through labored breaths.

I bite my lip. I'm not a big fan of slow. We're alone, we're in his bed, and every inch of my body is on fire. I want him to keep going. But I remember the way he's spoken of sex like it's something foreign to him, so I let him pull my shirt down, let him lie down beside me, let him link our fingers together.

"Oli?" I whisper. "Are you a virgin?" I hope it doesn't sound like I'm accusing him of anything, like there's anything wrong with him being a virgin on his nineteenth birthday. There definitely isn't.

He doesn't say anything, but when our breaths have leveled out between us, he nods, his head bumping my shoulder. He sets his hand on my stomach, fingers splayed, and I close my eyes.

"Okay," I say because there's nothing else to say. It doesn't bother me, and I can't help but look at him to see if it bothers *him*. But his eyes are focused up on the ceiling, his fingertip absently tracing a shape on my hip.

I want to ask him where this leaves us, if we're still just friends, but the room is quiet, nothing but the sound of our breathing, and for now, I'm okay with that.

APRIL

OLIVER

AMY, SITTING ACROSS the table, is wearing my headphones and smiling as she listens to Hunter Hunted. She tilts her head back, exposing the long column of her neck as it disappears down into her flannel shirt, and I feel like I'm going to combust.

We haven't talked about what happened at my party. We haven't talked about the fact that we made out in my bed or that I almost took her clothes off. We haven't talked about what it means for us and our friendship. The last time we had this discussion, she was pretty adamant that we're just friends, but does that still apply? Are we still just friends?

She bites her lip and slides the headphones off to hand them to me. Our fingers brush, and I take a deep breath to keep from diving across the table.

"I love it," she says. "But a musical genius you are not."

Just ask her. Just ask her what Wednesday meant. It's been three days. You guys can talk about it. It doesn't make you pathetic. Oh, who are you kidding? You are pathetic.

"This place is nice," she says, slumping down in the seat so she can put her feet up on the seat next to me. She smiles. "I can see you in this place, late at night, listening to music like the world doesn't exist." How does she do that? Know everything about me without me even telling her? "How's your dad doing, by the way?"

I shrug. "Still going to A.A. That's all I can ask, right?"

She sends me a *pretty much* look and finishes off her tea. "You have to get back to work," she says, slipping out of the booth. "The last thing I need is Brooke thinking I'm a bad influence on you."

I snort and slide out to stand beside her, slipping enough cash on the table to cover our food and a tip.

She looks down at the money and then back up at me. "I can pay for my own."

I wave her off, even though her comment is rocketing inside me. If she wants to pay for her own, does that mean this isn't a date and we're still just friends and I've managed to get my heart broken again without even trying?

But then, as natural as anything, Amy reaches over and laces her fingers with mine, leading me out of Charlie's and out onto the sidewalk. We walk toward Spirits. My entire body is tingling, with ground zero being the places where her skin is touching mine.

It's over too soon because we're in front of Spirits, and she's looking up at me with those dark brown eyes, and I'm fairly certain I would sell my soul if she'll look at me forever the way she's looking at me right now.

"When do you work next?" she asks, looking down at our still-linked hands. "I know you're off Sundays. Monday?"

I nudge the toe of her shoe with mine. "We could hang out outside of work." My stomach is rolling with nerves. That sounded casual, right?

She smiles up at me, the late morning sunshine making her eyes turn the color of milk chocolate. "Are you asking me out?"

"Fuck yes," I say because I'm in love with her, and I want to go on a date with her, and hold her hand, and whisper in her ear, and kiss her, and do other things with her, and if she says we're just friends, I might die.

But her smile gets bigger, so I drop her hand, grab her face, and kiss her. She kisses me back so enthusiastically, we start to tip over, and then we're laughing into each other's mouths.

"What about Tuesday?"

She nods and I kiss her again, finally letting her go so that she drops back on her heels. "Tuesday," she says, and then she turns and walks away, and I'm watching her go and willing my legs to stay put instead of following after her the way they want to.

I'm about to turn to go into Spirits when I catch sight of someone in the window across the street, inside the tutoring center. I'm not positive, but it seems like maybe they're watching me. It takes me a second, but then I can make out his face.

It's Amy's ex, Jackson, and his eyes are following after Amy and then traveling all the way back to where I stand. I want to laugh in his face, because he threw away something amazing, and now that amazing girl is mine.

I turn with a grin and go into Spirits.

AMY

When our AP bio teacher asks Jackson and me to stay after class, I think maybe she's going to assign us new lab partners after all.

But our teacher is frowning. And not that *darn teenagers bringing their drama to school again* kind of frown that teachers like to give but an *I'm not mad just disappointed* kind of frown, and I immediately start to panic because I have never done anything to receive that expression from a teacher.

"Amy, Jackson, I think we need to have a little conversation about taking this class seriously."

I frown right back at her. "What do you mean?"

Her eyes move to me sharply. I know she's not exactly my biggest fan, but whatever it is, it can't be that bad, can it? "I will not tolerate you sharing answers. I figured you were studying together, but I certainly didn't think you'd stoop so low as to copy each other's exams. . . ."

She's still talking, but my heart has stopped. When she finally ends her tirade, I say, "I don't know what you're talking about. I've never cheated on anything in my life."

Her eyes narrow. "Miss Richardson, you and Mr. Brody had almost identical answers on your essay questions, so don't you dare look at me and lie about this."

I see Jackson glance at me out of the side of his eye, and I know that I'm going to kill him. If I murder him, right here and now in this science lab, what are the chances they'll still consider my application for Stanford? There's no explanation other than that Jackson cheated off me, that he copied my test answer for answer thinking that she wouldn't notice. But there are two tests on the desk in front of her, both of them with the same grade, a ninety-six, and of course, since we share a lab table, there can only be one explanation.

"I swear, I didn't—"

She puts her hand up. "You'll both get zeroes for this exam, and you'll be separated at the next exam. If you ever pull a stunt like this in my class again, I will have you both suspended."

The tears start before I can stop them. I've never been accused of cheating, and all I can think about is losing valedictorian. My grades have to be perfect, and I can't believe I just lost everything. And because of Jackson.

Our teacher looks at me and sighs. "Oh, Amy. You don't need to be so dramatic. There will be other exams, believe me. Now move on before you're late to your next class."

I'm out the door before anyone says anything else, but I can hear Jackson on my heels. Outside, the halls are already mostly empty, the bell for second period looming.

"Amy, wait."

I spin around, and it takes everything in me not to scream, not to just turn into an animal, open my mouth, and emit a battle cry. "Get the hell away from me," I growl at him. "Haven't you fucked up my life enough?"

"I never thought she'd figure it out," he says, his voice a whine. "I changed words around so it wouldn't be obvious."

I laugh up at the ceiling, a hysterical sound. "Right. Because she's too stupid to figure *that* out. Well, I hope you're happy, because now I'm going to get a fucking B, and Petra is going to be val."

"You were already struggling."

I freeze. "What did you say?"

He almost looks embarrassed that he even said it, but it's too late to take it back now. "People are saying you probably weren't going to make val anyway because you've been struggling in calculus."

My eyes shoot to him. "Who told you that?"

He shrugs.

"Don't fucking shrug. If you're going to gossip about me, at least get your facts straight. I might have slipped, but I've been doing better." I can almost believe it, too, while I shout it in his face.

He rolls his eyes. "You're not going to get anywhere when you're spending your weekends with that guy's tongue down your throat for everyone to see."

I'm so shocked by what he says, I skip right over angry and straight to incredulous. "What?"

He gestures wildly. "That guy you were making out with in front of the tutoring center on Saturday. You should be at home studying, and instead, you're making out with randos on street corners."

It takes me a second to realize that he's talking about Oliver. That we did, in fact, kiss in front of the tutoring center. That he's admitting to watching us. I grind my teeth together and take a menacing step toward him. "Why do you even care? You're the one who broke up with me. You're the one who's seeing someone else. And *you're* the one who wanted to *have fun,* so why are you so concerned about where I am on the weekend? Oliver is none of your business and neither is my academic standing."

I'm about to turn and leave him there, but he reaches out, his fingertips brushing my elbow, and it burns me enough to stay put. "I just want us to go back to being friends," he says, and it is the most unbelievable thing he's ever said to me, because we were never friends. We were two people who had friends in common, who occasionally ended up in a room together, and then we were more, just like that. There was never time for friendship. Just dates and kissing and sex and a million other things I wish I could take back.

"We are not friends, Jackson. Not ever."

AMY

I HATE THAT I have to tell my parents that I'm going on a date with Oliver tonight. I hate it because I will never hear the end of their mocking and their teasing, and I groan because I don't think I can handle it. But Oli is going to pull up in front of our house in, like, ten minutes, and I can't just jump into a boy's truck without my mother asking a billion questions, so I might as well just get this over with.

I knock on their bedroom door, where they're inside, hiding from the twins and watching *Law and Order*.

"I'm going out tonight," I say, barely poking my head in the door so they can't see that I'm all dressed up. I'm wearing my favorite red dress, even though it's still cold out, and a pair of boots.

Mama crunches on a handful of popcorn she just pulled from the bowl sitting between her and Carlos, and smiles over at me. "I thought you were off today. Where are you going?"

"Actually, I'm going out with Oliver."

By the way they both whip around quick to look at me, it's like I just told them I'm going on a date with Charles Manson.

"Oliver?" Mama demands, and I'm already backing away from their bedroom door because I don't want to do this with them. I just want to go. "Oliver, from work?"

I nod and try to close the door slowly, until there's nothing but a sliver of light left. "Yes, that Oliver. We won't be out too late. Okay, bye."

"Amaría Valentina Richardson, you get your butt back in here."

I sigh and open the door all the way. "Mama, it's just a date."

Her face lights up. "A real date? Like, boyfriend/girlfriend?"

I roll my eyes. "This isn't the third grade."

"Where are you going?"

I shrug. "I don't know. He's just going to pick me up. He didn't say where we are going."

Carlos scowls. "I don't like the sound of that. Are you sure you can trust this boy?"

I shrug again because I trusted Jackson, and look how that turned out. "Yes, I trust him."

"And you're not going to do anything inappropriate," Mama pipes up.

"Right," I say, without adding that Oliver and I have been alone on a dozen different occasions, and we could have had sex all those times and they never would have known the difference. But they don't need to know that. The last thing I need is to be on a short leash from here on out, especially if Oliver and I *do* want to take things to the next level.

Mama narrows her eyes. "I don't know about this."

I sigh. "Mama, it's just a date. You never asked this many questions when it was Jackson."

She throws her hands up. "I knew Jackson. I don't know Oliver."

"Sure, you do. You met him at family dinner."

"That doesn't count."

I stand in the open doorway while she chews on her lip, both of us waiting for the other to speak. But I've said everything I need to say, and when I hear Oliver's truck pull into the driveway, I bolt down the hallway.

"See you later!" I call behind me.

AMY

OLIVER TAKES ME to Knucklehead Saloon, and I'm so excited, I throw open the door before he's even put the truck in park.

I've always wanted to come here, but it's not exactly the kind of place my parents are particularly eager to let me visit, as it's mostly a biker bar.

"Who are we seeing?" I ask, rushing around to Oliver's side of the truck and grabbing his hand to pull him along. Holding hands with Oliver feels so natural, like it's something we've been doing our whole lives.

Oliver has a smile on his face that I've never seen before, and he digs his heels in long enough to pull me to him and kiss me.

My stomach cartwheels. Kissing him feels natural, too, and we ignore the people moving toward the bar from the parking lot in favor of making out against the side of Oli's truck. His fingers skim my thighs, just barely skirting under the hem of my dress, and I'm suddenly very glad I wore a dress, even though it's still cold out. Oliver keeps me warm with his body pressed up against mine.

"We're going to miss the show," he says against my neck, and I sigh before pushing him away.

"Who are we seeing?" I ask again, and this time it's him pulling me along, my boots crunching along the pavement.

"An eighties cover band," he says. "They don't do under-twenty-one shows very often, so I bought tickets as soon as I saw. Hope that's your thing."

"Definitely my thing!" I have to shout at him because we've stepped just inside the bar, where it's balmy compared to the cold air outside. We stop long enough to show our IDs and get stamped as underage, and then Oliver is moving so confidently, I know he's been here before.

People are crammed against one another, and Oliver doesn't stop as we pass the bar and tables full of already tipsy middle-age show-goers. He keeps moving until we've walked right out another door, onto a patio, and the world seems to descend into magic.

A band is already onstage, singing "Hungry Like the Wolf," and I can't stop the smile that stretches my face. *This.* This is what I want, to feel this happy for the rest of my life. There are people everywhere, at long tables spread out across the patio and pressed against the railing of a second-story viewing area. Bright neon paints everyone's faces in pink, and twinkle lights are wrapped around the stair railings.

"Let's find a place to stand," Oliver says into my ear as he hands a guy two tickets, and then I'm dancing as we move onto the patio, finding a spot by the stairs to stand. Lights flash out at us, pink and blue and green, and I close my eyes as Oliver stands behind me, his hands on my hips.

I lean my head back, rest it on his shoulder, and say into his ear, "How could you be so sure I was going to be down with an eighties cover band, since I have such inferior music tastes and all?"

He rolls his eyes, and then his hot breath in my ear makes me shiver. "You date me, you date cheesy Duran Duran covers."

I laugh loud, since no one can hear it over the music. "Am I dating you, Oli?"

He nips my earlobe. "I don't take girls I'm not dating to cheesy eighties concerts."

I crane my neck to look up at him, at the curve of his jaw and the stubble across the cleft in his chin. We listen to the band for a long time, some songs I recognize from listening to them with Mama or Jackson, and some I don't recognize but really like. After a while, we squeeze over to the bar and Oliver orders us waters before we move through the shuffle back to our spot.

But a group of leather-clad women are now leaning against the railing where we were standing, so we climb the stairs and find a spot on the balcony, against the golden twinkle lights, looking down at the band from up high. I love watching their fingers move over the guitar necks. I always wanted to learn how to play something, anything, but especially the guitar, and my heart aches for it again now, more than ever.

I sip my water and look up at Oliver. He's not looking at me, his eyes glued to the stage, but I've learned that just because Oliver isn't looking doesn't mean he's not paying attention. His thumb moves back and forth against my hand. He's holding it tight, his fingers wrapped firmly around mine, and I know he can feel that I'm looking.

"What is everyone going to think when they find out you've got the interior of a marshmallow?" I shout to him.

He looks down at me with only his eyes. "Are you going to tell people?"

I pretend to think about it. "What would happen if I did?"

He purses his lips. "I suppose I'd have to kill you."

I scoff. "You couldn't stomach murder, York."

He moves quick, sandwiching me between the railing and his body, and he's so tall, he blocks out everything else around me, until everything is his pale skin and his freckles and his Human League T-shirt. His hands press the railing on either side of my waist, and maybe he's trying to intimidate me, but all he's doing is making me want to jump his bones. His eyes bore into me and then drop to my mouth, but then the song ends and the applause begins.

OLIVER

I HAVE THE Lumineers playing as we drive down the highway. Amy leans her head against the fogged-up window and sings along. We drive right out of Kansas City, until the lights from the city are dim enough in the distance that we can see the stars.

I take her into Independence, to a quiet stretch of road far from where we live, and park beside a field. I know this spot from dozens of trips out to Independence, an open field, encircled by trees, but open to the night sky right above where we sit. It's the perfect spot for stargazing.

"Why, Oli, are we parking?" she asks, one hand on her chest.

"Yes, *Grandma*, I guess you could say that."

"And will there be . . . necking?"

I grit my teeth. "God, I hope so." I reach into the back seat for the blankets I brought with me while Amy gets out of the truck.

"Here." I hand her one of the blankets, and she immediately wraps it around herself, and I'm immediately sad to not be able to see her in her red dress anymore. I leave the truck running, the Lumineers playing out the open windows, and we climb into the bed of the truck after I spread a blanket over the cold metal.

Maybe the whole stargazing thing is a bit of a cliché, but Amy is pressed against my side, her warmth seeping into my bones. I can feel every soft inch of her, so I don't give a damn how cliché it is.

"You're like a space heater," she says, pressing her nose into the place where my neck and shoulder meet, and I shiver at the touch of her icy skin.

"No, you're just so tiny you don't produce any body heat."

"True." She wraps her arms around one of mine and holds it against her body, and I have no clue how she can be cold when my entire body is on fire.

"Want to lie down?" I ask, and she nods.

We look up at the stars, pointing out the few constellations we know as we listen to the music. She puts her head on my shoulder, and I look down at her, those dark eyes of hers so close that I feel like I can see every pigment in them in the moonlight. It isn't much different from looking up at the stars.

"You make me want more," I whisper, and her eyes widen. I shake my head, realizing how that sounded.

"More?" she asks.

I run a fingertip along her jaw. "You make me feel like maybe I have a future."

She's much less bashful than I am, reaching up to press her hand against my cheek. Her skin is cold, and I turn to press my mouth against her palm, breathing steam into it. "Of course you have a future, Oli."

I shake my head. "I can't even be honest with my mom about not going to school. You have so much to offer, and I'm just here. With nothing to give."

A crease appears between her brows. "Oliver York, you have so much to give. What is it going to take to make you realize that?"

I want to tell her that hearing it come from her mouth is one step toward believing it could be true, but instead, I kiss her and hope she understands.

OLIVER

SOMETIME LATER, Amy decides she wants a hot dog, and half an hour and a trip to a drive-through later, we're sitting in the cab of the truck, quiet as we eat.

Amy slips out of her boots and puts her feet up on the dashboard as she takes a bite out of her hot dog. Her dress rides up her thigh, and my palms start to sweat. Outside the front windshield, the Missouri River is swaying hard in the wind. We're parked on the edge of the beach, the windows cracked. There are goose bumps crawling up Amy's arms.

"So, is this a normal first date for you?" she asks, a tomato clinging to the edge of her mouth. She swipes at it with the back of her hand.

"Never been on a date." I lick relish off my finger.

She stops chewing and looks over at me. "Never?"

I shrug, watching the waves in the moonlight. "I've dated girls. But most of the girls I dated just wanted to make out or go to parties or watch TV. Nothing so . . . official. I've never been good at all this."

She pops the last bite of her hot dog into her mouth. "You're a tragic case," she says, her cheek all puffed out with food.

We sit, quiet, without music for the first time since we met. Just us and the sound of the waves.

"I come here sometimes, when I don't want to go home," I tell her. Her darkly painted fingernails, her delicate skin, her red dress—it all shines in the dark, the whole world just shadow and light. "It's better with you."

She sits for a minute, a slight smile on her face, and then she says, "Okay. Music time. I haven't gotten a shot in a while. Seems like a good time to win."

What Amy turns on breaks the silence so completely that it's almost startling. "The Strumbellas," she shouts over it. She's turned it up so loud that I'm pretty sure the people driving by on the highway can probably hear it through our rolled-up windows.

And then she's dancing in her seat as the song picks up even higher, throwing her arms over her head and wiggling around so enthusiastically that all I can do is laugh.

When the song ends, she collapses against the seat like that one dance took everything out of her, and I lean across the console to kiss her. Against her mouth, I say, "That was adorable, but you're going to have to do better than that."

AMY

I DON'T MEAN to fall asleep on the way home, but it's late, and I'm so relaxed as we bump our way back into Kansas City, that I can't keep my eyes open.

I jerk awake when we come to a stop in front of my house, and I realize it's because Oliver has pressed his hand to the inside of my arm, the slightest of pressures to wake me up.

"Did I bore you?" he asks, but he's smiling, and I kiss him before climbing down out of the truck, my boots dangling from my fingers.

"Thanks for the best first date ever," I say, my hand curled into the open window.

His eyebrows go up. "Does that mean there's going to be a second date?"

I bite my lip. "Guess you'll just have to ask me and see."

And Oliver's smile rivals the brightness of the moon.

OLIVER

"You have one new message. First new message from phone number . . ."

I scowl at my phone while Brooke putters around behind me in her office. She's trying to reach over me to get to a stack of papers, and I reach out to grab them and hand them to her.

"Hello, Oliver, this is Matt with the admissions office at Missouri State University. We're calling to confirm your campus tour this afternoon at—"

I hang up and look at the clock on Brooke's computer.

Shit.

I forgot I was supposed to change my work schedule so I could drive out to St. Louis and tour the Missouri State campus, and now it's too late. I sigh. I'm so exhausted with trying to keep track of all the lies I've told Mom that I'm not even sure I give a shit anymore.

I delete the voicemail. Just one more thing Mom won't know about.

"Everything okay?" Brooke asks, leaning against the desk and absently flipping through the papers I just handed her. Even though Brooke has her issues with her parents and the stresses of running this place, this is the way she always exists in my mind: carefree and confident, taking care of her shit like an adult and living the life she wants.

"Brooke, can you teach me how to run a business?"

Brooke's eyes stop scanning over the page in her hand, and she turns to look at me. "Really?"

I shrug. "Only if you're cool with it. I want to learn how to do what you do. I want to learn how to have a place like Spirits."

Brooke grins. "Well, I can't take all the credit since Lauren's parents did most of the work, but . . ." She tosses the stack of papers onto the desk with a *smack* and leans back on her palms. "I'd be honored, Mr. York."

AMY

I ALMOST FORGET that it's gymnastics and karate night until Hector comes running out of his bedroom in his gi. He walks straight past me and to the fridge, where he pulls an already poured glass of milk from the shelf and swallows it in three gulps.

Mama tosses a loaf of bread and sandwich supplies on the table for dinner before rushing off to take care of something else, so I fix sandwiches for me and my kid siblings, all the while considering my options. My parents are usually gone for two or more hours when they take my brothers and sisters to their activities. That's usually time I use to revel in the peace of the house, but tonight I'm thinking about Oliver. I'm thinking about lying in his truck and looking up at the stars.

I take out my phone and text him.

My family is going to be gone for a few hours tonight. Want to come over?

They're all putting on their shoes when I get a text back.

Are you sure?

I laugh because when I first met Oli, I thought he was a badass. I thought he was the kind of guy who would quietly sit in the corner but rip you to shreds if you got too close. But now I know Oli is just a big softie, one who's afraid of getting me in trouble and saving himself for the right person, and my heart bursts when I think about it.

I'm sure. We don't have to do anything. I just want to be with you.

Maybe it's a forward thing to say, but I don't want him to be nervous about coming over. I don't want him to think I'm going to pressure him just because he's a virgin and I'm not. In the back of his truck, he kissed me and held my hand and ran his fingers along every inch of my exposed skin. And I'm okay if he just wants to do that again.

Leaving work now. Be there soon.

OLIVER

I GET HOME from work, planning to get straight into the shower. I want to be fresh when I meet up with Amy. I know she says we don't have to do anything, but I want to be prepared just in case we decide we're going to do something after all.

But I never make it to my room because Mom appears in the living room, and she's wearing an expression that says I'm in deep shit.

"Did you forget about something?" she demands, her arms crossed tight over her chest and her mouth the opposite of her big-gummed smile.

I just stare at her. I can probably assume this is about Missouri State, but it could be anything, honestly. "I'm guessing yes?"

She lets out an exasperated noise that kind of makes her sound like a horse. "You were supposed to tour Missouri State this afternoon, but instead, I got an email from their office because you never showed up for check-in."

"Why did they even contact you?" I demand, and I realize as soon as she scowls at me that that's definitely not the point.

"Because *I'm* the one who scheduled the tour, Oliver! I'm always the one who schedules the tours and contacts the admissions offices and forwards you the applications! You won't do it yourself!"

"Because I don't want to go!" I just blurt it out, and when I do, I wish I could stuff it back into my mouth. This isn't how I wanted to have this conversation. This isn't the time for it. But now she's looking at me like she doesn't know who I am.

"What are you talking about? You don't want to go to Missouri State? Then why didn't you say something?"

"It's not Missouri State," I say. I could build another lie, but this has to end. Might as well be now. "I don't want to go to college."

She freezes, her whole body going still and her eyes going wide like I just told her a meteor is about to crash right into our living room. "What?" she finally says, her arms stiff at her sides. "What are you talking about?"

"I'm talking about the fact that college isn't for me. I want to own my own record store, and I think I can do that if I stick with Brooke. I don't want to go to college."

"Where is this all coming from?" she asks. "You've never said anything to me about wanting to own a record store."

I throw my hands up. "Because the only time you talk to me is when it's about college. What about everything else? What about asking me about my girlfriend or about my job? Or about how Dad is doing? You don't care if I have friends. You don't care if I'm happy. You just care that I go to fucking college!"

She looks shocked for a second, but then her jaw tightens. "Don't talk to me like that. This isn't about us, Oliver. This is about you lying. Gap year, huh? I can't believe you. Were you just going to string me along and let me pay for everything while you lived comfortably, never growing up and never doing anything for your future?"

"Hey, I pay rent here!"

"Oh, give me a break, Oliver. Paying rent does not make you an adult."

I look at her, my mom's face so packed with shame and disappointment that my chest starts to ache. "I wasn't going to string you along," I say, insulted that she would even suggest it.

"But you were never planning on going to college." She says it with such finality that I know it's not really a question, but I answer it like it is.

"No, I was never planning on going," I say. Because it's the truth. Ever since all this started, the GPAs and the standardized tests and the applications and the transcripts, I've known that college isn't the place for me. Everyone was planning the next four years of their lives, and I was just waiting for the moment that they would move on and forget about me. And they did, right on schedule. I told myself I was still trying to decide, but I always knew.

I think of Amy, waiting for me in her empty house. She's a valedictorian, and she doesn't care if I go to college and get a degree. It doesn't matter to her. She thinks I'm worth something without all that.

"College is not going to make me successful, Mom. It's not some magical ticket to a successful life. There will be too many people, and the classes will be boring, and I'll be in debt for the rest of my life."

She crosses her arms over her chest. "But it's also an opportunity. And you will never make it anywhere in life without it."

"That's bullshit."

"Enough with the language."

I want to roll my eyes because I'm nineteen, and I can talk however I want, but she's already moved on.

"This is not how it works, Oliver. You will go to college, and you will get an education."

"No, I won't. You can't make me." I realize I sound like a child, and that just makes me even more mad. She's so fucking capable of turning me into a ten-year-old.

"Is this about your father?"

I bark out a laugh. "You mean my father, who gave up his entire life for us? My father who still wasn't good enough after sacrificing everything?"

"Your father who never made anything of himself. Ever. He could have gone to school, like I did, and gotten an education, but instead he decided that he was too good for all that. And now look at him."

We stare at each other, our mouths clenched, our eyes angry.

"You don't get to be the one that decides someone's not worth anything because they didn't make the choices you did." I know the words finally strike something in her because her eyes go wide, her mouth pops open a little, and I think maybe she's going to concede. Maybe she's going to finally tell me that I'm right, and that she's been judging the situation all wrong this whole time. But that's not how it happens at all.

Her eyes alight with fire, and she says, "I think it's time for you to find somewhere else to live."

"What?" Her words cause a pit to open inside me. Not because I don't want to leave, and not because I'm scared of not having somewhere to come home to. It's the fact that she's the one to pull the trigger. That she's kicking me out. My own fucking mother.

"Fine," I say, then turn and walk away from her so she won't know how upset I am. She's right. It's time for me to find somewhere else to live. I can feel her watching me as I pack a few bags, can feel the heat of her gaze as I grab a handful of clothes, an extra pair of shoes, things that'll get me through until I can come back and get the rest of it.

I gather my bags in my arm, sling my backpack on, and when I turn back to the door, Mom is blocking the way, and I wait. I wait for her to tell me that she didn't mean it. I wait for her to tell me not to go. We stand like that, looking at each other, until, with a downward curve of her mouth, she steps out of the way to let me pass.

AMY

I DON'T KNOW why I'm so nervous. It's not like it's the first time we've ever been alone together.

My heart thumps wildly when he knocks on the door, and I have it open in seconds, but what I find is not my Oliver, the one who smiles at me and holds my hand and lights up the whole world. This Oliver is frowning, his eyes exhausted and his body slumped.

"What's wrong?" I ask, stepping back to let him in.

He looks down at the carpet between our feet—mine bare, his in sneakers. He shrugs, and I'm worried, for just a second, that he's going to shut me out again. That he's not going to tell me.

But then he says, "My mom kicked me out."

"What? Why?"

"She found out about my college plans. Or lack thereof. Got really pissed. I don't know what I'm going to do." His voice breaks on the last word, and I put my arms around him, pressing up on my toes.

"It's going to be okay," I say in his ear, feeling the way he trembles against me. "Everything's going to be fine. My parents will let you stay here tonight."

His trembling subsides, and I feel him take a deep breath before he wraps his arms around me, lifting me up off my feet. "I guess I just wanted her to see me the way you do," he says. "Like I'm not a failure."

I wrap myself around him tighter, closing my eyes and feeling the plaster of his cast digging into my back. "You are anything but a failure, Oli. You just have to figure out what you want to do next."

He holds me like that for another minute, and then he lowers me back to the floor, until I'm craning my neck to look up at him again. "I'm here," I tell him, holding his face between my hands. "Whatever you need, I'm here."

His eyes search my face for a long time, and then he's bending forward, kissing me, pressing me back against the wall of our entryway until I can't breathe between him and the wall. Oliver has never kissed me like this before: urgent and desperate. It's scary and exciting, and I can't stop kissing him, holding him to me, letting his hands roam every part of me that he can find.

"I'm here," I say again.

I can't remember ever being this close to another person, ever feeling so wrapped up in someone else, so close that our bodies don't feel like two separate bodies anymore.

"I love you," I hear him say, low, under his breath, like he doesn't mean for me to hear him.

I close my eyes and press my face into his shirt, latching on to him. My heart is screaming, but I can't say it back. Because I'm not sure if what I feel for Oliver is love.

He makes a quiet sound against my neck and then spins us

around, moving toward the couch, where he lays me down gently and settles his weight on me. The urgency has faded, his kisses turning long and slow, and I can feel myself ready to cry because I want to love this boy. I want to feel this way, this feeling of safety and acceptance and something so kind and intimate, forever. I want Oli. My heart wants him.

So even though I don't say it back, I press my mouth to his and try to show him anyway.

OLIVER

I SLIP OUT of Amy's house when we hear her parents' minivan pull into the driveway, moving out the back door quick, even though my body feels heavy and drugged from almost an hour of Amy's mouth on mine.

I walk the two blocks to my truck, but as soon as I'm in it, I'm not sure what to do next. Amy offered to talk to her parents, insisting they would let me crash on the couch if I need to, but I have other options.

Really, I only have one option. The option that makes the most sense.

I drive to Independence.

Dad's porch light isn't on when I pull up in front of his house, but the lights are on inside. There's a good chance the porch light doesn't even work. It's kind of early, and his truck is still parked in the driveway, although he must be getting ready to leave for work soon.

As if on cue, the front door opens. Dad turns and props the

screen door open with his back while he locks his door. I watch him until he turns around and his eyes catch on my truck, parked against the curb. He frowns in my direction and then walks around the front of the truck, looking both ways before he steps into the street. He comes around the side and knocks on my window.

"Oli?" he says when I've rolled it down, letting in the cool evening air. "What's going on?" His eyes flit down to the bags on my passenger seat. It's hard to get used to him like this, clear-eyed and sober.

"Could I stay with you for a while?"

AMY

"Okay, well maybe I can text you on my lunch break," I say into my phone as people file into AP bio. I know I have to get off the phone before our teacher sees, but it's hard when Oliver sounds so sad, so lonely. He's been living with his dad for a few days, but he says it feels like years, and I can't even imagine. I wouldn't have any clue what to do if my parents kicked me out, other than sit on the floor and cry.

"You should come see me on my break."

Jackson drops down in the seat next to me, and I turn my face away, lowering my voice because I know that he's the kind of person to eavesdrop, and I really should have thought this through before having this conversation in AP bio.

"I can't come see you every time I'm off work. That completely defeats the purpose of my not having to work. I have homework to do."

He sighs. "Homework schmomework. I miss you."

I smile down at the table, scratching at the black surface with my nail. "I miss you, too. Maybe I can come over and hang out tonight. What time does your dad leave for work?"

He makes a humming noise in the back of his throat. "Not sure. I think he has a meeting tonight before his shift. I'll let you know."

"Okay." My voice has gone soft, the way all of me does when I talk to Oli. "Text me."

"Amy," Oli says loudly, like he's afraid I'll hang up before he can get his next words out. "I love you."

I open my mouth to say it back, want to say it back so bad, but Jackson shifts on the chair next to me, so I just say, "Bye, Oli," and hang up.

"You and your boyfriend are so cute," Jackson says as soon as my phone is back in my pocket.

"I would appreciate it if you'd mind your own business."

"Yeah? Well, I would appreciate it if you'd make your personal phone calls somewhere else." He turns away from me, and I just roll my eyes because he's acting like a fourth grader, and it's embarrassing. For him, not me.

"Did you get the answer for number five, because I struggled on it for like an hour," he asks, his voice completely normal, like we've been discussing homework this whole time.

For just a second, I stare at him. "You're kidding, right? What makes you think I'm going to help you after what you did?"

Jackson slams his book on the table, making me jump. "Because I apologized, and I really didn't mean to fuck things up for you." His eyes find mine, and there's something about the way he looks at me that has me completely rattled. His eyes drop, and I can't look away. "Because I need help."

I can feel myself wavering. Jackson has always had this *power* over me. I think about Petra offering to tutor me even though I've been awful to her. Does Jackson deserve the same kindness? Maybe. But I've never done to Petra what Jackson did to me.

I turn away from him slightly so that I don't have to look at his downtrodden expression anymore. "You should have thought about that before you acted like a jackass."

He sighs, but I don't turn to look at his face. Because I know myself well enough to know that I'll forgive him, and he doesn't deserve it.

AMY

I'M JITTERY. I want to go see Oliver. I want to feel his arms around me. When I get home, it's to all four of my siblings running around like chickens with their heads cut off and my mother shouting at them in Spanish. Carlos is in the living room watching TV as if he can't hear all the commotion, and I immediately plug my ears.

"Mama!" I shout, but with all five of them screaming, no one can hear me. "Mama!" Still nothing but now my mother is chasing my little brothers around with one of her wooden spoons, and I've completely given up trying to get anyone's attention.

I drop my bag by the door, kick off my shoes, and walk to the mailbox in my socks. I'm the only one in the house who gets the mail for some reason, and because of this, our mailman hates us immensely. There's always a week's worth of mail crammed into the box, and today is no different.

Today *is* different, however, because today, on top of our

stack of crumpled mail is a large white envelope, pristine and undisturbed.

For that, I will love my mailman forever.

My hands tremble when I reach in and pull out the envelope. I'm too scared to look at it and too excited not to. And when I finally peek at the return address, my heart leaps up into my throat.

It's from Stanford.

I decide immediately that I don't want to open it inside. I don't want all six of my family members breathing down my neck. So I stand there, my feet in the street, and rip open the envelope as cars drive by behind me.

Dear Amaría,

Congratulations! It is with great pleasure that I offer you admission to the Stanford University Class of 2025.

I hold in the scream.

But just barely.

Then, very calmly, I put the letter back in the envelope and hide it behind my back while I go into the house. Once I'm inside and certain no one is paying attention to me, I slip the envelope into my backpack and hike it onto my back while stepping into my shoes.

"I'm going to the library to study!" I call to no one in particular, and then I make a run for it.

AMY

I GO STRAIGHT to Oli's dad's house in Independence. I haven't actually been there yet but Oli sent me the address as soon as he moved, and

I plug it into the GPS on my phone. I don't see any vehicles besides Oli's truck in the driveway, and I pray that his father isn't home. I don't want to share this moment with anyone but Oli.

As soon as he opens the door, I throw my arms around his neck.

"Hey," he says, and I don't miss the fact that he's freshly showered, his hair still wet and his skin smelling like soap.

I push him away so that I can reach behind me to pull the letter out of my backpack. When I wave it in his face, his eyes go wide.

"Did you . . . ?" He snatches it out of my hand and his eyes scan over the page before he lunges at me, lifting me off my feet.

I laugh into his neck, but when he sets me down, the laughter fades and next thing I know, we're kissing. I'm not even sure who initiates it, but he lifts me off the ground, walking with me wrapped around him, down a hallway.

"Is your dad home?" I pull back to gasp.

He shakes his head and then covers my mouth with his again. I close my eyes and clutch him tight until I feel his bed beneath me. He's kissing me everywhere he can reach, and I'm trying not to shake with nerves.

"Are you sure?" I ask when he sits up on his knees to take his shirt off.

He nods and then he's on top of me again, his weight the most welcome pressure. "I love you," he says. "I want to. Do you want to?"

I nod. I let him take my clothes off and then watch him as he takes off his own. When he comes down on top of me and his hips find mine, I bite him on the soft curve of his shoulder.

And he whispers that he loves me over and over.

OLIVER

EVERYTHING SEEMS A little like bliss on Tuesday. I have a hard time focusing at work, choosing instead to daydream about Amy's skin, about Amy's arms around me, about the sound Amy made last night when her nails dug into my shoulder.

"Dear God," Brooke says to me when she comes into the stockroom to check on me. "Could you be any more obvious?"

My mood falters a little, but only a little because I don't think the actual apocalypse could kill my mood right now. "Obvious about what?"

Brooke leans against the wall, crosses her arms over her chest, and sends me an *oh please* look. "It couldn't be any more obvious that you got laid last night if you were wearing a neon sign. In fact, I think I have an *I got lucky* sign in the back of my car; want me to go get it?"

I roll my eyes, and my smile slips all the way. "Shut up, Brooke. It's none of your business."

Her eyebrows shoot up. "Wow. That was a defensive response. Must have been really special."

Special. What a mediocre word for what happened last night.

Brooke leans against the shelf beside me and smiles. "You know, it's nice to see you happy."

I send her a look. "It's not like I've been *distraught* in the past."

She shrugs. "Not far from it."

I sit down on the low shelf and mess around with a stack of vinyl. "Getting kicked out sucked, but at least now I don't have to pretend anymore. I feel . . . free."

Brooke sighs and sits next to me, throwing her arm around my shoulders. "Welcome to the adult world, Oliver. We're happy to have you. The only question now is, where do you go from here?"

My hand freezes, and my eyes slide over to her, and she must know, from the way her mouth is tilted in an uncertain expression, that she's asked me a question I don't know the answer to.

AMY

AFTER CLASS ON Wednesday, I decide to go past the admin office, and I'm a nervous wreck. My weekly trips to check on my rank quickly dissolved when I found out about the tie, mostly because I'm completely terrified to know. Like Schrödinger's Cat, if I never stop by to ask, I can be first in class as easily as I can be second.

"Amaría Richardson," Mrs. Grimes calls out to me through her open door. Like always, I take a seat across the desk from her, but I've never been this nervous before. For so long, I've been confident about my rank, and now I'm terrified.

She doesn't say a word. She knows why I'm here, and she immediately starts clicking around on her computer almost as soon as I've sat down.

She squints at the screen, her eyebrows furrowing deeply and her mouth pulled down into a frown. Then she writes the number down and slides it across the desk to me.

I've always known there was a chance that Petra was going to creep up on me. But I haven't dropped below the number one spot since halfway through junior year.

Today, the sticky note says *2*, and my stomach plummets into my shoes.

I just stare down at it, nodding, like my physical agreement with this particular event unfolding can make it hurt less. “Okay,” I finally say, my fist closing around the sticky note. “Okay.”

Mrs. Grimes looks at me with pity in her eyes, but she doesn’t offer her sympathies, which I’m perfectly fine with. It isn’t like she can say she’s sorry. She can’t be sorry to see some other student succeeding. And I guess I can’t be sorry, either. Petra worked for it, and so will I.

“Have a nice day,” Mrs. Grimes says quietly as I turn and walk out of her office.

I walk straight to the nearest girl’s bathroom and lock myself in the very last stall.

Second. I’m second. I can’t be the salutatorian. I have to be valedictorian or I’m not eligible for the Keller Scholarship.

I press myself against the wall, cover my face with my hands, and try not to cry. I will not cry over this. But I can feel the ache in my throat. I’ve worked so hard.

But I’ve been distracted.

Distracted by Spirits. Distracted by Oliver. Distracted by all of it.

Something has to change.

AMY

AT WORK, I smile up at Oli as best as I can, let him kiss me when no one’s looking, and then beg Brooke to put me in the back room when it’s time for my assignment. I don’t normally like the back room. I much prefer to work with customers. But today, I want to sit in the quiet, not have to look anyone in the eye, especially Oli.

Because I already know what I'm going to do, even though just thinking it makes my stomach twist so tight that I feel like I can't breathe.

The hours fly by, and when the door opens behind me, I know it's because the shop has closed. I don't turn around, and apparently, I don't need to.

"Something's wrong," Oliver says. "I can tell."

I don't know how he can tell, but isn't that always how it is with Oliver? I feel the hot tears run down my face before I even realize I'm going to cry, and I finally turn to look at him. He has his back pressed to the door, his entire body slumped like there's something heavy sitting on his shoulders.

"I slipped. Petra took top rank. I don't think I'm going to make val."

Oliver stares at me for a long time, and I can see the sadness in his eyes. Maybe he doesn't understand the merit behind making valedictorian, but he understands what it means to me. That much is obvious. That alone should make this easier. He should understand why I can't go on like this.

But then he's coming closer to me, putting his arms around me, and I feel the tears start all over again. "You still have time," he says quietly. "The school year isn't over yet. You still have to take finals."

I have to push him away, put distance between his body and mine, in order to think about what I have to say next. "It's not that easy, Oli," I say. And then I brace myself, looking away from him. "I think maybe it was a mistake to start seeing you."

That isn't what I meant to say, and I'm pretty sure immediately that it came out the wrong way, but there's no taking it back now, that much is clear from the look on Oliver's face. He looks like I just hit him.

"What?"

The tears are starting to well up again, and I have to cough them away before I can speak. "I'm in over my head, and I can't let anything come between me and making val. I can't lose this scholarship, Oliver. I've already gotten into Stanford."

A crease has appeared between his eyebrows, a distinctly confounded and possibly angry expression. "So, what, I'm just getting in the way?"

I sigh. "It sounds awful when you say it like that."

"How am I supposed to say it, Amy? I thought you were in this with me."

I take a deep breath, trying to calm down, trying to remember why I'm doing this. It's not about love or emotion. It's about Stanford. It's about my future.

"You're a distraction."

At that, he steps away from me, backing up until his back hits the door. "That's all I am?"

I want to scream. I feel like something is clawing at my throat. "Of course not."

"But you were able to date Jackson, and you were gunning for valedictorian then, too."

I have to catch my breath when he says it, because he's right. Sure, Jackson took up my study time, he made my life lose a little of its focus, but not the way Oliver has. Oliver consumes all my thoughts. He's all I can think about now that we're together, and it's started to turn everything else in my life into a haze.

"It's different" is all I can say. It's a sorry excuse.

"Right," he says, and I hate the way his voice sounds, cold and defeated. "Because you loved him."

I scowl. "Wait. What? No. Oliver that's not—"

"I get it," he says, and he's already started to open the door. "You have your perfect future planned out, and I wouldn't want to be the one to ruin it for you."

Panic starts to rise inside me, but I clamp it down because isn't this what I wanted? To end things? But I didn't want it to happen like this. But before I can say anything, try to stop him, he's left, closing the door behind him.

AMY

It's a long time before I can bring myself to step foot out of the back room, a long time before I can muster the courage to knock on Brooke's office door while also trying not to look at where Oliver is ringing someone up at the register, a long time before I gather the courage to tell Brooke that I quit, and that I'm not coming back.

OLIVER

I'm thankful that I'm closing with Brooke tonight and not with Amy. I'm thankful when Amy finally comes out of the back room, her purse in her hand, and leaves the shop.

Her eyes are red, her face blotchy, and I feel like I'm going to die. *What the fuck just happened?*

Yesterday, I was standing in that stockroom, thinking about how amazing it was to spend the night with Amy. How did we just break up in it? God, I say break up like that's really it. Amy was never mine. That much is clear now. No matter how I try, no matter how much of myself I give her, I'll never have all of her. I never wanted her to give up her chance at making it to Stanford, I just wanted *her*. But she wasn't willing to give me that.

It feels like needles in my skin and fire in my throat. I claw at my cast. When I look down and see her handwriting, I want to take a saw to it myself. I set my head against the counter.

I don't hear Brooke come up behind me. I don't hear her move over to me, don't know she's there until her arms are wrapped around me. I press my head against my arm, trying to hide as much as I can, but I don't push her off me.

"It's going to be okay," she says, and I don't know if she's saying it because she actually knows what happened or she's just guessing. Or maybe she has no clue at all. But it doesn't matter, because I don't believe it anyway.

I suck in a deep breath and straighten, looking down at her. "I'm fine." I clear away the lump in my throat.

"Oli, it's okay to—"

"Brooke, I'm sorry, but I quit."

Brooke looks stricken, but I don't try to explain myself to her. I just leave.

AMY

I SPEND ALL weekend in bed. I don't do homework, and I don't get up to eat and I don't do anything but stay in bed and listen to Oliver's

CDs. I still have so many of them. I'll have to return them eventually. But every time I think about doing that, I start to cry again because Oliver, rightfully, doesn't want to have anything to do with me.

On Sunday evening, I hear the doorbell and I know that I've forgotten about family dinner. I feel a stomachache coming on. I can't deal with anything right now, much less my entire family.

"Amy?" Mama says, and I roll over in bed so she won't be able to see that I've been crying.

"No," I say by way of an answer. I know it's, like, a cardinal sin in this house to miss family dinner, but I'm not doing it tonight. There's no way.

Mama opens my door anyway. "Amy, sweetie, you can't stay in here all weekend."

"Yes, I can," I groan and pull the covers over my head.

She sighs. "Honey, I don't know what happened, but you should put on some clothes and come say hello to your *tía y tío*." She doesn't say anything else, because she doesn't have to. I won't defy my mother, never have before, and she knows I'm going to get up and get dressed.

I put on sweatpants and a baggy T-shirt. She might get my presence, but that's all she's getting.

"Oh, Amaría," Abuela says when I'm standing in front of her. "*Mija*, are you sick?"

Heartsick, I think. But I just shake my head and load up a plate with rice and chilaquiles before cramming into a spot at the table. It's impossible not to notice that my entire family is looking at me with an amount of pity reserved for cheating spouses and dead pets.

"What?" I bark at them, my mouth full of rice, and they all look away.

But Mama doesn't look away. She takes a deep breath and then she says, "Everyone, Amaría got into Stanford."

I whip around to look at her, shocked, and I fully expect a commotion. I expect everyone to start talking all at once, the way they always do, the way I've become so used to. But instead, the entire table goes quiet. More than one person is looking at me with wide eyes, but nobody says a word.

And then finally, Abuela says, "You really are going to California?"

She says it so sincerely, with genuine curiosity, that I almost laugh. "Yes, Abuela. I'm really going."

She looks at me for a long time, her face completely expressionless, until, at the head of the table, Mama says, "Carlos and I are very proud, and she's going to be first in her class and get a good scholarship." She says it with such certainty in her voice that I can almost believe her, but even though she's clearly trying to make an effort, it's wasted now.

"Mama, I might not make valedictorian," I say, and the smile that Mama has plastered on her face slips.

"What?"

I shrug, and even though I have about twenty people staring at me right now in fascination, I speak only to her. "I lost the top spot. Petra might be valedictorian, and I won't be able to go to Stanford, because we can't afford it. They won't consider me for the Keller Scholarship without val."

Mama scowls. "That doesn't mean anything. There are other scholarships. There are loans—"

"Mama, Stanford is over seventy thousand dollars a year."

At the other end of the table, one of my cousins chokes on her food.

But Mama holds my gaze. "Amaría, you're going to Stanford. I don't know how we're going to get you there, but we will. I promise."

OLIVER

"SO WHY ARE you interested in working here at Charlie's?"

I'm trying to decide on the most respectful way to say, *I really need the money or my dad is going to kick me to the curb*, but I figure there's not a good way to go about that. So, instead, I say, "I'm really looking for a comfortable atmosphere and a place where I can get some good business experience." I don't add that I, in fact, already have a shit ton of business experience as I worked at Spirits for three and a half years.

The guy across the booth from me nods and jots something down on the tablet in front of him. He's short and round and has sweat stains on his blue button-up, and I'm pretty sure he's going to give me a job.

He smiles at me, his round cheeks pushing his glasses up when he shows his teeth. "Well, Mr. York. Everything looks great. We've been looking for a hardworking young person to help us bring some spirit to the team, and I really think you've got what we're looking for."

I nod and try not to feel like I'm being eaten alive from the inside.

AMY

IT'S THE WEEK before prom, and everyone on the prom planning committee is supposed to be prepping decorations. When I walk in, I'm so anxious, my fingers are trembling. My entire life feels like chaos right now, and I feel like everyone is watching my every step, waiting to see what I'll do next. In reality, chances are good that not a single person in the room gives a shit about me, unless they're looking for juicy gossip, of course.

I set up a station for making the table centerpieces, my back to the rest of the room so that I don't have to witness it when Petra finally shows up. But I know the second she gets there. I feel the way the tension stretches to cover all of us, and I can't resist glancing over my shoulder.

She walks into the room, her purse slung inside her elbow, her head held high, and an iced coffee in her hand. If I'm being completely honest, she looks incredible. Her face is completely made up, her outfit on point, and I can't take my eyes off her as she strides into the room, stopping to check in with people, moving around the room to oversee everyone. My heart races when I hear her heels clicking in my direction.

"How's it going, Amy?" she asks, and I'm surprised at how civil the question sounds coming out of her mouth. There's not an ounce of smugness in her voice, even though I know she knows about her rank. She's almost more obsessive about checking than I am.

"Great," I say, my voice shaking. I clear my throat. "I just have to finish wrapping ribbon around the candleholders."

She nods, her eyes on the centerpiece instead of me. "And did you ask the hotel about using real candles?"

My mouth goes dry when her eyes finally land on me. "Yeah. They said no fire. So I got the fake ones." I scramble around on the table until I find one of the plastic tea lights I bought at the store, but by the time I find one to show her, she's already clicked away from my table. And I find myself sitting there, watching her with a plastic candle in one hand and a swatch of ribbon in the other.

I turn to go back to what I was doing, but I can still hear what's going on behind me, despite the music that someone has turned on that echoes through the room. I try to just focus on my work, hot gluing the ribbons with a single dot of glue around the candleholders.

And then people are filtering out, everyone excited to go home for the weekend and before I know it, I'm alone with Petra, and as much as I hate being here, I hate being home more. Every inch of my house reminds me of Oliver. Not to mention how weird Mama has been since family dinner. So I'd rather be here, placing a single battery-operated tea light into every candleholder.

But then Petra leans against my table, holding something out to me. I glance down at her hand. Two prom tickets. I can't bring myself to take them.

Petra wiggles them in my direction. "You reserved two, right? I figured I'd bring them to you so you don't have to deal with the lines this week." When I still don't take them, Petra sets them on the table in front of me. "Are you still going with Jackson?"

The thought seems so preposterous right now that I snort. "Absolutely not. Jackson and I . . ." I don't even know how to explain it. We're not together, and we're not friends anymore, not after what he did. Just lab partners, I guess. "We're not going to prom together."

Petra leans back on her hands and looks straight ahead at the open doorway. "Looks like you have an extra ticket then. Who're you going to take?"

"Um. I probably won't go, I guess." I don't even have a dress. Prom has been the last thing on my mind.

Petra looks down at me, her eyebrows crooked in confusion. "Are you kidding? It's senior prom. You can't just *not* go."

I can't help but wonder why Petra cares anyway, but instead I say,

"You're the one who said I should eliminate anything getting in the way of school. That includes prom."

She shrugs. "I didn't think you'd really go through with it."

That makes me scowl harder. "Well, thanks for the vote of confidence. Anyway, thanks for the tickets, but honestly, you might as well just throw them in the trash."

I'm done with the centerpieces, and I start to load them in a box, ignoring the fact that Petra still hasn't moved. She's quiet as I finish, stacking the boxes one on top of the other and then sliding them in her direction. As president, she has to deliver them to the venue on prom day.

But I catch sight of the look on her face, contemplative but also maybe a little . . . devious? "What?"

She looks down at the tickets and smiles. "You know, I haven't gotten mine yet."

I reach down and pick up the tickets. "Then take mine. You can pay me back or whatever." Like I care.

She reaches out for the tickets but then keeps one and extends the other in my direction. "Or we could go together."

I raise an eyebrow at her, not taking the extended ticket. "What are you talking about?"

She shrugs and the ticket that's still held out to me waves gently. "I'm talking about the fact that I'm not letting you skip prom because of this valedictorian thing. Either you're going to make it or I am, and either way, it shouldn't keep you from every experience senior year has to offer. You only get one prom, and you only get one prom date. So, what do you say? Be my date?"

I reach out slowly and take the corner of the ticket between my fingers. "Why would you want to go with me?" I know Petra has friends, girls that she sits with at lunch and goes out with on the weekends. I've seen them together in the halls and at the mall sometimes.

Petra rolls her eyes. "Because we're friends, you idiot. Meet me outside the doors at eight." She reaches down, grabs the boxes of centerpieces, and walks out the door.

AMY

IT'S THREE DAYS until prom, and I'm in a department store, searching for a dress I can afford. Since Carlos got a job, I've been shoving my paychecks into a shoebox in my closet to save for Stanford—California living isn't cheap—but I scraped out a little money to pay for a dress, and now I'm wandering around a department store with Mama, Gabi, and Mari. Well, I suppose more accurately, I'm wandering around the store while my sisters run between the racks, yanking on tulle skirts and silk sashes that hang to the ground while Mama chases after them.

"Girls!" she shouts, taking off down a row, and I take the opportunity to duck into the fitting room alone. I have three dresses, one that's pink, one that's lavender, and one that's black and white, and I hang them all on the hook beside me.

I decide to go for the lavender one first. It takes me a second to struggle into it, but when I'm finally zipped in, I stare at myself in the mirror.

The dress is perfect.

But I feel wrong.

I'm supposed to be excited.

But I'm not excited. I'm exhausted. I can't sleep, and I don't have any energy, and every time I close my eyes, I see the devastated twist of Oliver's mouth when he asked if he was only a distraction.

The song on the speakers in the store changes, and my heart ramps up in my ears. I recognize the song immediately, feel the way my body responds to it within seconds of the opening notes playing. It's the Ed Sheeran song that Oli and I kissed to all those weeks ago, sitting on top of the counter, pressed together like there was no tomorrow.

I should have known then. I should have known this would happen. I could feel the dread of it in my stomach the morning after, when I woke in my bed and realized that Oliver might feel something real for me. I should have listened to my gut. I should have let Oliver go on in peace.

But instead, I ripped him apart.

Now, I'm in a puddle on the dressing room floor crying, and Mama is banging on the door. "Amy!" she shouts. "Baby, let me in!"

But I can't move. I wrap my arms around myself and press my head to the plastic partition that separates me from the changing room beside me. I can't hear Mama anymore, but I hear the jangling of keys and then the door flies open.

Mama crouches on the floor beside me, pulling me into her arms, and here in the safety of them, I cry harder.

OLIVER

"A BITE TO eat then?" Dad asks as he climbs into my truck. Ever since that first meeting that I went to with him, he hasn't asked me to come to another one, but I've insisted on driving him to them when I get the chance, just so I know he's going to them. Maybe it's not right of me to assume that he'll cannonball off the wagon if I'm not there to keep him in line, but I don't feel like I can completely trust him yet, and he must not trust himself too much either because he never protests.

Surprisingly, Dad reaches out through the open window and waves at a few guys standing against the curb, talking while they smoke. I didn't know he had friends. I've never known my dad to have friends other than bartenders.

"Sure," I say, pulling out of the space I've been sitting in for almost half an hour and turning the car toward the lot exit. "But not Charlie's. If I have to eat there again, I'll be sick."

Dad sighs. "Why'd you have to go get a job at my favorite place, huh? There's about a million cafés in Kansas City."

He's shaking his head and hanging his arm out the open window, but I'm still sitting in the parking lot, the truck still in reverse, and my headlights pointed toward the parking lot of the mall. There's a tiny curving road that loops around the mall, and we're sitting on the other side of it, my taillights pointed toward Grand Boulevard, where traffic is building up.

And I'm frozen because there she is. Amy. The mall is crowded, the parking lot teeming with people, and she's walking down a line of cars with her mother and her two little sisters, carrying a plastic-wrapped dress, long and flowing and a shimmering blue color.

A prom dress.

Amy is going to prom.

Does she have a date? Is she going with Jackson? Does she even remember that I'm alive, or has she already forgotten all about me in favor of all the things in her life that aren't getting in the way of her future?

"Oli?" Dad's voice catches my attention, and I clear my throat before putting the truck into gear and driving out of the parking lot. But we get stopped at the light leading out to Grand Boulevard, and I can see Amy in the rearview mirror. I clutch the steering wheel when I see Amy's mother put her arm around her and say something in her ear. Amy's head is down, and there's something off about her, something strange in the way she's standing.

"It's a green, Oli."

I push my foot to the gas before I've even looked at the light. My hand slips on the gearshift, and we stall. I restart the car amidst the noise of the cars honking behind me and pull onto the road like nothing happened.

Part of me hoped my dad would just let it go, the way he's always let it go, never really asking me about myself beyond the basics, but he says, "I knew something was off about you lately, but I didn't think it had to do with a girl."

I grip the steering wheel and refuse to look at him. "Don't worry about it."

Dad snorts. "Don't worry about it? At this rate, you're going to break that other arm all on your own." I don't look at him still, and he lapses into silence for a long time before saying, "Want to talk about it?"

It's my first instinct to say no, to refuse my father any information about my personal life. I don't like opening up to people, and even Brooke, my best friend, doesn't know absolutely everything about what happened between Amy and me. Nobody knows how I really felt about her, how much it hurts now that she's out of my life. And I intended to keep it that way.

But things have changed; my dad has changed.

So instead, I tell him everything as we drive home.

AMY

I AGREE TO let Carlos drop me off at prom. Jackson wanted to do the whole limo thing, but seeing as how he's not my date anymore and Petra wanted to meet at the hotel, I don't bother with anything so fancy.

So that's how I end up pulling up in front of prom in my parents' minivan. I'm surprised by the nerves that flutter through my stomach when everyone who's outside, waiting for dates or getting fresh air, looks over at me as I climb out.

I got used to being ignored. When I was with Jackson, people were always trying to make an effort, always trying to pretend like they liked me even though it was dreadfully obvious that they didn't. And when we broke up, I became a ghost, floating through the halls of the school like I wasn't even there.

And now here I am again, with all eyes on me because I'm walking up to Petra by the door. There's a bit of whispering as Petra smiles at me and then laces her arm through mine.

"Well, Amy, don't you look dashing?"

I laugh because, honestly, it's nice to be with Petra and not be talking about grades or class rank, and I realize, with a kind of clarity that's almost tragic, that I don't even really know anything about Petra. I don't know what she likes to eat or what kind of movies she watches. I don't know her middle name or where she went to elementary school before the two of us merged in the same middle school.

I only know that she's class president, president of the student council, number one in our class, and most likely going to Yale. I don't even know if she got in. Because I've never asked.

I grip her a little tighter, and we take a picture inside the door, below a string of balloons that spell out CLASS OF 2021 that I helped put up this morning. Petra presses her cheek to mine, and I can feel her grin as the flash goes off.

The room is full of people, dark, with lights shining in patterns on the walls and the dance floor, which takes up half the room. The other half of the room is full of round tables with white tablecloths, the little plastic candles in their holders in the center—the ones I made last week.

Petra and I go straight for the dance floor. I'm not much of a dancer, but when we join her friends on the floor, it doesn't seem to matter. Petra grabs one of my hands and a girl I only know from glances in Petra's direction in the hall grabs my other hand, and I'm suddenly dancing with a group of four other girls to a rap song I don't know, and it feels amazing. We dance through a few songs, until a slow song starts, and then the girls, all of us sweaty, our perfectly styled hair a little worse for wear, scatter in different directions.

"Hungry?" Petra asks, nodding toward the refreshments table.

"Uh, sure. I'm just going to run to the restroom."

She nods and wanders off, and I find the bathroom, alone. Inside, there are girls everywhere, but very few of them are actually using the restroom. Most of them are fixing their makeup or lamenting torn dresses, and one girl is crying into her cell phone while two girls drape themselves over her in sympathy.

I do my best to squeeze into a stall and then find an unoccupied sink at which to wash my hands before holding my dress up off the floor so that nobody in the tiny space accidentally steps on it.

I push out into the hallway, feeling like I can breathe again, until I get back to the room where the lights are pulsing in time with the music, and see Jackson. Word on the street is Jackson also came to prom alone. I know this only because two girls were talking very loudly in nutrition and food science last week about Jackson's very public break up, and from the fact that Jackson is currently leaning against a wall and acting as a spectator all by himself, I would say the word on the street is sound. Even still, Jackson looks like a groom on his wedding day. He's wearing a tux that looks absolutely perfect on him, his hands tucked into his pockets, looking so handsome it's a little unreal.

I'm still standing there, outside the bathroom, when Jackson's eyes travel over the room and find me. The music is loud, but just for a second, it seems too quiet, and I look away quick. Over by the refreshment table, Petra has two clear plastic cups full of punch, and she's talking to one of the girls who was dancing with us. My eyes wander back to Jackson and find that he's still watching me.

"Excuse me." A girl in a knee-length silver dress nudges past me, and I move out of the way to let her pass.

I look around for an open table. That's the thing about not having friends: You never have a place to sit. Every table is occupied, and even though there are empty seats here and there, they're sandwiched between people I don't know, people I would never sit with outside this room. I finally find a spot, on the other side of the room from where Jackson was leaning against the wall, but when I take a seat and look back over, he's gone.

I sit and wait for Petra, watching people go crazy on the dance floor and scrolling through my phone for lack of something better to do. As I scroll through Instagram, my eyes catch on my own face, and I stop. On the screen, Oliver is singing karaoke in front of a group of people, and I'm watching him with a giddy look on my face.

I'm fairly certain I actually hear my heart rip in two. That was the night I knew I liked Oliver, as more than just a friend, even though I didn't want to admit it to myself. I watched him go up on that stage and sing the Cure in front of all those people, and I felt butterflies in my stomach.

The caption reads: *#tbt to when our very own ex-assistant manager sang the Cure for karaoke night. Karaoke night was a huge success! If you want another one, let us know in the comments. 20% off for anyone who sings!*

My brain gets caught on one word: *ex-assistant.* Where did Oliver go?

"Dance with me, Ames."

I spin around in my seat and find Jackson's hand stretched out toward me. For a second, I just stare. Behind Jackson, I can see Petra, still standing by the refreshments table, her eyes on us. She looks disapproving. *It's one dance*, I want to tell her. *One dance can't hurt.* I hope she can hear my thoughts as I look from her to Jackson, to the face I know so well, and slip my hand into his.

He pulls me straight to the dance floor, and I'm in his arms so quick, and it's like this is the way it's supposed to be. I'm supposed to be here with Jackson, we're supposed to be together, and it feels so natural as we sway to a slow song. I smile into his neck, loving his long, strong arms around me, despite everything. I missed them, I missed him. I press in closer to him, smelling the cologne that clings to his shirt.

"I can't stop thinking about you," he says, his voice so low and hot against my ear that I think maybe I misheard him.

I pull away from him. I always thought Jackson was tall, but I've spent so long looking up at Oliver that it's strange to have to look a little lower, into Jackson's pale green eyes. "What?"

"Amy." When he says my name, my eyes drift down to his mouth, his perfect lips, the tiny cleft in his chin. "I'm still in love with you."

My hands drop to my sides. "Jackson—"

"I know you're with that guy, but this is killing me." He takes a step back and scrubs his hands down his face. He looks beautiful doing it. I hate that he looks so beautiful.

I squeeze my hands into fists. I lose my train of thought when his eyes focus on me again. He's standing too close to me, and I have to remember how to get words from my brain to my mouth. "We broke up. *You* broke up with me."

He throws his hands up and they fall to his sides again with a *smack* against the fabric of his tuxedo pants. "I fucked up. I know that. I get that. I didn't mean to hurt you. I was just feeling . . . I don't know . . . wrong. But *this* feels right. I want you back, Amy."

He's there in my space, and I don't know how to do anything but look at him and remember everything, the way he held me when I was freaking out about applying to Stanford, the way he would bring me my favorite ice cream when he knew I was studying, the way he'd kiss me so gently, just a flutter against my lips.

"Amy," he breathes. "We keep coming back to each other. It was always supposed to be us. I know you know that." His eyes drop down to my mouth, and I see it coming, but I let it happen anyway. He leans in and kisses me.

My relationship with Jackson was never perfect. He may not

have always said the right things, and he may not have been there for me every time I needed someone, but when Jackson kissed me, the world always disappeared.

So even though it makes my chest hurt, I kiss him back. Because it's Jackson.

"Amy," he breathes again, this time against my mouth, and it's enough to pull me back to reality. We're at prom, and Jackson is kissing me, and even though it feels good, and even though I miss everything Jackson and I had, I don't want to kiss Jackson anymore. I don't want to be Jackson's girlfriend.

"No," I say, pushing against him. He pulls away, his eyes confused, and I wipe at my mouth. "I don't want to get back together, Jackson." If I got back together with him now, I would always know it was because I didn't want to be alone. But it's not Jackson I want.

Jackson's face shifts, going from confused to disbelieving in seconds. "Why not? We belong together."

I take a step back from him and sigh. "We don't belong together, Jackson. I don't . . . I don't love you anymore." It takes everything in me to finally make myself say it, but as soon as I do, I know it's the truth. I haven't loved Jackson in a long time.

People are starting to look at us, probably because we're dissecting our relationship in the middle of the dance floor, but I don't care, and it doesn't seem like Jackson does, either.

"You weren't happy with me," I say. "And nothing is going to change. If we get back together, you'll still wish we hung out more, and I still won't be able to give you as much time as you want, and then we'll just break up again. And—"

I can't bring myself to say it, but I don't have to. Jackson knows.

"And you're in love with him."

I shrug, looking down at my feet. At his shiny shoes and my silver heels. "It's not really about him." This is only partially a lie. Maybe if I had never met Oliver, if I'd never kissed him and had sex with him and fallen in love with him, then getting back together with Jackson would seem like the right thing to do, even if it wasn't. But now that I know what it's like to feel what I feel when I'm with Oliver, I can never go back.

"Isn't it?" Jackson asks, coming closer to me.

"That's not all of it, but you're right, I do love him," I say, still not looking at Jackson. Because it's so strange for him to be the first one to hear it. I couldn't say it to Oliver, but I can say it to Jackson. I can admit it to him, and maybe that's because it doesn't matter if Jackson knows the truth or not. It doesn't change anything.

"Can I just ask you a question?"

I finally look up at Jackson, and it stings, the hurt in his eyes. I guess I thought it would be easy for him to move on since he was the one who did the breaking up. But apparently I was wrong.

"Yeah."

"Why is it easier for you to be with him than to be with me?" It takes me a second to understand what he means, but when I do, I almost feel sad. When I was with Jackson, Stanford was always my number one priority, but when I was with Oliver, he became as important to me as college and scholarships and class rank. Jackson was never quite enough to make me lose focus.

"I guess because he doesn't ask me to change." I don't want to start a fight, and I don't know if my answer will hurt Jackson's feelings, but it's the truth.

Jackson puts his hands in his pockets and nods down at the floor. "That's a good reason."

It is. It's a good reason. And being too busy is a terrible reason to break up with someone. Just like Jackson wasn't right to dump me because I was too busy, I wasn't right to dump Oliver for the same reason. It wasn't Oliver's fault that I slipped. It was my own. Oliver believed in me, always, and he liked me when nobody else did, and he made me feel like I could be myself, no matter what.

I love Oliver, and I suddenly need him to know it. I need to tell him he's all I think about, and he's all I want.

I push up on my toes and kiss Jackson on the cheek. "Thanks, Jackson," I say, even though I'm not sure he knows why I'm thanking him. But it doesn't matter. I rush off the dance floor and up to Petra, who, somehow, is still standing beside the refreshments table, watching me.

"What the hell just happened?" she asks.

"Do you think you could give me a ride to Independence?"

AMY

I ALMOST COULDN'T remember how to get to Oliver's dad's place, but I'm finally standing on his front porch. It feels like the whole world is made of water, and I can't take in a full breath without the threat of suffocation, but I can do this. I know I can. I can do anything.

I reach out and knock.

For a lingering second, I think maybe nothing is going to happen. I don't see Oliver's truck in the driveway, but I know there's a garage in the back, and I'm hoping it's parked there.

But it isn't Oliver that opens the door. It's his father, dressed for work in a pair of coveralls, with a bottle of Jack Daniels dangling from his first two fingers. I stare down at it because I can't quite bring myself to look him in the eye. Other than the red hair, Oliver doesn't look anything like his dad, who's large-framed and beefy, a red beard covering most of his face. But the eyes. The eyes are the same.

He unlatches the screen door and leans against the doorjamb. "It's Amy, right?" he asks, and even though Oliver told me his dad is Scottish, I'm surprised to hear such a thick accent.

"Yes, I'm Amy. Is Oliver home?"

"Oh, girlie. You are barking up the wrong tree. Oli's at work, and even if he wasn't, I wouldn't let you into this house after what you done to him."

It's such a shock to hear these words out of his mouth, that I look up at the house, at the black numbers nailed to the siding, as if I've somehow stepped up to the wrong house. This house must belong to a different Oliver.

"I just—" I start, but Oliver's father cuts me off.

"You just what, honey? You came to tell him you messed up and you did wrong and that you love him?"

I grip the fabric of my dress in my hands, refusing to be intimidated. "I do love him."

His father snorts. "Look, let me tell you something maybe no one else ever has." He glances over my shoulder, his eyes going glassy. "True love doesn't exist. But you know what does exist? Sadness. Heartbreak. Reality. Your bills and your taxes and your fucking dead-end job, and Oli's in the midst of figuring that out. So why don't you just go back on home, because I'm not letting you in this house, and I'm not telling him you were here, and I'm not telling you where he works."

I'm surprised to feel anger rise in me, and I know that what I have to say is completely out of line, but I say it anyway. "What would he say if he saw you like this? What would he say if he knew you were drunk after all the work he's put in—"

"All the work *he's* put in?" He takes a step toward me, and I scuttle back away from him, until I've taken one step off the porch, and now this man is towering over me, and I hear a car door open behind me, know that Petra is getting out and maybe coming toward us. "Oli's been off wooing you, hasn't he, while *I* dealt with this? You don't know the first thing about me."

"And you don't know the first thing about me," I say, my chin coming up. I hope I look more confident than I feel. "Maybe I've let Oliver down, but you're not exactly the poster child for being there for him."

He lets out a stuttering, wet laugh. "You're right on that count. But he's here with me, now, isn't he? And you, you're going to run on home, and you're never going to see him again, because whatever pretty picture you have in your head about true love, it's all bullshit." He makes a shooing motion with his hand, and surprisingly, I step the rest of the way off the porch.

I want to cry. I want to cry for myself, for letting Oli go, and for Oli, who's hurt and will be so disappointed when he finds out his dad is drinking again. I want to tell him that I'm disappointed in him, too, even though I don't know him, but I don't have the words.

It's too late anyway. He speaks over me. "I've fucked up a lot by Oli. I've been an awful father. But if there's one thing I know, it's that he doesn't deserve to have his heart eaten by the likes of you."

As angry as I am, I know his father is right. At least in this one thing. Oliver deserves better than me. I just nod, taking another step back.

"And don't you come back looking for him," he says. "He doesn't love you."

I'm shaking as I turn back to the road, and even though I can still hear him yelling after me, I keep walking until I'm back in Petra's car.

"Are you okay?" she asks, getting back in, but I just shake my head, and before I know it, I'm crying, and Petra has her arms around me, rocking me back and forth in her prom dress.

OLIVER

WHEN I GET home from Charlie's, Dad's truck is gone. He's probably already at work. I walk past the empty driveway and up the front steps, but I stop when I'm in front of the door, staring down at the welcome mat that I can see between the spaces between my keys.

There's glitter stomped into the brown fibers. I blink down at the shimmering doormat for a long time before unlocking the door and going inside.

I drop down onto the couch and kick my shoes off before turning on the TV, but unlike Mom, Dad doesn't pay for cable or streaming TV or anything like that, so there are exactly four channels, three of which are airing news programs, and the last that's airing a documentary about pumas. I turn the TV back off and stare down at the carpet, aware, painfully so, that I'm right back where I was four months ago, before I met Amy, and I had something to be excited about.

At least then I had Spirits.

But I can't walk in there now without thinking about her, so even though Brooke is a little pissed at me for leaving, it's better that I quit.

I tug my phone out of my pocket to order a pizza when I see that Brooke tagged me in some photo on Spirits's Instagram account. I sigh. The only reason I got a stupid account is because Brooke made me. She said that as the assistant manager, I had to do social media stuff, so I periodically took pictures of albums I thought were great and posted them, but that pretty much ended a few months ago.

My stomach clenches when I see the picture Brooke posted.

#tbt to when our very own ex-assistant manager sang the Cure for karaoke night.

I don't know why she's doing this to me, but seeing that picture, me doing karaoke for Amy, is enough to make my insides feel like they're on fire.

OLIVER

I start driving to Hassey's before I even really know what I'm doing. Honestly, if it weren't for Dad, I wouldn't even know where to look for a bar in Kansas City, but as it is, I know how to get to Hassey's as easily as I know how to get to Spirits. The turns from Dad's house to the bar are burned in my brain, but this is my first time driving them in this order.

I can't remember ever stopping to look around in Hassey's, an Irish pub that only feels Irish because the owner, Carson, is from Kilkenny. Mostly, I was just pointed in the direction of my father, often slumped over the side of the bar, and then hauled him out to the truck without a second glance. But tonight, I take it in, the smell of alcohol and cigarettes, the neon lights behind the bar, the sound of cue sticks striking billiard balls.

"Fergus ain't here, man!" Carson calls from behind the bar.

"I know," I say, stepping up to the bar and having a seat. "I came to have a drink." I don't drink often, mostly at parties and other social engagements, should I find myself at one, but I've always been careful. Tonight, I can't help but wonder, I can't help but think that maybe my dad has had it right this whole time.

I try to think about beers and cocktails, but honestly nothing comes to mind. And then Carson leans his elbows on the bar and looks at me.

"You're mad if you think I'm serving you anything."

I grind my teeth together. "I'm almost twenty." A lie. I have eleven whole months before I turn twenty.

Carson scoffs. "It's not because you're a teenager, Oli. It's because you know better."

I spin the barstool I'm on away from him. "Fine. I'll just get something at the liquor store."

"No, you won't," he says behind me.

I stop, halfway off the stool, and look at him over my shoulder. "What makes you so sure?"

Carson has a ghost of a smile on his lips when he says, "Because you've seen what happened to your dad. And I know for certain that you're the reason I haven't seen Fergus around here in a while."

I stare at him for a long moment, until he has to turn away to help someone else at the bar, and I slide slowly off my stool because I know he's right.

AMY

"Amy?" Mama says, her mouth hanging open when I finally walk in the door that night. It's sometime around midnight, and the bottom of my dress is brown from the grime of walking along the concrete, the hem dragging around me. "What happened?"

She grabs my face, but I pull her hands away and drop my shoes by the front door. "I'm fine. Just a bad night."

She takes my hand and squeezes it. "Baby, you just tell me what you need, okay?"

I don't know what I need. "I just want to be alone," I tell her, even though it immediately makes her mouth turn down in a frown. I hike up my dress and shut myself inside my bedroom, immediately pulling the gown off and replacing it with my favorite sweatpants and an old t-shirt. I sit at my computer, my legs pulled up in the chair with me, and I think about everything Oliver's dad said.

Why couldn't it have been Oli who opened that door? Why couldn't he have been home? Why couldn't he have been standing in front of me so that I could tell him everything, so I could beg his forgiveness?

Someone knocks softly on my door, and Mama pushes it open and tiptoes in. "I know you said you want to be alone, and I respect that, but I thought maybe this would cheer you up." She reaches out and hands me a small white envelope, and I recognize it immediately. My tickets to the Lumineers concert. I asked that they be mailed to me because I like having real tickets instead of just a barcode on my phone at the door. They must have come in the mail today.

"Thanks." I take them from her, and once I feel the weight of them in my hand, I have an idea. I can see the shape of the tickets inside. *Our* tickets.

"Amy, are you okay?" Mama asks from behind me.

I'm still staring down at the envelope in my hands, but then in a hurry, I reach out and rip a piece of paper from my printer.

If Oliver's father thinks I'm just going to give up, he's seriously mistaken. I am not the kind of person who just gives up. I am the kind of person who fights for what she wants, and well, I want Oliver. More than anything.

AMY

ON SUNDAY, I go to Spirits.

The shop isn't open yet, but I bang on the door anyway because I know Brooke is inside. Brooke is always inside.

"We're closed!" I hear her call from the other side of the glass, but I bang on the door harder, until I see her head pop out of the office. I see the moment she realizes it's me. Her eyes go blank, her expression unpleasant. I know Brooke is angry at me, but she's my only hope.

She walks to the front door and unlocks it, planting a hand on her hip and not letting me inside. "What do you want?"

I've already been shown down by one person, and there's no way I'm going to let Brooke take me out, too, so I shove past her, and once I'm inside the shop and Brooke has closed the door with a huff, I say, "I need a favor from you."

Just like I expect it to, Brooke's expression dissolves into disbelief. "What in the world makes you think I would do any favors for you?"

I knew she would say that, too.

"Brooke, I know you hate me. And I don't blame you. And I

know you don't owe me anything. But"—I stop, emotion that I'm not expecting rising in my throat—"But I need your help."

Brooke's mouth twists. "You think I'm going to help you get Oli back?"

I nod. "Yes."

Her expression is one of disgust now. "What the hell makes you think that?"

I reach out and slap the envelope in my hand down on the counter beside me. "Because you believe in true love."

I see her anger slip, just for a second. Because I see right through her. I've seen her and Lauren together. I've seen the way they look at each other. I know she believes in love.

"You don't have to do much," I say when she's silent. "All you have to do is give him this letter." I pick up the envelope and hold it out to her. When I sat down and thought about it last night, this was the only way I knew I was going to be able to say what I needed to say without anyone interfering. I know that Oliver will read it, even if he wouldn't listen to me if I was standing right in front of him. I know he'll read it. Because it's me. And it's Oliver. And he has to.

Brooke stares down at the envelope, and I can see her jaw working as she contemplates. Her fingers twitch, and then she sighs huge and rips the letter off the counter. "Fine," she says. "But only because I know better than anyone that Oli was head over fucking heels in love with you, and if nothing else, he deserves closure."

I feel light explode in my chest at her words, even though I think she has it all wrong. I'm not looking for closure. I'm looking for forgiveness.

"Thank you," I whisper because all the emotion in my chest is too much.

"But I swear to fucking God, Amy, if you hurt him again, I will rip your heart out with my bare hands."

I smile because I won't. I know I won't.

OLIVER

I'M NOT SURE what I'm doing here, sitting in the back row of the sanctuary, watching the back of Mom's head as she nods along with the sermon in the third row. I've been orbiting the church every Sunday since I moved out. It's impossible not to. I've been going to this church every Sunday since I was four, and old habits die hard.

But I'm not just here for the sermon, I know that much. Because when the service ends and everyone rises from their seats to leave, I stay where I am. I stand at the end of the pew, right against the aisle, and wait for Mom to come.

And she does. She's wearing a bright yellow dress, and for just a second, I'm afraid she's not going to see me because she's looking down at her feet as she walks, speaking to no one. But at the last minute, just as she's about to pass, her head comes up and she sees me, and for a second, it's almost as if she doesn't recognize me. And then she rushes toward me, her arms outstretched.

I let her hug me, but I already know this isn't going to go the way she thinks it is. She takes my hand, and I follow her out into the parking lot, where the sun is warm and spring is in full bloom.

"Mom," I start, but she speaks over me.

"Oh God, Oli. I'm sorry. I'm so sorry. I was so wrong. I know that. I was just so angry at you. But it's time for you to come home. We can figure all this out. Just please, come home."

I'm already shaking my head before she's done speaking, and I can see the horror growing on her face before I've even spoken. "Mom, I'm not moving back in. That's not why I'm here."

My mother's mouth is still hanging open. "Why not? You can't live with your father forever."

"I won't," I say. "But you were right. I'm not the person you wanted me to be, and that's fine, but that means that I can't live with you anymore, not when that comes with so many stipulations."

Her mouth finally closes, and I can see the resignation on her features when she realizes she's lost. "Oh, Oli. I never meant to make you feel like you weren't the person I wanted you to be. There's absolutely nothing wrong with the person you are. I love who you are."

I smile at her. "And I appreciate that. But it doesn't change anything. I'm not going to college, and I'm not moving back in. I just missed you."

She's quiet for a long time and then she moves forward and wraps her arms around me. "Okay, Oli," she says. "Okay. If that's what you want."

I want to tell her that I have no idea what I want. I don't really want anything anymore. I'm empty inside and when I look into my future, all I see is black.

She strokes my hair. "Come on. Let's get some grub."

OLIVER

BROOKE'S CAR IS parked in my driveway when I get home that evening. The sun is almost down, the light shining on her silver hatchback, and I'm surprised at how excited I am to see her. I've missed her a lot.

She's not in her car, and when I unlock the front door, I find her in the living room, talking to Dad. The TV blares in the background, the Royals game, and when I shut the door behind me, Dad mutes the TV.

"Brooke, hey," I say when she hops up off the couch. "Were we supposed to hang out today?"

She sighs. "No. Look, Oli, normally I would be totally opposed to this kind of thing, as, despite my previous actions, I don't 100 percent believe in friends interfering in their friends' shit, but I . . . I have something for you."

Brooke is holding out a long white envelope to me, and when I reach out to take it, she says, "it's from Amy," and I almost drop it. "She's been trying to get a hold of you," she goes on. "But, you know, new cell and all."

I feel the weight of my phone in my back pocket. It feels heavier somehow. Mom stopped paying my cell phone bill, and I had to get a new phone, a new number, everything.

"She even came here, but um . . ." Brooke trails off and when I look up, her eyes are on Dad. He looks guilty as fuck.

"Did she come here?" I ask him.

He can't meet my eye. "She came a few nights ago. Wearing a fuckin' ball gown like Cinderella or something."

Prom. She must have been dressed for her prom. I can't even imagine her here, all dressed up in that blue dress I saw her carrying. "Why didn't you tell me?"

He sighs and his head falls into his hands. "Oh, Oli. Don't hate me."

I don't hate him but if he doesn't start talking, I might kill him.

"Oli," he says again, finally looking up at me. "I was drunk. I'm so sorry. You weren't here, and I was lonely, and I just started drinking. By the time she came, I was halfway through a bottle of Jack. I was an asshole to her, completely and totally. I'm sorry."

I can't even look at him but now that I'm holding this letter in my hand, I realize it doesn't matter. What my dad did or didn't say doesn't matter. Because he didn't scare her away. She still wrote this letter. She still has something to say to me.

I tear my eyes away from the letter and look at my dad. "I want every fucking bottle of alcohol you have hidden in this place," I tell him. And when he doesn't move, I say, "Now."

He scrambles off the couch, and I hear him rummaging in different parts of the house while I sit on the couch. My hands tremble, and even though it would probably be smarter to wait until Brooke is gone to open it, I tear at the envelope.

Dear Oliver,

I realize that you probably don't want to hear what I have to say. And I get it. I fucked up. I'm not going to pretend I didn't. But I want to apologize. I'm sorry for hurting you. I'm sorry for making you feel like you weren't good enough. I'm sorry for throwing away our friendship. And I'm sorry for not realizing sooner that I'm in love with you.

You're not a distraction, Oliver. I need you to know that. I was getting in my own way and blaming it on you, and I'll regret that forever. But I don't blame you anymore. You were the one who kept me going when I didn't even have faith in myself.

Do you remember when we talked about Plato's Cave, that night in your truck? Well, I'm the people in the cave who are facing the wall. I'm the people who mistook the shadows of the objects for the real things. I'm the people who were terrified when reality was right in front of them. I thought what Jackson and I had was real. I thought that was love, but I didn't know what the real thing looked like until I met you. No one has ever really seen me before, not the way you do. No one has ever accepted me just the way I was, and I'm sorry I tossed that aside like it didn't mean anything. It meant everything.

Maybe what your father told me is right. Maybe true love doesn't exist. But, Oli, I love you. And if you never want to speak to me again, I understand, but it's not going to change anything. You're still my best friend, and I'm still in love with you.

I miss you.
Amy

My hands are still shaking when there's no letter left to read, and I can't explain the pain in my chest. It's want and also hurt and also confusion. When I open the envelope to put the letter back in, I see that there's something else there. It's my ticket to the Lumineers concert. After everything, I forgot all about it.

"What did she say?" Brooke whispers.

"That she loves me," I say because it's the easiest way to sum it all up.

Brooke nods, like this is obvious. "And what are you going to do?"

I set the envelope on the couch between us and stand, Brooke craning her neck to look up at me. "I'm not going to do anything."

I'm actually surprised by the look on Brooke's face. After I told her what happened between Amy and me, she was so angry, I thought she was going to kill Amy. But now here she is, with this look on her face like she can't believe I just said that. "But, Oli—"

"There's a reason I don't spend much time with people," I say, "and it's not because I'm mean, and it's not because I don't like people, and it's not because I'm a loner. It's because people tear you apart. And I've been torn apart enough. I gave Amy everything I had, and there's nothing left."

Brooke's eyebrows crease in. "I'm sorry," she whispers.

I smile at her. "Don't be. It doesn't matter anymore. What's done is done. I've moved on, and she will, too. Because that's real life."

Just then, my father reappears. He slams five unopened bottles of liquor down on the coffee table. It's all whiskey, and I'm so shocked that I don't say anything for a full minute. "What the hell is all this, Dad?" I finally ask. "When did you get this?"

My father looks like he's near tears. "Here and there. None of it's open. That bottle of Jack was the first one since I quit, I swear. All this is just in case."

I reach out and snatch up a bottle. "*Just in case* doesn't exist. *Just in case* isn't an option anymore." I gather the bottles in my arms and head for the door, ready to smash them all on the pavement outside when

Dad says, "I'm sorry about the girl. I thought I was doing the right thing. I wanted to keep you from getting hurt again."

I open the screen door without looking back at him. "Whatever you told her, you were right."

AMY

I'M NOT SURE what I was expecting. I gave Oliver the concert ticket in hopes that he would meet me there, but the concert isn't for another month, and I guess I was hoping he'd read the letter, forgive me, and show up at my doorstep.

But that doesn't happen.

I spend the rest of April focusing on my schoolwork. My break up with Oliver plunges me into motion. Once the sadness is over, I barely take a breath between student council, volunteering on the weekends, and getting ahead on homework. I feel like a machine.

Staying busy keeps the sadness away, even when it kills me a little to walk by Spirits on my way to the tutoring center, where I've been working part-time. Every time I'm inside, I have to avert my eyes. Looking at Spirits is just as painful as looking directly at the sun.

While everyone else celebrates the end of senior year, I spend it locked away, because making valedictorian is the only thing I have left.

OLIVER

I SPEND THE rest of April in a haze. It's hard to explain it, really. I go to work at Charlie's, I come home and make sure Dad isn't drinking, I go to church with my mom on Sundays, but at the end of every day, I lie in bed, staring up at my ceiling, wondering.

Wondering what would happen if I just left.

What's holding me here?

Dad hasn't had a drink that I know of since that incident, Mom seems to be doing just fine without me, Charlie's will find another waiter as easily as they found me. I fantasize about getting in my truck and driving until I don't recognize anything anymore. I imagine leaving Kansas City and going to Boston or New York or L.A.

MAY

AMY

WE GET THE call at the end of the month, in the middle of last period.

"Amy," my teacher says. "You're needed in the office."

Everyone's eyes are on me as I grab my stuff and head for the door, but I already know what's going to happen. All my other responsibilities, all my clubs and duties, are over. School is almost over. Finals have been taken. There's only one thing left.

Petra is already waiting when I get to the administration office. She's got her hands folded in her lap and her legs crossed beneath her chair, and I take the seat next to her.

We sit in silence for a second. We've been hanging out a lot since prom, since I cried in her car. Studying in the library after last period, eating lunch together in the cafeteria, planning last week's ice-cream social to mark the end of student council.

She reaches over and takes my hand.

"You nervous?" she asks.

"No, my palms are always this sweaty."

She laughs, and I suddenly regret so much. I regret all the times I didn't tell Petra that she was the closest thing I had to a friend, all the time we spent fighting instead of being friendly. I think it would have been nice to have her on my side. I open my mouth to tell her these things, but the principal's door swings open, and his eyes go back and forth between us before finally deciding on me.

"Amaría, why don't you come in?"

I stand, and he steps out of the way to let me through. I was nervous before, but now I feel like I'm going to be sick. I've been working toward this for four years. Four years of hard work and dedication, and when he sits in front of me, his mouth a solid line, I already know what he's going to say.

I fucked up, letting everything else in my life get in the way of this. It's irreparable, that much I'm sure of.

"You seem to think you already know what I'm going to say." Principal Cohen's face is completely impassive.

I shrug. "I had a rough semester. I didn't do my best, so I don't expect to get valedictorian."

His whole face seems to crease. "Your grades tell a different story. And your standing doesn't just depend on you. It depends on Miss Johnson, too. And it seems you both had a hard time this semester. I even hear from your AP biology teacher that you cheated on a test."

A surge of anger rushes through me. "I didn't cheat on that test. Jackson copied off me."

He holds up a hand. "What's done is done, I'm afraid. But in the end, it doesn't matter. Even with a zero on that test and what you *think* was a bad semester, you still pulled out quite far ahead of everyone else. So, you better start writing your speech."

I stare at him for a second. "I . . . I got it?" I stammer.

Principal Cohen smiles at me. "Yes, Amy. Congratulations."

I'm going to cry. I can feel it starting in my throat, pressing against my eyes, but when Principal Cohen reaches across the desk to shake my hand, it knocks me out of my shock.

"Thank you," I say.

He lets go of my hand and sends me a confused expression. "You have no one to thank but yourself."

That settles in my brain as I open the door and see Petra in her seat right outside. Her head comes up, and it only takes a second before she's standing up, grinning at me.

"Damn, you have the worst poker face," she says, and her words cause the dam to break. I stand in Principal Cohen's doorway and cry. I feel Petra's arms come around me, smell her laundry detergent on her shirt, and I hug her back.

"I'm sorry," I say when I pull back, wiping away the tears. "You worked hard for it, too."

She bites her lip and nods. "That's true. But you won it, fair and square, and that's all I could have asked for. A true competitor. And honestly, I'm just relieved."

I look up at her. "Relieved that I got it?"

"Relieved that it's over."

I know exactly what she means. We swap places and she closes the principal's door behind her, even though it's useless now. We both know what he'll say to her. Standing in the office, quiet since all the office attendants are getting ready to go home, I pull out my phone and grip it hard.

All I want is to call Oliver. I want to tell him about this, I want to tell him that I love him, I want to tell him that I couldn't have done any of this without him.

I already know what will happen when I call the number that's saved in my phone.

I've called it a thousand times. Maybe more.

But I dial anyway.

We're sorry, the number you have dialed is no longer in service. Please hang up and try again.

OLIVER

"I'M SO GLAD you're here," Mom says as she puts a plate of lasagna on the kitchen table in front of me. "This place is so quiet without you. What's it like living with your father?"

I shovel some pasta into my mouth and shrug. "It's loud. Dad listens to his music louder than I do. Plus, he's been playing again."

Mom's eyes go wide. "His guitar? Really?"

"Must be because he's sober."

Her eyebrows shoot up further, but she doesn't comment.

After a long time, she says, "Is everything okay?"

I take a sip of my water. I came here for a reason, to talk to her about Dad, and now it's time. "Dad told me, you know, about his parents and why he moved here. He told me everything."

Mom doesn't look angry, she just looks tired. "That story doesn't exactly paint me in a good light." She sighs, and for the first time I feel like she looks her age. "When I was younger, I had this idea that there was some kind of fairy tale love, and if you tried hard enough you were guaranteed a happy ending. And, unfortunately, your father paid the price for me being such an idealist."

"You don't believe in any of that anymore?"

"No." She doesn't even hesitate.

"When did you stop believing it?" I hope she can't see that these questions are more than just questions. That there are things that have been going around and around in my mind for the past month.

I don't know what's real anymore, and I don't know what's worth working for anymore. Don't even know what I'm doing.

"Despite what your father thinks, it wasn't him that made me stop believing in happily ever afters. It was me. He gave up everything to come here and help me raise you. And he got here, and we didn't have money, and he didn't have his band, and he was working all the time, and we were never together. He gave up everything. He came here, and all he got was an ordinary life with an ordinary person, and it wasn't the fairy tale that we thought it was going to be. I still wanted him even when he started to drink, but I could see that we were destroying each other. I was destroying him. So I stopped believing in all of it because we did everything the way all the storybooks tell you to, and all it did was ruin our lives."

This, at least, I understand. Because I feel like I did everything right, and look where it got me.

"Oli," she says, and I look up at her. "If I could do it again, I would. I want you to know that. I don't know if fairy tale romances exist, but I know that you can be happy. I know that real happiness exists as long as you're not afraid to go after what you want."

"What if I don't know what I want?"

She shrugs. "What makes you happy?"

I shake my head. "I don't know. Maybe nothing anymore."

She laughs. "Nothing? What about the way your eyes light up when you put your favorite CD in the stereo in your car? Or the way you smiled for a week after you took that job at Spirits? Or the way I knew you wanted to date that girl you worked with before you even told me her name?"

Her words send a jolt through me, but she keeps talking.

"I'm sorry I made you believe there was only one road to take in this life. I just saw what happened to your father when he gave up his future, and I didn't want that to happen to you."

"Can't give up what you don't have." I mutter the words, but she hears them anyway.

"Oliver, you have a future. I don't know what it is or who it's with or where it's going to take you, but it's there and it's up to you to make it a good one."

I can't stop myself from thinking about Amy, as if I've stopped thinking about her even once since she sent me that letter. It's under my pillow, always there because I still don't know. I don't know what to do.

"You make me believe in happily-ever-afters, Oli. You make me believe maybe I did something right."

My heart is pounding, the way your heart pounds when you've made up your mind, when you know what you want, when you know you're going to go after it.

JUNE

AMY

I SIT IN my assigned ticketed seat, and my leg bobs up and down. We've been through two openers, and so far there hasn't been any sign of Oliver. I keep checking my phone even though I know I won't recognize his number even if he does call or text me.

Every time I see movement at the end of the aisle, I spin around thinking that maybe it'll be him, but it never is. I check the time on my phone. I look up an itinerary to see exactly what time the Lumineers will be taking the stage, and I only have three minutes left.

I can't even pretend not to be upset when the music starts, and the seat next to me is still empty. The Lumineers are my favorite band, but as everyone else stands up, I sit in my seat and try not to cry. I guess the idea that maybe today would fix everything has kept me going more over the last month than I thought it has. Maybe he wasn't calling or texting or showing up at my front door, but I still had this tiny little bit of hope that he would show up at this concert. And now that he's not here, my heart is even more shattered than it already was.

I take a deep breath and stand with everyone else. I close my eyes, and I listen to the music. With every song, the muscles in my body start to loosen. Not everything can be perfect every time, not even a concert.

I breathe in the smell of sweat. The floor vibrates with each pulse of the drums. I smile to myself, feeling the buzz in my veins that only music gives me, like I'm alive. Really and truly alive.

And then they melt into my favorite song, "Stubborn Love."

I remember that cold night, my and Oliver's very first date, sitting in the back of his truck, wrapped in a blanket together and looking up at the stars while this song played through the open windows. A tear makes its way down my cheek. I feel like an idiot, crying in the middle of a concert, where anyone might see.

They're moving into the final chorus when I feel something brush against my hand. My first reaction is to jerk away because I'm surrounded by strangers, and I certainly don't want to be touched by any of them. But when I open my eyes and look down, I see a hand tilted tentatively toward mine, a very familiar hand. And I'm completely crying before my eyes even make their way all the way up the six feet and four inches of Oliver York, standing beside me.

He has this look on his face like I shouldn't be surprised to see him standing here. Like there's no reason at all why he wouldn't have come. Like this, holding my hand after not seeing each other for almost two months, is a completely average occurrence.

He just holds my hand, and I let the tears get crusty on my face while I listen to the rest of the concert, feeling so alive, it just might kill me.

AMY

HE DOESN'T SAY anything while we walk to his truck. He doesn't say anything while we drive out of Kansas City and into Independence.

He doesn't say anything as he pulls onto the same quiet road where we parked during our first date and stops the truck. And as the gearshift rattles with the hum of the engine and the Colourist plays softly in the background, Oliver looks at me, and I know he's waiting for me to speak first.

"Oli, I'm sorry. I'm so sorry. I wish I could take it back. I wish I could undo it."

He doesn't say anything, just watches me spill my guts as we sit beside a field of tall grass, watching it sway in the wind.

"It wasn't about you. Any of it. I was just freaking out because I was so scared that I was going to lose what I've been working so hard for, and I thought the only way to stop it was to cut out everything in my life, and that meant punishing you for something you didn't have any control over. I thought you were the thing holding me back, but you weren't. I was holding *myself* back. You were the thing pushing me forward."

I stop talking because none of the words coming out of my mouth seem to make it any better. They're just building up and not clarifying anything.

"I love you, Oliver," I say because it's the only thing that means anything. "I love you, and I want you, and I don't want anyone else. All this time you were worried about being a fuckup, and here I am, the biggest fuckup of all."

"You're not a fuckup."

But it's a lie, and I think we both know it. "I won't hurt you again, Oli," I say, looking up at him. "I swear. I never meant to hurt you, and I swear on everything I am that I won't hurt you again."

He's watching me, and I just want him to say something,

anything. I want him to tell me he forgives me. I want him to tell me he loves me. I want him to say that he never wants to see me again and this night was just like what Brooke said, closure. Because that would be better than his mouth not moving, not saying anything.

But he still doesn't say anything, just leans forward and kisses me. I'm too relieved to be embarrassed that I'm crying into his open mouth, that my tears are getting his face wet, too, as he pulls me across the console and onto his lap, and I hold on to him as tight as I can because I'm never letting him go again.

OLIVER

"I missed you," I say against her mouth, the thing I've wanted to say since I saw her standing alone at the concert, swaying to the music, looking every bit like that girl I fell in love with in the stockroom at Spirits. Amy and I have only been friends for a few months, but in the time we've been apart, I've felt like I lost a limb, and I didn't even know it until I was holding on to her again.

"I missed you, too," she says, wrapping her arms around me and burying her face in my neck.

I wish I could explain to her how everything feels different. But I don't know how to put into words how I feel, like I'm jumping off a cliff and hoping to fly, and I'm taking her with me. Like the way I love her has shifted, into something quiet and solid.

I pull away from her so she'll look at me, and even though I didn't really plan to say any of these things on a dark road in Independence with her straddling me like this, I want to say it.

"I've been in love with you since almost the day we met. I've never felt like this before. I feel like I handed you my fresh, beating heart and maybe that wasn't fair. Maybe it's not fair to put all your hopes into a single person and think they can be everything you need them to be. I looked at you, and I saw my future, and that was too much to push onto one person."

She shakes her head and presses closer to me. "But I'm okay with that. I *want* you to see me in your future, Oli."

I bite my lip. "It wasn't right of me to put that pressure on you. You're not responsible for my happiness." I think of my parents. I think of the expectations they had for each other, the expectations they had for themselves. "It's not going to be perfect. It's never going to be perfect, but I've seen what happens when you walk away, and I think we can do better than that."

Her eyes are wide, her chin wobbling. "I love you," she whispers, and I feel like every inch of my skin, every cell in my body, is screaming out for her. She presses her forehead to mine and then sighs against my lips. "I have to go home. Mama has been extra worried about me, and if I'm late, she'll panic."

I nod at her, but everything inside me mourns her touch as she pushes off me awkwardly and climbs back into her seat. She puts her seat belt back on while I start the truck, and when I reach for the wheel to make a U-turn, she reaches out a hand, putting it on my arm, stopping me.

When I look at her in the dark, I see something brewing in her eyes. "Come to California with me."

OLIVER

Brooke leans against the front counter and smiles at me. "Well, well, well, if it isn't my favorite employee. What's cookin', sweetheart? Did you come here hoping I'll take you back?"

Hoping isn't really the word I would use. More like, *expecting*. "Yep," I say, "but you'll have to forgive me. I can only work through the summer."

Brooke narrows her eyes. "Is that your way of telling me that you're going to Missouri Baptist after all, and you can't manage a part-time sales position while you're a full-time student? Because that is just so not like you, Oli."

I grin at her. "No, that's my way of telling you that I'm moving to California with Amy at the end of the summer."

It's hard to shock Brooke. But when I say this, her mouth falls open. "Are you . . . are you serious? You're leaving?"

I shrug. "Don't you think it's time?"

She laughs and shakes her head. "So I guess all that romantic gesture garbage worked on you then, huh?"

"You know me," I say. "I'm quite the romantic."

She narrows her eyes at me again. "You don't have to tell me that, Oliver York. You've never been able to fool me."

I laugh because I know she's right. "I love her," I say, "and maybe fairy tales are bullshit and maybe I'm making a huge mistake, but when I look at her, I feel like maybe I have something to offer."

Brooke's expression of suspicion melts away, and she sighs. She reaches for her phone, and then I'm just standing there, watching her scroll through something, a thoughtful expression on her face.

"What are you doing?" I finally ask.

Her eyes slide up to mine. "I have some contacts in California. I'll make sure you have a job by the time you get there. And you better start looking at buildings for us because I wasn't kidding about Lauren and me moving Spirits out there someday."

I wrap my arms around her and lift her off the ground.

"Oliver," she screams in my ear. "You know I'm not a hugger. Put me the fuck down!"

AUGUST

AMY

OLIVER AND I lie flat on our backs on the floor of Oliver's new apartment and stare up at the spotted gray ceiling. Oliver reaches over with just the tips of his fingers and laces them through mine.

"Is it everything you imagined?" he asks me.

I'm quiet for a long time. No. This isn't how I imagined it. When I imagined moving to California, I imagined being alone. I imagined being terrified but keeping my head held high because that's what I've always done. Never did I imagine Oliver here with me.

This is so much better than I imagined.

But I don't say any of that. "I guess maybe I expected you to have carpet. I don't even know why."

"Carpet is old-school."

"Apparently."

I turn my head to look at him, and he turns his head to look at me, and his green eyes seem to shimmer in the light of the afternoon sun streaming in through the window. I reach out and run my fingers along his jaw as he reaches for his cell phone.

"What are you doing?" I ask, letting my hand drop back to my side.

"Trying to win a contest," he says, and I roll toward him, trying to snatch his phone away. He holds it out of my reach.

"You're never going to win!" I shout, climbing on top of him in an attempt to reach his phone, but Oliver's arms are so much longer than mine.

"Just cave to my musical genius already," he says, and I put my face against his neck and laugh as he wraps his arms around me. He clicks around on his phone, and then Ed Sheeran starts to play from his tiny speakers.

"Are you trying to seduce me?" I ask him, pushing up from his chest and smiling down at him.

"Technically, I'm trying to let Ed Sheeran seduce you," he says, and I laugh again, but this one is swallowed up as he leans up to kiss me.

SONGS AMY AND OLIVER LISTENED TO IN *ALL OUR WORST IDEAS*

"DO YOU REALIZE??" BY THE FLAMING LIPS

"CERTAIN THINGS" BY JAMES ARTHUR

"EVERY LITTLE THING SHE DOES IS MAGIC" BY SLEEPING AT LAST

"MOLLY" BY THE FRONT BOTTOMS

"ST. PATRICK" BY PVRIS

"POISON & WINE" BY THE CIVIL WARS

"HALLELUJAH" BY JEFF BUCKLEY

"WANNABE" BY THE SPICE GIRLS

"AIN'T NO SUNSHINE" BY BILL WITHERS

"FRIDAY I'M IN LOVE" BY THE CURE

"SHE IS LOVE" BY PARACHUTE

"YELLOW" BY COLDPLAY

"PARKLIFE" BY BLUR

"COME ON EILEEN" BY SAVE FERRIS

"I FOUND" BY AMBER RUN

"VARM" BY KRISTIAN KRISTENSEN

"MAPS" BY THE FRONT BOTTOMS

"NEXT IN LINE" BY WALK THE MOON

"LOVER, PLEASE STAY" BY NOTHING BUT THIEVES

"LET'S GET IT ON" BY MARVIN GAYE

"SHIRTSLEEVES" BY ED SHEERAN

"SLOW IT DOWN" BY THE LUMINEERS

"FLASHLIGHT" BY THE FRONT BOTTOMS

"SATURN" BY SLEEPING AT LAST

"GHOST" BY HUNTER HUNTED

"HUNGRY LIKE THE WOLF" BY DURAN DURAN

"STUBBORN LOVE" BY THE LUMINEERS

"SPIRITS" BY THE STRUMBELLAS

"WE WON'T GO HOME" BY THE COLOURIST

"DIVE" BY ED SHEERAN

ACKNOWLEDGMENTS

One of my favorite things about working in this industry is how, with every book, my list of people to thank gets longer and longer.

First, always, my God, who has given me this job and these experiences and all of the people in this section. I am truly, truly blessed.

A huge thank-you to everyone at Swoon Reads. Jean Feiwel, for letting me write another book for you. Lauren Scobell and Emily Settle, for being tireless and always supportive. Kat Brzozowski, for believing in my stories and always being patient with me when I have a billion questions. And for excellent guinea-pig content, which always helps the editing process. Also, Rachel Diebel, Ilana Worrell, Kelsey Marrujo, Katie Klimowicz, and Raymond Ernesto Colón, for working hard for me and the other authors at SR. Everyone else at Swoon Reads, especially those who have helped make this book possible without ever having known me. Your hard work is endlessly appreciated.

Swoon Squad. You guys know how much you mean to me, and I won't get sappy, but I would be lost without you all. Thanks for always having my back and being the most supportive group of people I've ever known. A special thank-you to squad members Katy Upperman and Claire Kann, for listening to me complain and always being wonderful friends and coworkers. Dallas Area Kidlit group: it has been an absolute honor to be in this with you guys for the last year. And especially Karen Blumenthal and Polly Holyoke, for always being willing to share your wisdom with me and not letting me hide in the background. Upperclassmen, you have been endless help and support for me, and it's a joy to know and be a part of you. And lastly, my Electrics, my ever-constant group who always has fierce advice and never-ending virtual hugs. Love you guys.

The majority of this book was edited at my home away from home: the library. Endless gratitude to the Smith Public Library, the Sachse Public Library, the Richardson Public Library, the Grand Prairie Library, and the entire Plano Library System for giving me a place where I feel comfortable enough to work on draft after draft, especially the lovely people at Smith who always kindly looked the other way while I ate prohibited Starburst by the handful. Also, thanks to all of the librarians and bloggers I've met over the last three years who have been supportive and kind. This industry wouldn't run without all of you. And, of course, the readers. Thank you for caring and for leaving kind comments and just sharing your enthusiasm. It is so, so lovely.

This book took a village of extremely kind people who took time to help me with details, and I am extremely grateful to that village. Jacqueline Fane, Sean Enfield, and Jonathan Upchurch, for sending me music to help drive the story forward, with a special thank-you to Chris Fluitt, who spent way too long trying to educate me on jazz (sorry the jazz chapter got cut), and Scott Fane, who introduced me to the Front Bottoms. As you've probably figured out, they became integral to this story. Christina Babu, for sharing your knowledge with me on the valedictorian race. De Vickery and Cherelle

Sparkman, for standing by me while I wrote this book in the lobby of Snoopy's. If you had ever asked me to please turn off my music, I never would have gotten through that awful first draft. Stephanie Crowe, for being an excellent beta reader and always being up for talking about books. Aiden Thomas, for sharing your knowledge on Spanish grammar rules with me. You're a star.

The village it took to make this book is nothing compared to the village that it takes to keep me moving every day. Kathy, there were many days in there when I was squirreled away in my office working while you were making sure the house and my husband were taken care of. Thank you for that. Meghan, you spent hours helping me brainstorm this book and listening to me moan and groan and just generally being my support system any time I needed it. There are no words for how thankful I am that you're in my life. Yoon, I love love love you. Thank you for always putting me back together when I fall apart. Any book I've ever written wouldn't exist without you telling me I could do it. Mom, you gave me books and music and movies that you loved and then told me to find what I loved, and for that I am forever grateful. Thank you for letting me be me and always being willing to love that person. And Jeremy. There are really no words. If anyone has been beside me through the absolute best and the absolute worst, it's you. You're in every love interest I write because I wouldn't know true love if it weren't for you.

**Check out more books
chosen for publication
by readers like you.**

  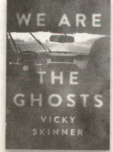 

DID YOU KNOW...

READER · APPROVED
Swoon READS

readers like you helped to get this book published?

Join our book-obsessed community and help us discover awesome new writing talent.

1 **Write it.**
Share your original YA manuscript.

2 **Read it.**
Discover bright new bookish talent.

3 **Share it.**
Discuss, rate, and share your faves.

4 **Love it.**
Help us publish the books you love.

Share your own manuscript or dive between the pages at **swoonreads.com** or by downloading the **Swoon Reads app.**